DIAVLO

MY FIRST FRIEND

DIAVLO

MY FIRST FRIEND

HENRY DOES

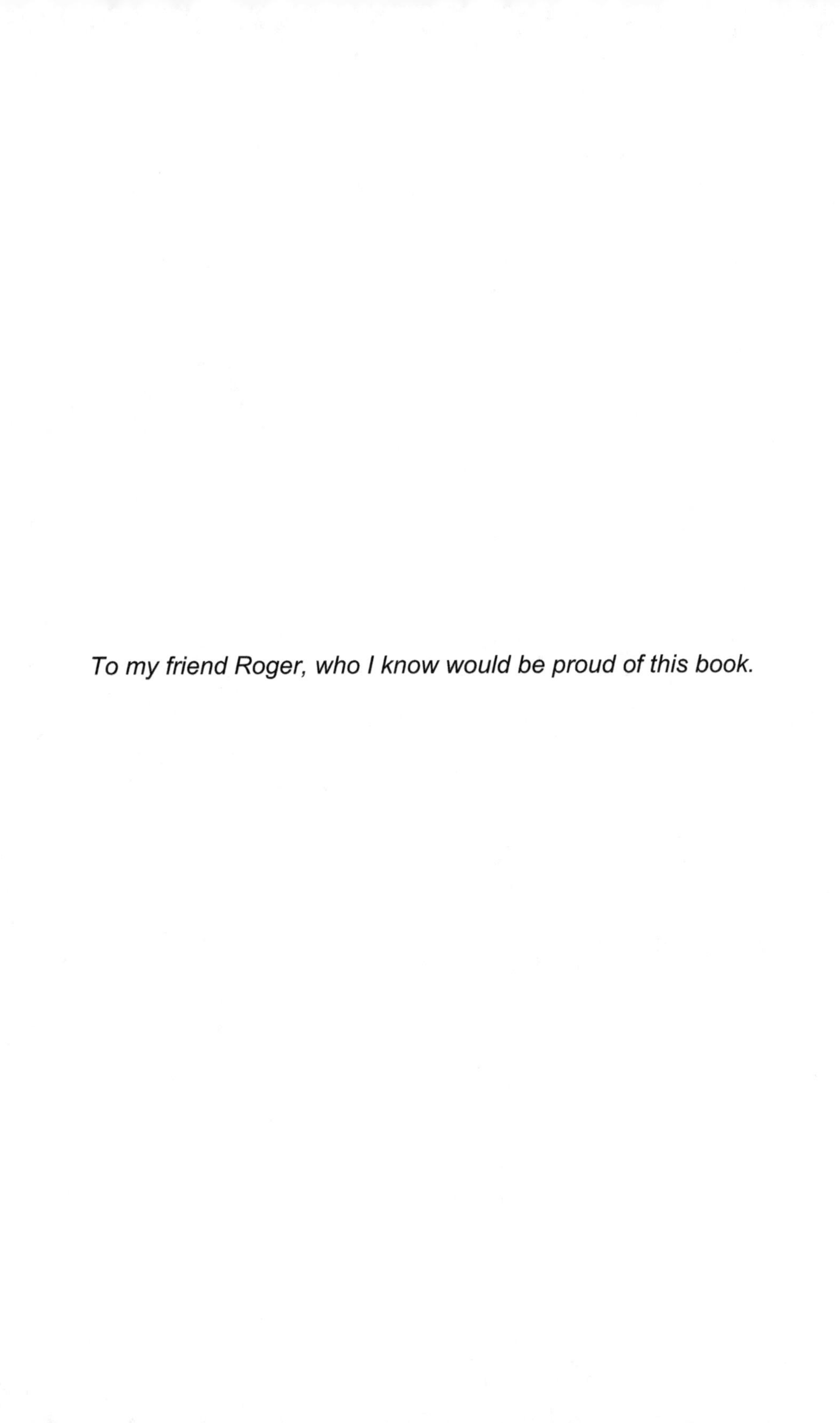

To my friend Roger, who I know would be proud of this book.

TABLE OF CONTENTS

PROLOGUE

June 11, 2032

The world was quieter now. Too quiet. The haunting silence of empty streets and abandoned cities echoed the unimaginable cost of the Third World War. Eighty percent of humanity had perished, leaving behind a planet scarred and broken. Nations once mighty had crumbled under the weight of nuclear fire, biological devastation, and unrelenting despair. Yet, amidst the ashes of the dead and dying, a single man had risen to forge a new world order—Hank Johnson.

Two months ago, Hank did the unthinkable. Through means unknown to all but himself, he had convinced the fractured remnants of humanity's leadership to lay down their weapons, dismantle their borders, and unite under one banner. The era of divided nations had ended. In its place stood a unified Earth, a single nation governed by what Hank declared to be a council of cooperation and peace. The war that had ravaged the world was over.

Most of the survivors hailed Hank as a saviour. They whispered his name with reverence, calling him the man who had saved humanity from annihilation. Statues were being built in his honour, and cities in ruins now bore his insignia as a beacon of hope. Few questioned how he had achieved such a monumental achievement. Perhaps they didn't want to. After years of suffering, the promise of peace, however fragile, was enough to quell any curiosity. The details of Hank's methods, his rise to power, and the sudden capitulation of world leaders were left shrouded in mystery. For most, it didn't matter.

But not everyone accepted this miracle. In the shadows, far from the adoration of the masses, a secret group of investigators had been piecing together a different narrative. These individuals, drawn from the remnants of intelligence agencies, military operatives, and rogue scientists, had long been tracking Hank's rise to power. His unexplainable influence, the enigmatic nature of his leadership, and his ability to sway entire governments without resistance had raised questions too dangerous to ask aloud.

For years, their inquiries had yielded little more than scraps of speculation and vague rumours—until recently. Several days ago, an ally deep within Hank's inner circle had leaked information that changed everything. Evidence suggested that Hank had not simply united the world by diplomacy or charm. He had been hiding something, something powerful and terrifying, within the walls of his luxurious mansion in Sydney, Australia.

The tip was specific yet cryptic: "The answers are in the vault." The informant couldn't say more without risking exposure, but it was enough to set the wheels in motion. The investigators, operating privately and without the backing of any government, launched Operation Pegasus— a covert mission to infiltrate Hank's heavily fortified estate, retrieve the hidden evidence, and uncover the truth behind his unification of the world.

The stakes couldn't have been higher. If Hank's rise to power had been legitimate, the investigators risked shattering the fragile peace that held the world together. But if their suspicions were correct—if Hank's unification of Earth was built on something darker, something monstrous—the world's salvation might have come at a far greater cost than anyone could comprehend.

The team chosen for the mission represented the best of what humanity had left. Marcus Kane, a former MI6 operative with a reputation for achieving the impossible, led the group. His team included Elena Vasquez, a tech prodigy capable of breaching any security system; Dimitri Volkov, a hardened ex-special forces operative from Russia; Kira Yamada, a master of stealth and reconnaissance; Jackson "Jax" Monroe, a demolitions expert with surgical precision; and Aminah Sahal, an intelligence analyst who had pieced together the fragmented puzzle of Hank's rise.

Their mission was clear: infiltrate the mansion, locate the evidence, and escape undetected. But clarity didn't equal simplicity. Hank's mansion was said to be impenetrable, protected by cutting-edge technology and guards loyal to him alone. Yet, the team had no choice. The truth about Hank Johnson, the man the world hailed as its saviour, had to be uncovered—even if it destroyed what little remained of humanity's hope.

And so, on a cool June evening, under the cover of darkness, Operation Pegasus began.

OPERATION PEGASUS: THE BREAK-IN AT HANK JOHNSON'S MANSION

The moon hung low over Sydney, its pale light reflecting off the glass walls of Hank Johnson's mansion. Situated high on a hill overlooking the city, the mansion was an architectural marvel of the new age—sharp angles, blackened steel, and towering glass panels that seemed to pierce the sky. But for all its beauty, it was shrouded in mystery, much like the man who owns it. Hank Johnson, the enigmatic leader who had united the fractured remains of humanity under one nation after the Third World War, was now the most powerful person on Earth.

But tonight, a shadowy team of elite operatives had gathered to infiltrate his stronghold. For years, whispers of Hank's mysterious past had circulated among the remnants of old governments and private agencies. His meteoric rise to power, his uncanny ability to sway the most stubborn of leaders, and his seemingly inexhaustible resources all pointed to secrets buried deep within the mansion.

23:45 PM

The team was in position. Led by Marcus Kane, a former MI6 operative turned independent investigator, the team comprised some of the world's finest covert specialists:

- Elena Vasquez, a tech prodigy from Argentina who could hack into anything with a signal.
- Dimitri Volkov, a Russian ex-special forces operative who had defected after the war.
- Kira Yamada, a reconnaissance and infiltration expert from Japan, known for her unparalleled stealth.
- Jackson "Jax" Monroe, an American demolitions and breaching expert with a penchant for precision.
- Aminah Sahal, an intelligence analyst from Kenya who had pieced together the puzzle that led them here.

Each of them carried personal scars from the war—lost families, broken countries, and the gnawing guilt of survival. But tonight, they had one goal: retrieve the hidden documents rumoured to reveal Hank Johnson's past.

23:50 PM

"Team, focus," Marcus said through the encrypted comms as he crouched near the mansion's perimeter wall. The mansion's security system was state-of-the-art, designed to repel even military-grade intrusions. Elena was already working on disabling the perimeter alarms. Her laptop emitted a faint glow as her fingers danced across the keyboard.

"I've got the outer defences," Elena whispered. "But the internal systems are adaptive AI. I'll need to be inside to shut them down completely."

"Understood," Marcus replied. "Kira, lead the entry. Dimitri, cover her."

Kira nodded, her movements fluid as she scaled the wall with barely a sound. Dimitri followed, his eyes scanning for guards. The mansion's staff had been dismissed for the night—a decision that was rarely made, and one that made the team uneasy.

23:55 PM

Inside the mansion, the air was eerily still. The operatives moved silently through the opulent hallways, their black uniforms blending into the shadows. Elena plugged a small device into the wall, bypassing the mansion's AI security layer by layer.

"I'm in," Elena whispered. "You've got ten minutes before the backup system kicks in. Move fast."

"Kira, Dimitri, secure the study," Marcus ordered. "Aminah, keep tracking the blueprints for hidden rooms. Jax, hold position here and watch for any surprises."

The team split, each moving with military precision.

00:05 AM

Kira and Dimitri reached the study, a cavernous room filled with bookshelves, holographic displays, and a massive oak desk. It was an anachronism, filled with objects from a world that no longer existed. Kira scanned the room with a thermal sensor.

"There's a cold spot behind the east wall," she reported. "Looks like a hidden compartment."

"Found something," Aminah's voice crackled through the comms. "Blueprints show an underground vault. It's directly beneath the study."

00:10 AM

As Jax kept watch near the entrance, his comm buzzed. "Heads up, we've got movement. Security drones are reactivating. Elena, can you stall them?"

"I'll try," Elena said, her voice tense. "But the AI is learning my patterns. I can't hold it for long."

"Move faster," Marcus urged.

00:12 AM

Dimitri and Kira found the access point to the underground vault—a hidden lever disguised as a book on the shelf. The shelf slid back, revealing a staircase descending into darkness.

"Found the way down," Dimitri reported.

"Careful," Marcus said. "This feels too easy."

00:15 AM

The team regrouped at the staircase and descended cautiously. The vault was lined with steel walls and lit by faint, flickering lights. At the centre was a glass case containing a collection of documents, photographs, CDs and what appeared to be old cassette tapes. On top of the glass case there was a little square, the only way to open it.

"It's locked with some kind of biometrically triggered mechanism. Look," said Aminah.

She pointed to the small square panel embedded on the top of the case. It was about the size of a playing card, its smooth surface glinting faintly under the dim light.

"Dimitri, let the blood from the vial we were given touch the panel. That should open it," said Marcus.

As the blood hit the panel, a faint click echoed in the room. The glass case unlocked with a soft hiss, and the lid lifted slightly, releasing a chilling draft that made the group shiver.

"Is this it?" Marcus asked, his voice low.

Aminah scanned the contents. "These are the records we've been looking for—dates, locations, names. Some of this aligns with what we were looking for… but it doesn't make sense. There are references here to a time before the Third World War even began."

00:20 AM

Suddenly, the lights in the vault flickered violently, and the sound of heavy footsteps echoed above.

"Drones are in the house!" Jax shouted through the comms. "We've got company!"

"Grab everything and move!" Marcus barked.

00:22 AM

As the team scrambled to gather the documents, a deep, mechanical voice echoed through the vault.

"You shouldn't be here."

The operatives froze.

"What the hell was that?" Dimitri growled, raising his weapon.

The room seemed to shudder as the temperature dropped. Kira glanced at Marcus, her face pale. "We're not alone."

00:25 AM

Elena's voice crackled through the comms. "Guys, the AI… it's not just adaptive. It's aware. It knows you're there."

"Get us out!" Marcus shouted.

"I'm trying!"

00:27 AM

The footsteps above grew louder, accompanied by the hum of drones and the unmistakable sound of reinforced doors slamming shut.

"Too late," Jax muttered. "We're trapped."

00:30 AM

As the team prepared for a confrontation, the lights in the vault went out completely, plunging them into absolute darkness. Before they could react, a low rumble echoed through the room, followed by the sharp sound of mechanisms whirring. Suddenly, a section of the wall slid open, revealing a hidden corridor. The lights within the corridor flickered sporadically, casting eerie shadows along the narrow passageway.

"Who did that?" Marcus hissed into the comms.

"Not me," Elena replied, her voice trembling. "I'm locked out of the system. This isn't us."

"We don't have a choice," Dimitri said, his weapon raised as he stepped toward the corridor. "We need to move. Now."

"Grab everything!" Marcus ordered, taking the glass case with all the material inside.

The team hurried into the corridor, the air damp and cold. The flickering lights created an unsettling strobe effect, but the passage was narrow and clear. Their comms were filled with tense breathing and the faint hum of machinery in the walls.

00:33 AM

"This feels like an escape tunnel," Kira observed as they moved deeper into the passage. "But who activated it? And why?"

"Doesn't matter," Marcus said firmly. "Keep moving. We can figure it out later."

After what felt like an eternity, the corridor opened into a larger tunnel system. The air was fresher, and the distant sound of water dripping echoed around them. They followed the tunnel until it finally led to an exit hidden in the dense foliage outside the mansion's perimeter.

00:45 AM

Emerging into the cool night air, the team paused to regroup. The mansion loomed behind them, its silhouette eerily quiet. No alarms sounded, and there was no sign of pursuit.

"How is this possible?" Elena whispered. "Someone must've known we were in there."

"Enough," Marcus said, cutting her off. "We'll speculate later. Right now, we need to stick to the plan. Extraction point is at 01:00 AM. Let's move."

01:00 AM

The team arrived at a secluded airstrip just outside Sydney. A small, unmarked jet waited on the tarmac, engines humming softly. Marcus gave the signal, and the team boarded swiftly, securing the glass case in the cargo area.

As the plane taxied down the runway and lifted into the night sky, the tension in the cabin began to ease, but the weight of their discovery remained heavy.

02:15 AM – Onboard the Plane

The team sat in a dimly lit cabin, the hum of the jet's engines filling the silence. Marcus opened the glass case and began laying out the material on the table in front of them.

"Let's figure out what we've got," he said. "Aminah, start organizing these by date. Elena, see if you can digitize any of this."

The documents were old, some yellowed with age. Among them were handwritten notes, photographs, CDs and cassette tapes labelled with dates.

Aminah sorted the papers methodically. "This goes back farther than I expected," she said, holding up a document dated 1987. "This is the year of Hank's birth."

Dimitri leaned in. "Why would he have hidden all this evidence, possibly incriminating himself? Did he think no one would ever find it if he gathered it all in one place?"

"Possible," Aminah replied, "but look at this." She unfolded a fragile piece of paper. "It's a report about a remote village in Peru. A massacre. The date matches the year Hank supposedly went missing when he was a child."

Marcus frowned. "What else do you see?"

Elena was scanning a stack of photographs. She froze, her face pale. "Guys… look at this." She handed the photo to Marcus. It showed a boy, no older than seventeen, standing in the middle of a street, wearing a tuxedo covered in what appeared to be blood. His eyes were dark and hollow.

"That's Hank," Kira whispered, leaning closer.

02:45 AM

Aminah continued organizing the documents, pulling together a series of entries that appeared to be journal pages. She read aloud:

"My first friend is my shadow friend. He doesn't have a name—he doesn't like names."

The writing was scrawled, childlike, and the entries were dated from the 1990s.

"These are Hank's," Aminah said, her voice shaking. "He must've written these as a child. But what does he mean by 'the shadow'?"

"Whatever it is," Dimitri said grimly, "it's been with him for a long time."

03:15 AM

Elena began analysing the cassette tapes, feeding a random one into a portable player. The tape crackled to life with static, then a chilling voice—a child's voice—spoke.

"I don't remember everything. But… my first friend, my shadow friend told me. You know, the one I told you about before? I think he killed them."

The team exchanged uneasy glances as the recording continued. In the background, faint, guttural sounds could be heard, almost like growls.

03:30 AM

"This isn't just about Hank," Marcus finally said, breaking the silence. "Whatever happened to him in his childhood, whatever this 'shadow friend' is, it's tied to everything—his rise to power, his ability to unite the world. It's not natural."

"Are we saying he's… not human?" Kira asked cautiously.

"Not necessarily," Aminah replied. "But there's more to him than we've been told. And if this 'shadow friend' is real, it could be the reason for everything."

03:45 AM

The plane continued its journey into the night, carrying the team and Hank's secrets they had uncovered. As they pieced together Hank Johnson's past, one thing became clear: this was only the beginning.

BIRTH

Hospital Birth Report
Date: June 2, 1987
Time: 7:10 AM

Mother's Information:
Name: Mary Ann Johnson
Date of Birth: August 27, 1960
Address: 205 Ann Street, New Farm, Brisbane
Medical Record Number: 284736159
Gravida: 1 (second pregnancy)
Para: None
Blood Type: O+
Physician: Dr. Robert L. Greene

Labor and Delivery Summary:
Onset of Labor: May 31, 1987, 8:30 PM
Duration of Labor: 7 hours and 15 minutes
Delivery Type: Vaginal
Complications: None noted
Anaesthesia Used: Epidural

Infant Information:
Infant Name: (Baby Boy) Hank
Date and Time of Birth: June 2, 1987, 7:10 AM
Gender: Boy
Weight: 3.29 kilograms
Length: 48.26 centimetres
Apgar Scores: 1 minute - 8, 5 minutes - 9
Head Circumference: 34.29 centimetres
Blood Type: O+

Postpartum Condition:
Mother's Condition: Stable
Infant's Condition: Stable
Breastfeeding Initiated: Yes

Discharge Instructions: To be provided upon discharge

<u>Notes:</u>
No notable complications during labour or delivery. Both mother and infant are in good health. Paediatric assessment is scheduled within 24 hours.

After delivery, it was observed that the infant did not cry immediately. Instead, he extended his arms upward and focused his gaze on the ceiling, as if looking at something specific. The nursing staff noted that he seemed intrigued, possibly by the light fixture. They also remarked that they had never witnessed such behaviour before.

Mary Ann Johnson's Diary
June 5, 1987

It's been three days since our little Hank was born. I still can't believe he's here. I'm overwhelmed by how happy I feel, more than I ever imagined. Hank has been an absolute angel – he's such an easy boy. I was prepared for sleepless nights and all the challenges everyone told me about, but he's settled into things so smoothly, almost as if he's been here all along. He's sleeping well, and even at night, he's not giving us any trouble. It's a blessing I wasn't expecting, and it's made these first few days easier than I could have hoped.

I can't stop looking at him. There's something so perfect, so pure, in every tiny detail of his little face, his tiny fingers, his gentle breathing. Feeding him feels like our little ritual, something that's just between us. He's nursing well, and I'm grateful my body is able to provide for him like this. I was nervous about breastfeeding, unsure if it would come naturally, but with him, it's been such a smooth, almost instinctive connection. I feel so close to him during those moments – it's like we're in our own little world.

June 6, 1987

Today, I woke up feeling so grateful – not just for Hank, but for Michael too. He's been such a steady, loving presence. I feel like I'm seeing a whole new side of him, a softer side I didn't know was there. He's been taking care of everything, making sure I have what I need, and watching over Hank and me with such tenderness. I don't think I could do this without him. It feels like we're stronger, more connected than ever before. Every time he holds Hank, my heart swells. I see a glimpse of the father he's going to be, and it fills me with so much hope and gratitude.

In the quiet moments, when it's just the three of us, I feel like the luckiest woman in the world. Hank has brought us closer, and I can already see the love Michael has for him in his eyes. It's beautiful. These are the days I'll remember forever, the beginning of our life as a family.

June 15, 1987

Today was quite an eventful day. Mom and Dad came over to visit Hank for the first time since he was born. They were absolutely thrilled to meet their new grandson – the smiles on their faces when they saw him were unforgettable. They kept saying how healthy he looked, with those chubby little cheeks and bright eyes. It made me feel so proud and relieved to see their happiness.

They brought Sanson, their boxer, along with them. Sanson is a four-year-old bundle of energy and mischief. He's always loved children, so I thought it would be fine for him to meet Hank. The weather was cool and pleasant, with a light breeze drifting through the open window, and it felt like the perfect day to spend together as a family.

We all enjoyed a nice lunch together – my favourited quiche, which Mom was sweet enough to bring. It's been so long since I tasted it, and it was just as delicious as I remembered. Michael kept going on about how he needs the recipe, and we all laughed. It felt so warm and easy, like old times.

But something strange happened. After lunch, we let Sanson sniff Hank, just for a few seconds, thinking it would be a sweet introduction. Hank was lying peacefully in my arms, and Sanson leaned in, curious. But suddenly, he let out a deep, low growl and stared right at Hank with this intense look. Hank's eyes grew wide, and then he started crying, a sound I hadn't heard before, full of fear. It broke my heart a little.

We were all shocked. Sanson had never done anything like that around other babies or children. Mom and Dad were just as surprised and kept saying he must have been startled or confused. They quickly took him out to the balcony to calm him down. Poor Hank needed a few minutes to settle, and I held him close, trying to soothe him.

It was such an unexpected moment. Sanson has always been the gentlest dog with kids, but I suppose Hank is still so new, and maybe Sanson just didn't understand what he was sniffing at. I'm still not quite sure what to make of it. But as I look at Hank now, sleeping so peacefully, I feel a sense of calm again. There's so much to learn and experience each day, and I'm grateful to have my family with me through it all, even when things don't go quite as planned.

CSBNC Australia Newspaper
June 28, 1987
By Cameron Whitaker

Headline: U.S. Vice President Killed in Plane Explosion After NATO Summit in UK

Red Alert Issued as Terrorist Attack Claims Lives of U.S. Vice President and Staff

In a shocking and tragic turn of events, a plane carrying the Vice President of the United States was destroyed in an apparent terrorist attack on British territory, killing the Vice President and all members of his staff on board. The explosion occurred just hours after a successful NATO summit in the United Kingdom, where representatives from allied nations gathered to strategize in response to the ongoing tensions of the Cold War. The U.S. Vice President, whose name is being withheld pending official announcements, had been actively participating in discussions aimed at strengthening Western alliances and addressing Soviet influence in Eastern Europe.

The explosion has sent shockwaves through the international community. U.S. officials, in conjunction with British authorities, have launched an immediate investigation to determine the perpetrators of this heinous act. Intelligence agencies from several NATO member countries have been placed on high alert, and enhanced security measures have been implemented across key government facilities and transportation hubs worldwide. The British Prime Minister and U.S. President have both condemned the attack, calling it a "cowardly assault on democracy and freedom."

Reports from military officials confirm that the Vice President's plane had just departed from a secure airfield in the UK when the explosion occurred mid-flight. Witnesses in nearby towns described hearing a loud explosion and seeing a fireball in the sky. Rescue operations were promptly dispatched, but authorities quickly confirmed there were no survivors.

The United States has declared a period of national mourning, and flags are being flown at half-staff across the country in honour of the fallen Vice President and his dedicated staff. This devastating loss comes at a critical time in global politics, with tensions between NATO and the Soviet Union at an all-time high. The incident has raised questions about the security of high-ranking officials and sparked renewed concerns about potential vulnerabilities in transportation protocols for government personnel.

Although no group has yet claimed responsibility for the attack, both the U.S. and UK are taking the incident very seriously. "We will not rest until we find those responsible for this tragic and unjust act," stated the U.S. President in an address to the nation. "This is not just an attack on one individual or one country, but an attack on all of us who stand for freedom, justice, and peace."

Military and intelligence forces worldwide remain on high alert, and discussions have begun within NATO regarding additional security measures and possible responses. European leaders have expressed their condolences and pledged their full support for the investigation. The NATO alliance has vowed to continue its mission undeterred, standing united against any threats to peace and stability.

As the investigation unfolds, questions are being raised about how this attack was possible despite extensive security protocols. Security experts are speculating that the attack may have involved sophisticated planning and possibly internal assistance, though no evidence has been confirmed.

The world watches and waits as officials work to uncover the truth behind this devastating attack. In the meantime, security agencies urge the public to remain vigilant.

Mary Ann Johnson's Diary
July 13, 1987

It's hard to believe that it's been over a month since Hank came into our lives. Time feels so different now – it's like the days are passing in a soft, warm blur. I feel so lucky; Hank has been such an easy baby. He hardly ever fusses, and he's sleeping well through the night. I almost can't believe it myself. Cheryl keeps telling me how rare this is, especially since she had her hands full with her three boys. She can hardly believe how smoothly things have been going for us, and I have to admit, part of me finds it a bit unusual too. Not that I'm complaining – I'm so grateful, truly. It's just… I don't know, surprising.

One thing that's been a joy to watch is how Hank and Michael seem to have this special bond. There's something so beautiful in the way Michael holds him, talks to him, and makes him laugh. It's almost as if they're in their own little world sometimes. I'm grateful that Michael is such a wonderful father, but a small part of me can't help but feel… left out. I know it's silly, but I miss the way things were before. Ever since Hank was born, Michael's been dedicating all his time to work and to Hank, which I love about him – he's so devoted. But there's barely any time left for me. No dinners, no quiet moments just the two of us, no lingering affection. I feel selfish even writing it, but maybe I'm a little jealous. I miss feeling like I was a part of his world too.

Hank has been making the cutest little noises lately, especially after he's had a full meal. It's almost as if he's trying to talk to me. He gurgles and coos, waving his tiny hands in the air, his little fingers stretching like he's trying to reach for something. Sometimes, when I'm preparing milk or meals, I can hear him in his bassinet, just making soft sounds to himself, like he's having his own little conversation. It's so endearing, and I find myself watching him, wondering what's going through his mind.

The paediatrician says it's perfectly normal and there's nothing to worry about, that some babies just like to "talk" early on. But there's something about it that feels… special. He's only a month old, but he's already so full of personality. I can't wait to see who he grows up to be, to hear the words he'll say one day. For now, I'm treasuring every coo and gurgle, and hoping that as he grows, I'll find my place again in this new family dynamic.

July 15, 1987

Today was a lovely day with Hank. He's starting to really enjoy solid foods, or at least the bits he's allowed to have. His absolute favourite so far is mashed banana – he can't get enough of it! And of course, he still loves his milk. I think he'd drink it all day if I let him! I've noticed that if he gets a good feeding at night, he sleeps so soundly afterward. It's such a relief to see him happy and healthy, resting peacefully. I treasure these quiet moments with him, his soft little breaths as he drifts off in my arms.

But today wasn't all light. Michael told me something that's been on his mind, something I hadn't even been aware of until now. He shared the news about the recent tragedy with the U.S. Vice President – how he was killed in that terrible explosion at the end of June. It sounds like something out of a nightmare, but apparently, the investigation now suggests that UK officials might be involved. I can hardly believe it, and it feels like something so unimaginable. They're calling it an act of treason, and the U.S. has even presented evidence to NATO. There's talk of NATO possibly removing the UK from the alliance. The idea seems so surreal; I never thought things could come to this.

Hearing these kinds of things makes me anxious about the future. I usually try to avoid these heavy topics, but now, with Hank in my life, it's even harder to ignore. I worry about what kind of world he's going to grow up in. I know there's only so much I can do, but I hope and pray that these conflicts can be resolved.

For now, I'm holding onto what's in front of me – Hank's little giggles, his sleepy sighs, and the simple joy of watching him grow. It's all I can do to keep my focus here, on this life we're building together. I hope the world beyond our doors can find some peace soon.

CSBNC Australia Newspaper
October 11, 1987
By Cameron Whitaker

Headline: NATO Expels United Kingdom Over Shocking Assassination Plot

UK Prime Minister Accused of Conspiracy in U.S. Vice President's Assassination; Calls for International Trial as UK Denies All Charges

In an unprecedented decision that has sent shockwaves through the international community, NATO has officially expelled the United Kingdom from the alliance. The expulsion follows startling revelations that the UK Prime Minister was allegedly involved in orchestrating the assassination of the United States Vice President, an act which, according to sources close to NATO, was initially intended to target the U.S. President.

This explosive accusation stems from the recent capture and interrogation of several individuals believed to be directly involved in the June 28 attack. The assassins, now in NATO custody, reportedly confessed that their orders originated from the highest levels of the UK government, with the Vice President's tragic death described as a miscalculation in a larger scheme aimed at taking the life of the President of the United States.

The findings have shocked NATO member states, leading to swift and decisive action to sever ties with one of the alliance's founding members. NATO officials released a statement condemning the alleged betrayal as a "grievous violation of trust and an act of hostility that cannot be tolerated within our ranks." Representatives from NATO countries expressed deep regret at the decision, emphasizing that it was necessary to protect the integrity and security of the alliance.

In response, the United Kingdom government has vehemently denied all allegations. The Prime Minister's office issued a formal statement calling the accusations "outrageous and unfounded," and accusing NATO of acting on false information. British officials insist that the alleged confession was obtained under questionable circumstances and lacks credibility. The UK has demanded a formal trial to present its case, claiming that the true masterminds behind the assassination are more likely enemies of both the UK and the U.S., specifically the Soviet Union.

The Prime Minister addressed the nation in a televised broadcast, urging British citizens to remain calm and stand united in the face of what he described as an "international conspiracy designed to sow discord between allies." He asserted that the UK would seek to clear its name on the global stage, appealing to neutral parties to oversee an impartial investigation.

This rift has created an atmosphere of uncertainty across Europe and beyond, with many questioning what impact this division will have on the already fragile balance of power amidst Cold War tensions. The Soviet Union, for its part, has remained silent on the matter, though many speculate that it stands to gain from the disruption within NATO.

The expulsion of the UK from NATO marks a turning point in post-World War II international relations, as this is the first time a major Western power has been ousted from the alliance. With trust among allies at an all-time low, world leaders are now grappling with the implications of this crisis on global security.

As the UK prepares to mount a defence and NATO braces for potential fallout, all eyes remain on the political chessboard. The coming weeks will be critical in determining whether a trial will proceed and if any path to reconciliation exists, or if this marks the beginning of a deepening divide between once-close allies.

HIDE AND SEEK

Mary Ann Johnson's Diary
December 2, 1987

Six months. I can hardly believe it's been six months since Hank was born. Time has flown by in a way that feels surreal, and yet it's been filled with so many beautiful little moments. Ever since his first month, Michael and I have celebrated each "month birthday" with a small party for Hank, inviting just close family and friends. It's become a bit of a tradition, but we agreed that this month would be the last. Six months feels like a good place to end these little parties, though part of me will miss them.

For Hank's half-birthday, we decided to do something special. We went to one of my favourite restaurants, Baddie's, in New Farm on Brunswick St. I've always loved the atmosphere there, warm and cozy, perfect for family gatherings. We invited my sister Cheryl and her three boys – Dean, who's now 10, Shane at 12, and Matthew at 15. It was a full table, but it felt wonderful to have everyone together, and Hank seemed so delighted by all the attention. He's come a long way in just six months; he can roll over now, reach and grab for things, and he even responds to his name! He was so curious about everything around him, especially his cousins. Watching him interact with them was such a joy; he seemed to get along with them effortlessly.

The evening was going perfectly until the waitress brought out Hank's little birthday cake. Just as she was walking toward our table, she tripped, and the cake fell right to the floor. She was mortified, apologizing over and over, saying she felt something grab her right leg, even though there was no one nearby. It was strange, but accidents happen. We reassured her it was fine and ended up buying another cake. Hank was too young to notice the mishap, thankfully, and everyone else just laughed it off.

After dinner, we all went back to our apartment for a cup of tea to wrap up the evening. Dean, Shane, and Matthew took Hank into the visitor room to play while the adults chatted. But then, another strange incident happened. Dean came out of the room in tears, clutching his thumb, saying it felt numb. My heart stopped for a moment, worried something had happened to Hank. But as it turned out, Dean's thumb was the problem – it was broken. Shane and Matthew insisted they'd been focused on their Monopoly game and didn't see what happened, but Dean claimed his thumb felt numb right after Hank let go of it. Cheryl quickly scolded Dean, telling him not to blame a baby, and after a bit more prodding, he admitted the truth: he had fallen and broken it himself. Poor kid, though, it must have been painful, and we got him some ice and bandaged it up as best we could until they could go to the hospital.

Once everyone left, Michael and I stayed up a little later, watching the news while Hank slept peacefully beside us. The world feels like a darker place these days, especially after the assassination of the U.S. Vice President back in June. Tensions between the U.S. and the UK have only escalated since then. They're sanctioning each other over immigration policies now, and it's so surreal to think that UK citizens are no longer allowed into the U.S. It makes me anxious, thinking about the kind of world Hank is growing up in. I can only hope that things will calm down and that some sense of peace will be restored.

For now, I'm holding onto these moments with Michael and Hank, grateful for this little bubble of warmth and love we've created together. As I watch Hank sleep, I feel a fierce hope that the world will become a better place for him. I want him to grow up safe and happy, without the shadow of these conflicts looming over him.

Chat between Dean and Matthew Coopla
December 2, 1987

Dean and Matthew had a secret way of communicating once they were supposed to be asleep. Their mom, Cheryl, had a strict rule: no talking or whispering after bedtime. She had an uncanny ability to hear even the faintest sounds from their room, so talking was out of the question. To get around this, the brothers came up with a clever solution: passing paper notes.

After the lights were out, Dean and Matthew would each tear a piece of paper from their school notebooks, scribbling their messages carefully in the dark. From their beds across the room, they'd crumple up each note into a small ball and toss it to each other. They'd listen carefully for the soft sound of paper landing, then reach out to grab it, unwrapping each note as quietly as possible.

They'd been doing this for a while, becoming almost experts at this silent note-passing system. It was their little secret, a way to share thoughts and stories when they were supposed to be fast asleep. And tonight, after everything that had happened with Dean's broken thumb, they had a lot more to talk about than usual.

[Paper note from Matthew to Dean]
Dean, are you okay? How's the thumb? Did the doctor fix it all right?

[Paper note from Dean to Matthew]
Yeah, it's okay. The doctor said it should heal in a few days. Still hurts a lot, though. I probably won't sleep tonight.

[Paper note from Matthew to Dean]
Mom was really mad tonight, huh? I know you didn't just fall and break your thumb. You can tell me what really happened.

[Paper note from Dean to Matthew]

I had to tell her that! She was so mad, and I got scared. And besides, would she even believe me if I told her Hank broke my thumb?

[Paper note from Matthew to Dean]
So… it really was Hank? You can trust me, Dean. What actually happened?

[Paper note from Dean to Matthew]
Honestly, I'm not even sure myself. But… yeah, it was Hank. At least, I think it was. After he let go of my thumb, it was like something I couldn't see grabbed it and squeezed really hard. It hurt so much I started crying.

[Paper note from Matthew to Dean]
Whoa… that's weird. Maybe it was just the adrenaline or something. Or… what if Hank has some kind of power? Like Professor X or Jean Grey from the X-Men comics?

[Paper note from Dean to Matthew]
I don't know, Matt. It's just… confusing. I don't want to think about it anymore.

[Dean stopped sending Paper notes after this]

Mary Ann Johnson's Diary
December 24, 1987

Tonight, we're at Cheryl's house in Logan, getting ready to spend Christmas Eve together. It's different this year. Normally, we'd go to our parents' place in Toowoomba for Christmas, but with Cheryl going through her first holiday alone since the divorce, we wanted to be here for her. It's not easy for her, especially this time of the year. I know she feels the weight of it all, and we couldn't let her spend Christmas without family around. Still, Logan has a bit of a reputation—some people call it "trashy"—but that doesn't matter to us. Cheryl's place is cozy, and it's home for her and the boys. That's all that matters.

The evening went by smoothly. Hank was thrilled to be around his cousins and spent most of the night trying to stand up. It was hilarious watching him – he has no real strength for it yet, but his determination is amazing. He wobbles and falls with a big grin, and every attempt seems to make him giggle even more.

His favourite game, though, was watching his cousins as they played hide and seek. He would track them with his little finger, pointing and following them as they dashed from place to place. Michael joined in, picking Hank up and moving him around so he could "follow" the boys better. The sound of Hank's laughter filled the room – pure, joyful, and infectious. It's moments like this that make my heart so full.

Dinner was delicious. Cheryl outdid herself with a beautiful roasted chicken and vegetables, and she even had ice cream for dessert. Hank was exhausted after all the excitement and went to bed right after. Michael tucked him in, and once the boys were asleep, it was just Cheryl and me left in the living room with the TV on. The news was playing in the background, going on about this whole UK-US tension. They keep hinting at a possible war, but I can't believe it. Who would want a war between two countries like that, especially with the Cold War still looming over us? The world already feels tense enough.

After a while, Cheryl turned to me and opened up about how hard it's been, raising her boys on her own. I could see the sadness in her eyes, and it broke my heart. She admitted she misses her husband sometimes, even though she knows he wasn't good to her or the kids. The truth is, he was a violent man, and she had to go to the police to get him out of their lives. I know she made the right decision, but it hasn't been easy for her, especially around the holidays. She looked at me and said, "I hope Michael is always there for you, Mary Ann. You're lucky to have him."

Then she gave me this advice that I didn't expect. She told me not to have more children – that one is enough. "Imagine three if Michael's not around one day," she said. "You should be prepared for anything." I don't know if she's right, but her words stayed with me. I can see she's speaking from a place of pain and worry, and I can't blame her. Raising a family alone has made her so strong, but it's also taken a toll.

Tonight, as I lie here with Michael and Hank nearby, I'm feeling grateful. Grateful for this little family of mine, for Michael's love, and for the laughter Hank brings into our lives. But Cheryl's words are there, lingering in my mind. Life is unpredictable, and maybe, in some way, I do need to be prepared. For now, though, I'll focus on the love we have, and hope that we'll always be there for each other.

Chat between Dean and Matthew Coopla
December 24, 1987

[Note from Dean to Matthew]
Did you see what Hank did tonight?

[Note from Matthew to Dean]
No, what are you talking about?

[Note from Dean to Matthew]
When we were playing hide and seek, I was hiding behind a chair, and Hank was watching. The chair... it moved, Matt. Hank moved it with his mind. I swear I saw it!

[Note from Matthew to Dean]
Haha, are you serious? Dean, come on. Hank's a baby! Babies can't move things with their minds. You probably just imagined it.

[Note from Dean to Matthew]
I did NOT imagine it! I know what I saw. I'm going to test him tomorrow. You'll see – everyone will see!

[Note from Matthew to Dean]
Alright, Professor X. Good luck with that. Now go to sleep – Mom's gonna hear us if we keep this up.

[Dean didn't send any more notes after this, and Matthew quickly went to sleep]

Logan Police Department
Incident Report
December 25, 1987
Time: 8:45 AM
Officer: Sgt. John Wilkins
Report No.: 87-1225-04

Incident Location:

65 Wesby Street, Logan

Incident Type:

Child Endangerment - Reported Disturbance Involving Minor

Summary:

At approximately 8:30 AM on December 25, 1987, the Logan Police Department responded to a report from a concerned neighbour regarding a potentially dangerous situation at 65 Wesby Street. The caller reported witnessing a young boy dangling a baby from the balcony of the two-story residence.

Details of Incident:

Upon arrival at the scene, officers observed that the situation had already been defused by the adults in the home. The child, later identified as Dean Coopla (age 10), had been holding an infant, referred to as Hank Johnson (6 months old), over the balcony railing. The baby was reportedly crying during the incident. Family members, alerted by the commotion, had rushed to the balcony and retrieved the infant from Dean's grasp before any harm occurred.

As is standard procedure in cases of child endangerment, we conducted an initial interview with the suspect, Dean Coopla. During the interview, Dean displayed signs of distress, crying and visibly shaking. He had a noticeable cut on his left shoulder. When asked about the injury, Dean claimed that the infant, Hank, had inflicted the wound by sending a knife towards him using "mind powers." Dean further explained that he had been attempting to provoke Hank into displaying these alleged abilities by shaking him. Dean stated that, out of frustration, he took the baby to the balcony and threatened to drop him if he did not "show his powers" to the others. Dean later clarified that he may have intended for Hank to "fly" using his supposed abilities. The boy was visibly remorseful and apologized repeatedly during the interview.

The adults present, identified as Mary Ann Johnson (mother of Hank), Micheal Johnson (father of Hank) and Cheryl Coopla (mother of Dean), were also interviewed. The situation was highly emotional, with Mary Ann reportedly yelling at Cheryl. It was noted that both women are sisters, adding a family dynamic to the incident.

Upon further inquiry, Cheryl Coopla disclosed to officers that she had recently gone through a divorce from her ex-husband, an individual she described as abusive. Given the young age of Dean and the emotional toll of the family's circumstances, it is plausible that this traumatic event may be affecting his behaviour, which is not uncommon in cases involving recent familial separation or trauma.

<u>Conclusion and Actions Taken:</u>

Dean Coopla was released to his mother, Cheryl Coopla, following the interview. Both parents were advised to seek professional counselling for the boy to address any potential emotional or psychological distress that may have arisen from the recent family changes. No charges were filed at this time, but a report has been documented for future reference should further incidents occur.

This case will remain on file with the Logan Police Department. The family has been referred to local child welfare services for additional support and guidance.

Officer's Signature:
Sgt. John Wilkins
Logan Police Department

Mary Ann Johnson's Diary
December 31, 1987

Tonight, we're getting ready to go to a New Year's Eve party at one of Michael's friends' place in West End. I feel a little nervous, to be honest. Ever since that incident at Christmas with Cheryl and the boys, I've been wary about taking Hank out. It was such a frightening experience, and I still can't shake the image of Dean holding Hank over the balcony. But Hank seems perfectly fine – if anything, he's as happy as ever. He keeps making those silly little faces and babbling to himself, so sweet and innocent. I remind myself that we can't shelter him forever, and he deserves to be part of celebrations. He's safe with us, and tonight should be a night of happiness, not fear.

Michael has been so excited for this party, and I think he needs a break too. His work has been demanding lately. He works for the Australian government, specifically with Medicare, reviewing and shaping new policies. It's an important role, and I'm proud of him. He's been so committed, putting in long hours to ensure that people have access to the healthcare they need. Sometimes I feel like the weight of the world rests on his shoulders, and tonight is a chance for us both to unwind and step away from it all, even if just for a few hours.

On my end, I've found myself turning to the newspapers more often, reading every article I can find on the conflict between the US and UK. I can't explain why, but it's become almost an obsession. There's something about knowing the details, understanding the gravity of it, that makes me feel more prepared, more aware. But it's also left me with a sense of dread. I worry that one day I'll open the paper to see headlines announcing an escalation, something that could potentially reach our shores and impact us here in Australia. I want Hank to grow up in a safe world, a place free from fear and conflict. It scares me to think of the world he might inherit if this situation spirals out of control.

As for Cheryl, I haven't seen her since Christmas. I still hear bits and pieces from Mum, who mentioned that Cheryl is taking Dean to see a therapist. She even sent her apologies, and I don't hold any grudge against her – I know she's struggling and that Dean needs help. But after everything that happened, I think I just need some time to process it myself. It's hard to shake off the memory of that day, and I think a little space is best for now.

Tonight, though, I'm determined to put my worries aside. It's New Year's Eve, after all, and I want to welcome the new year with hope, not fear. I'll hold my little Hank close, stand by Michael, and let myself feel the joy of the moment. Here's to a fresh start, and to the hope that 1988 brings peace, safety, and happiness for our little family and the world beyond.

THE TRIP

CSBNC Newspaper
February 26, 1991

Headline: UK Joins Soviet Union After NATO Expulsion, Cold War Tensions Reach New Heights

By Cameron Whitaker

In a stunning and unprecedented development, the United Kingdom has officially aligned itself with the Soviet Union, signalling a dramatic escalation in Cold War tensions. This alliance follows the UK's expulsion from NATO in 1987, after allegations surfaced accusing British officials of involvement in the assassination of the U.S. Vice President. The controversial move to partner with the Soviet Union has effectively shattered any remaining hopes of diplomatic reconciliation between the UK and Western allies.

The world watched as UK Prime Minister Robert Hastings and Soviet Premier Ivan Petrov signed a formal treaty in Moscow earlier this week, a symbolic and political act solidifying the UK's place within the Soviet sphere. The treaty establishes mutual defence commitments and increased economic cooperation, effectively making the UK a prominent player in the Soviet-led bloc. This alignment is viewed by experts as a turning point in the Cold War, ushering in a new phase of division and confrontation between East and West.

The ramifications of this shift are profound. For decades, the UK was a cornerstone of Western alliances, working in close coordination with the U.S. and European allies on matters of defence, economy, and foreign policy. Now, with this new allegiance, the UK has become one of the most significant powers to align with the Soviets, raising the stakes for both NATO and non-aligned nations.

U.S. officials have reacted with grave concern, describing the new alliance as a "dangerous betrayal" and warning of severe repercussions for global stability. Talks of peace, which were already fragile, now appear completely destroyed. Any hopes of diplomatic negotiation or easing Cold War tensions have been dashed, and the atmosphere is one of heightened anxiety and uncertainty. NATO has called for emergency meetings to address this shift and discuss how to respond to this unprecedented alliance.

Political analysts speculate that this alliance could spark an arms race unlike any the world has seen before. With the UK's industrial capabilities and intelligence expertise now accessible to the Soviet Union, Western leaders worry about the potential for new military advancements and increased espionage efforts. Intelligence agencies in both the U.S. and Western Europe are reportedly on high alert, anticipating a wave of Soviet-backed influence and activity.

Public sentiment around the world is one of fear and unease. Many wonder if this move is the final step toward open conflict, and if the geopolitical landscape will ever be the same. In London, Moscow, Washington, and beyond, citizens are bracing themselves, questioning what the future holds and how close the world may be to a direct confrontation.

For now, the world can only wait and watch as alliances shift, tensions mount, and the familiar dividing lines of the Cold War are redrawn. What lies ahead is uncertain, but one thing is clear: the world has entered a new, darker chapter in its history, and the road to peace feels further away than ever before.

Mary Ann Johnson's Diary
March 1, 1991

It's been almost four years since I last wrote in this diary. I can't believe it's been so long. Life just swept me up, day after day, and before I knew it, my little Hank is nearly four years old. But today, I feel like if I don't write something, I'll go mad. The news lately has me so anxious. I read in the paper about the UK joining the Soviet Union, and my heart sank. I never thought it would come to this, that two nations once so close to us would become enemies. The world feels like it's spiralling, and it scares me to think of what might happen next. Writing it down helps, somehow. Maybe by putting my fears on paper, I can clear my mind, at least for a little while.

Michael has been trying to lift my spirits. He told me he wants us to take a holiday this year, somewhere far from all the headlines and bad news. He mentioned Peru, of all places – Machu Picchu. I have to admit, the idea of being high up in the mountains, surrounded by history and beauty, sounds like exactly what we need. Even Hank is old enough for an adventure overseas. It's time for us to see a world beyond our small circle here.

Hank is growing so quickly. He speaks in full sentences now, his little voice filling the house with questions and stories. I know many parents start thinking about preschool or kindergarten at this age, but I'm just not ready. Maybe it's selfish, but I love being home with him, watching him discover the world at his own pace. And if I'm honest with myself, I still feel a lingering fear from that Christmas in 1987. What happened with Dean shook me deeply, and even now, I can't quite shake the hesitation about letting Hank be around other children too much. That incident changed so much for all of us, especially my relationship with Cheryl. We're still sisters, of course, but it's not the same.

The last time we spoke, Cheryl called me late at night, her voice thick with tears. She told me that Dean had gone to live with his father. She said it was for the best – that Dean had become too difficult to handle and that her mental health was suffering. She admitted she wasn't coping well, and though I tried to offer support, there's still a part of me that holds back. I don't want to feel that way, but something in me needs that distance, that safety.

I hope this trip Michael has planned will be good for us. Maybe a change of scenery is exactly what we need, a chance to escape the shadows of the past and the weight of the present. I want Hank to see a world full of beauty and wonder, a world worth exploring. And perhaps, somewhere along the way, I'll find a way to put these fears to rest.

Redflight Trip Planner: Machu Picchu, Peru
Dates: May 1 - May 14, 1991

Travelers: Mary Ann, Michael, and Hank Johnson

May 1, 1991 - Departure Day
Flight: Depart from Brisbane, Australia, to Lima, Peru (Layover in Los Angeles)
Airline: Qantas Airways
Flight Time: Approx. 20 hours including layover
Accommodation in Lima: Hotel La Hacienda (1 night)

May 2, 1991 - Arrival in Lima
Morning: Arrive in Lima, Peru
Activity: Relax and recover from the flight, brief sightseeing in Miraflores neighbourhood
Accommodation: Hotel La Hacienda, Lima (1 night)

May 3, 1991 - Travel to Cusco
Flight: Lima to Cusco (1-hour flight)
Airline: LATAM Peru
Accommodation: Hotel Monasterio, Cusco (2 nights)
Activity: Rest and acclimate to the altitude; light exploration around Cusco's Plaza de Armas

May 4, 1991 - Explore Cusco
Morning: Guided tour of Cusco – Sacsayhuamán ruins, Qorikancha Temple
Afternoon: Visit local markets and explore the historic centre
Evening: Relax at the hotel

May 5, 1991 - Sacred Valley Tour
Tour: Full-day tour of the Sacred Valley
Stops: Pisac Market, Pisac Ruins, Ollantaytambo Fortress

Accommodation: Overnight in Ollantaytambo at Hotel Pakaritampu (1 night)

<u>May 6, 1991 - Travel to Aguas Calientes</u>
Morning: Train from Ollantaytambo to Aguas Calientes (gateway to Machu Picchu)
Train Service: PeruRail Vistadome
Accommodation: Inkaterra Machu Picchu Pueblo Hotel, Aguas Calientes (2 nights)
Afternoon: Free time to explore Aguas Calientes, relax at the hotel

<u>May 7, 1991 - Visit Machu Picchu</u>
Morning: Early bus to Machu Picchu for sunrise view
Activity: Guided tour of Machu Picchu ruins (approx. 3 hours)
Afternoon: Free time to explore the site on their own, take photos
Evening: Return to Aguas Calientes, relax at the hotel

<u>May 8, 1991 - Second Day at Machu Picchu</u>
Activity: Optional visit to Machu Picchu again (second entrance ticket) or hike up to Huayna Picchu (advanced booking required)
Afternoon: Train back to Cusco
Train Service: PeruRail Expedition
Accommodation: Return to Hotel Monasterio, Cusco (1 night)

<u>May 9, 1991 - Free Day in Cusco</u>
Activity: Relax, visit any missed sites, and shop for souvenirs
Accommodation: Hotel Monasterio, Cusco (1 night)

<u>May 10, 1991 - Return to Lima</u>
Flight: Cusco to Lima
Accommodation: Hotel La Hacienda, Lima (2 nights)
Afternoon: Visit the Larco Museum and Barranco district in Lima

<u>May 11, 1991 - Lima Exploration Day</u>
Activity: Full day to explore Lima – Plaza Mayor, Cathedral of Lima, Magic Water Circuit

Evening: Farewell dinner in Lima

<u>May 12, 1991 - Departure Day</u>
Flight: Lima to Brisbane (Layover in Los Angeles)
Accommodation: Overnight flight

<u>May 13-14, 1991 - Arrival in Brisbane</u>
Arrival: May 14, 1991 – Return home

Cassette Recording Transcription
May 7, 1991

Location: Hotel Room, Cusco, Peru
Recorded by: Mary Ann Johnson

Soft click of the cassette recorder turning on. There's a slight rustle as Mary Ann adjusts the microphone and settles down beside Hank, who's nearly four years old. The background hum of the hotel room, faint street sounds from Cusco, and a sense of coziness fill the space.

Mary Ann: (softly) "Okay, Hank, we're recording. Can you say hello?"

Hank: (excitedly) "Hello! It's me, Hank!"

Mary Ann: (laughing) "That's right, it's you! Do you know where we are right now?"

Hank: (pauses) "Cusco!"

Mary Ann: "That's right, clever boy! And did you like the tour we went on today?"

Hank: (enthusiastically) "Yes! There were biiig rocks, and they told stories! And we saw the place where they used to have gold. So much gold, Mommy!"

Mary Ann: "I know! It was amazing, wasn't it? And what was your favourite part?"

Hank: (thinking hard) "Hmm… the stones that are like a puzzle! They fit together with no gaps. The man said it's magic."

Mary Ann: *(laughing softly)* "Well, maybe a little magic and a lot of skill. And did you like the llamas?"

Hank: *(giggling)* "Yes, they're funny! They have big teeth! Can I ride one, Mommy?"

Mary Ann: "Maybe one day, sweetheart. We'll have to ask a very nice llama if he'll let you." *(pause)* "Hank, are you happy you came here with Mommy and Daddy?"

Hank: *(excitedly)* "Yes! I like the big mountains, and it's so high up!" *(lowers voice, almost like he's sharing a secret)* "And he is… always taking care of us."

Mary Ann: "Oh?" *(curious, trying not to sound too startled)* "What do you mean by that, honey?"

Hank: *(turns slightly, looking off to his side as if addressing someone else)* "He's just here… over here." *(points next to him)* "Right there, Mommy. Why don't you say hi to, Mommy?"

Mary Ann: *(quietly, with a hint of concern)* "Hank, who are you talking to?"

Hank: *(smiling, as if it's the most normal thing in the world)* "My friend. He says he likes the mountains too."

Mary Ann: *(hesitating, slightly startled)* "Oh… okay. And what's your friend's name?"

Hank: *(shrugs, like he's thinking)* "I don't know. He didn't say yet. But he's nice, Mommy. He says he's just watching us."

There's a pause, and Mary Ann's voice is just the tiniest bit shaky when she speaks again.

Mary Ann: "Well… that's… that's nice, sweetheart." (tries to keep her tone light) "Do you want to say goodnight to your friend now? Daddy's almost done with his shower, and we should probably get you to bed soon."

Hank: (nods, speaking off to the side again) "Goodnight, friend!" (giggles softly) "He says goodnight back, Mommy."

Mary Ann: (clears throat) "Alright then, Hank. Can you say goodnight into the recorder, so you can listen to this when you're all grown up?"

Hank: (cheerfully) "Goodnight! Goodnight, Mommy! Goodnight, Daddy!"

Mary Ann: (laughing softly) "Goodnight, my little adventurer." (pause, as if collecting herself) "Alright, I think that's enough recording for now." (clicks off the cassette recorder)

The tape ends with the faint click of the stop button.

Mary Ann Johnson's Diary
May 9, 1991

Today was such a wonderful day for us, a day of freedom and exploration here in Cusco. It's been so refreshing to be away from everything and to just focus on the three of us. We spent hours wandering through the colourful souvenir shops, picking up little trinkets and gifts to bring home for family and friends. I found a beautiful jumper for Cheryl; I think she'll love it. I feel like being here, far from home, has given me a sense of calm. I've been able to let go of some of the tension I've been holding, and I feel ready to talk to my sister again, like things could be normal between us.

But as much as I've felt at peace, there's still something nagging at me about Hank. I've started noticing him talking to this "imaginary friend" of his, more often than I'd realized. Maybe he's been doing it for a while, and I just hadn't paid attention before. Michael insists it's normal, that lots of kids have imaginary friends at this age, but I can't help but feel a little responsible. Hank doesn't have real friends his age – he's been so sheltered, just with me most of the time. I've kept him from the world because of my own fears, and I wonder if that's why he's turned to this imaginary companion.

I told Michael that as soon as we're back home, I'll enrol Hank in kindergarten. It's time for him to be around other kids, to play and learn outside of our little bubble. It scares me, the thought of letting him go, even for a few hours a day. But I know it's what he needs, and it's what I need to do for him. He deserves to have friends, real ones, and I have to trust that he'll be safe and happy.

For now, though, I'm going to enjoy these last few days here in Cusco with my family. I'll keep the worries in the back of my mind and focus on the joy of seeing Hank's little face light up with wonder at every new thing. This trip has been good for us, and I'm grateful for every moment.

Newspaper Ojo
May 11, 1991

[Translated to English]

Headline: Australian 3-Year-Old Missing at Cusco Airport

By Juan Gutierrez

A three-year-old Australian boy named Hank Johnson has been reported missing in Cusco. According to statements from his mother to local police, the child was taken without her or her husband noticing while they were at the Cusco airport, preparing to depart for Lima. From there, the family was set to return to Australia to go home. Hank's disappearance occurred on May 10 around 9:15 am in the morning.

The Cusco police have launched a thorough investigation to find the boy. Authorities have not ruled out the possibility that the child may have been abducted. "We are considering all possibilities," said the local police captain. "We will not ignore the possibility that this is a case of abduction."

While the parents are devastated, they have begun offering financial rewards to local residents in the hope of obtaining any information that may lead them to their son. The police, for their part, assure that they are working tirelessly to locate the child and gather clues that could shed light on his whereabouts.

The disappearance of Hank Johnson has shocked both tourists and residents in Cusco. Authorities are seeking the community's cooperation and ask anyone with information about the boy to contact the police immediately.

Note from Maria Camargo to Pedro Camargo
May 12, 1991
[Translated to English]

Pedro,

I read the newspaper this morning, and now I know more about the
boy. His name is Hank, he's three years old, and he's from Australia.
Just as we thought, his parents are foreigners. The plan is still on track;
in a few days, you need to contact them and demand the money. Make
it a high amount, enough to get us out of this miserable life and make
us rich. They'll pay anything to get their little boy back.

The English classes we took when we were kids really paid off. But
I have to tell you, this kid is… strange. I tried to tell him that I'm his
mom's cousin and that she asked me to take care of him for a little
while. But he didn't believe me, not one bit. He keeps insisting that his
"friend" – some imaginary friend, I assume – told him I'm keeping him
away from his mom without permission. He's too young to understand
what's really happening, but he's not buying my story at all.

Honestly, I think there might be something wrong with him mentally.
He keeps talking to this "friend" who seems to be besides him. I've been
giving him fruit and milk to eat, and while he cried at first, he's actually
calmed down a bit, almost like he thinks he's safe. It's unnerving. He
even told me that his "friend" would hurt me if I didn't let him go.

Of course, nothing has happened, but I'm leaving this note for you,
just in case he says something similar to you. Don't be alarmed if he
starts talking about this invisible friend. He's just a kid with a wild
imagination, probably scared and confused.

Take care of things from here, and don't forget the plan. We need to
act smart, and in a few days, we'll have all the money we need.
— Maria

Note from Pedro Camargo to Maria Camargo
May 15, 1991
[Translated to English]

Maria,

I'm leaving you with the child. I've done everything possible to get money out of his parents, but it's not working. Their response to the police's advice is to hold back any payments. I've got a friend in the police who's pushing hard for the parents to release the funds, as he's expecting a cut, but there's no guarantee they'll give in.

It might be best to get the baby out of Cusco. The place is swarming with surveillance, and it's becoming harder to keep him hidden. Consider taking him to our leader in Bolivia – it could be safer and easier to manage there.

As for the kid, he's not causing immediate problems, but I've noticed, like you said, he's behaving strangely. He talks to himself, says odd things to his imaginary friend. I overheard him telling this invisible friend not to hurt me, claiming his parents will be coming for him soon. He's not right in the head.

I also checked the little bag the baby had with him—why didn't you? There's a cassette recording in there, some sort of tape. Maybe it's valuable. I haven't seen many of these around in Cusco. I gave it to the kid for now since he seems to enjoy playing it. It's just stupid conversations between him and his mom, nothing important, but it keeps him entertained.

If the parents don't pay soon, the cartel might decide to use the child for other purposes, like they've done in the past. It's best for everyone if they cooperate. I don't want to deal with a mentally unstable child anymore.
– Pedro

Newspaper El Popular
May 17, 1991

[Translated to English]

"Hope for Hank: Cusco Unites to Find Missing Boy"

By Raymundo Alanoca

The search for missing child Hank Johnson continues as new developments confirm the boy has been abducted. Police are tirelessly working to locate the child, who vanished days ago while traveling in Cusco with his family.

Two days ago, a chilling note was left at the hotel where Hank's parents are residing, specifying the ransom amount demanded by the kidnappers. According to sources close to the investigation, the amount requested is a staggering $1 million USD. This confirms what many feared: Hank has not simply gone missing but has been taken by individuals intent on profiting from his safe return.

The Cusco community has risen to the occasion, demonstrating an incredible spirit of solidarity. Local citizens are actively collaborating with authorities, forming organized groups to search for the boy around the clock. Volunteers patrol the streets, scour remote areas, and check potential hiding places in hopes of finding clues that might lead to Hank's recovery.

Police Chief Arnaldo García commended the community's efforts during a press briefing. "The people of Cusco have shown unwavering support. Every extra set of eyes and ears makes a difference. Together, we stand a better chance of bringing Hank home safely."

Hank's father, Michael Johnson, has been seen speaking to the public and joining the search efforts firsthand. Witnesses report seeing him walking through streets, parks, and nearby areas, tirelessly looking for his son. However, we cannot say the same for Hank's mother, who has not left the hotel since the boy went missing.

Hotel workers say that she is in a fragile mental state and prefers to remain in her room. Disturbingly, she reportedly believes that her son was abducted by demons in Cusco. According to her statements, she is convinced that Hank has been communicating with these dark beings since they arrive in Peru. While her condition raises concerns, we pray for her recovery and hope she finds strength during this difficult time.

As the hours stretch into days, anxiety grows among both residents and tourists in the city. The parents of Hank, understandably distraught, are doing what they can, despite their different approaches. Authorities urge anyone with information, no matter how insignificant it may seem, to come forward immediately.

For now, the search continues, and hope remains strong in Cusco. The eyes of an entire community—and a nation—are on this case, united in their determination to find Hank and bring him back to his family.

Stay tuned for further updates as this story develops.

If You Have Any Information:
Contact the Cusco Police Hotline: (084) 234-567

Note from Maria Camargo to Pedro Camargo
May 18, 1991

[Translated to English]

Pedro,

I can't do this anymore. I'm tired of taking care of the boy. He drives me insane with that recording of him and his mother—it's the only thing he ever plays, over and over. I can't stand listening to it anymore. And I can't even leave the house. There are people everywhere looking for him. It's impossible to go outside without feeling like someone is watching.

Today, I was contacted by the policeman you're working with, the one you sent. He came to the house, said who he was, and I believed him. He told me things about you that only I would know, so I trusted him. He looked at the boy, saw how he talks to himself, and agreed— he's mentally ill.

He said he'll come again tomorrow to take me and the boy out of Cusco and into Bolivia. I didn't know he was also working for the cartel. Is he a leader in the cartel? Why didn't you tell me? What am I supposed to do now?

I need answers, Pedro. I can't keep doing this.

– Maria

Cassette Recording Transcription
May 19, 1991

[This recording contains conversations that were originally in Spanish, as Maria and the policeman were likely speaking in their native language. Only select portions of the dialogue have been translated into English for clarity. Some sections may retain a level of ambiguity due to the original language used.]

Cassette Audio Begins with static, followed by muffled noises of movement and faint voices. The hum of a car engine grows louder. The voices become clearer.

Maria: (whispering nervously) "Is everything ready? Are you sure no one will notice us leaving? There are people everywhere during the day."

Policeman: (calm but stern) "It's fine, Maria. We're doing this at night for a reason. No one's looking for him now. We'll take him to the station where the bus is waiting. I hired it myself—it's safe, no questions asked."

Maria: (hesitant) "I don't know… I don't like this. What if someone finds out? The parents—"

Policeman: (interrupting) "They won't find out. You want to stay locked in that house forever with this… this thing? This is the only way out. Once we get to Bolivia, he's not your problem anymore."

Suddenly, the faint voice of Hank can be heard from the back seat.

Hank: (softly, almost eerily calm) "Mom and Dad aren't coming, are they?"

Maria: (startled) "What? What did he say?"

Policeman: (sighing) "Ignore him. Kids talk nonsense when they're scared."

Hank: (whispering to himself) "I think you're right."

Maria: (snapping) "Who is he talking to? He's been like this for days. He's... definitely not normal."

Policeman: (annoyed) "He's a kid, Maria. Kids make up imaginary friends. Focus. We're almost there."

The hum of the car grows louder. Tires crunch over gravel as the car speeds up.

Policeman: (speaking quickly) "We'll take a side road to avoid any checkpoints. The bus will wait near the old station."

Maria: "And you're sure the driver—"

Policeman: (cutting her off) "I told you, I hired him. He's one of ours. Now stop worrying."

Hank: (louder this time, voice unsettling) "You want to do it anyway."

Maria: (panicked) "What? What is he talking about? Hank, who are you talking to?"

Hank doesn't respond. The car falls silent except for the engine and the faint sound of static from the cassette. The tension is palpable.

Policeman: (gritting his teeth) "This kid gives me the creeps. We just need to—"

Suddenly, on the recording, there's a loud, jarring sound as the car jerks violently. The screeching of tires follows, making it clear the vehicle is swerving out of control.

Policeman: (shouting) "What the hell?! Something's pressing the gas—Maria, I can't—!"

Maria: (screaming) "Watch out! The tree—!"

The sound of a devastating crash fills the recording. Glass shatters, metal crunches, and both adults scream in pain. Then silence, broken only by the crackling of the recording and faint groans.

Maria: (whimpering in agony) "My legs… I can't move… Help me, please…!"

Policeman: (groaning, disoriented) "What… the hell just happened?"

The sound of a car door creaking open. Heavy footsteps as the policeman stumbles out.

Policeman: (panicked) "The kid… where's the kid?"

The sound of Maria gasping sharply.

Maria: (weak, horrified) "He's… he's floating… Oh, God, he's floating! Hank, stop! STOP!"

Hank: (calmly) "I'm leaving now."

Policeman: (yelling from the distance) "What the hell is he? Why isn't he hurt? HOW ARE YOU NOT HURT?!"

Hank: (calm but chilling) "My friend helped me. He says you should stop now, or he'll hurt you. Like he hurt Maria. I can't stop him anymore."

Maria screams in the background, choking on her breaths.

Maria: (fading) "Please… help me…"

Her voice cuts out abruptly. The policeman breathes heavily, his steps quickening as he fumbles for something.

Policeman: (shouting) "I don't know what the hell you are, but you're not getting away!"

The sound of a gun being cocked.

Hank: (calm but chilling) "You shouldn't do that."

Policeman: (shouting) "You, dev…"

A blood-curdling scream pierces the air, cutting off the policeman mid-sentence. The sound of a body collapsing follows. Then silence. Only the faint hum of the night remains.

The recording cuts off abruptly.

Newspaper El Popular
May 21, 1991

[Translated to English]

"A Dark Mystery: Hank Johnson Found Safe Amidst Disturbing Deaths"

By Juan Gutierrez

After days of fear and uncertainty, 3-year-old Hank Johnson has been found alive and unharmed by locals near an old bus station south of the city of Cusco. The boy was reportedly sitting calmly on one of the station's dilapidated seats, seemingly waiting for someone.

However, what should have been a moment of relief for the community was overshadowed by a gruesome discovery nearby.

Near the old bus station, police uncovered a horrific scene. Inside a bus, a decapitated man—later identified as an old bus driver—was found. Not far from the bus, a crashed car revealed further tragedy. A policeman was discovered dead, his back completely crushed, while inside the wreckage lay a 40-year-old woman who had suffocated to death, her legs broken from the impact of the accident.

Police Chief Arnaldo García described the scene as "terrible and deeply disturbing," adding that there is currently no explanation for the bizarre events surrounding the accident. Despite the horrifying circumstances, the boy was left unharmed, which only deepens the mystery. Investigators are working tirelessly to determine who could commit such heinous acts while sparing the child.

The boy has since been reunited with his parents. When questioned by police in the presence of his parents, Hank was asked about the events at the bus station and the deaths. His only response was chilling:

"My friend helped me." When pressed on who this friend was, Hank simply pointed to an empty space next to him.

The parents, visibly shaken, explained that their son had suffered a terrible traumatic experience and insisted he was too young—just three years old—to process what had happened. They prohibited the police from asking further questions and are now making immediate arrangements to return to their home in Australia.

Police speculate that the deceased individuals may have been the boy's kidnappers. However, their identities remain unknown, as the forensic investigation is still ongoing. When pressed by the media about the dead policeman, Chief García stated, "He was likely following the perpetrators and died trying to protect the child. For us, he is a hero."

While the identities of the woman and the bus driver remain unknown, authorities assured the public that they will notify relatives once forensic results provide more clarity.

As Cusco begins to return to normal, locals pray that this disturbing case does not deter travellers from visiting the region and the world-famous Machu Picchu. Tourism remains vital to the area, and the people of Cusco are eager to move forward from these tragic events.

Stay tuned to El Popular for updates as this mysterious case continues to unfold.

If You Have Any Information:
Contact the Cusco Police Hotline: (084) 234-567

Forensic Report
May 22, 1991

[Translated to English]

Prepared by Cusco Forensic Department
Case No.: 1991-CU-0521

Subject: Forensic Analysis of Fatal Accident Near Old Bus Station, South of Cusco

Incident Summary:
On May 20, 1991, three deceased individuals were discovered near an old bus station south of Cusco following a reported accident involving a crashed car and a parked bus. The victims were identified as:

- Maria Camargo, 40 years old, found deceased inside the crashed vehicle.
- Alfredo Mamani, 67 years old, discovered inside his bus, decapitated.
- Gonzalo Padilla, 48 years old, a police officer, found deceased near the crashed vehicle.

The following report details the forensic findings for each individual.

1. Maria Camargo

Condition of Body:
- Found seated in the passenger seat of the crashed car.
- Both legs were severely fractured, consistent with the impact of the crash.

Cause of death:
- Asphyxiation due to restricted airflow caused by trauma to the chest and ribcage during the accident.

Postmortem findings:
- No signs of struggle or defensive injuries. The injuries suggest she was conscious for several minutes before succumbing to her injuries.

Additional Notes:
- Seatbelt was not fastened.
- No traces of alcohol or drugs were found in toxicology tests.
- Bruising consistent with pressure on the chest indicates she likely experienced difficulty breathing post-impact.

2. Alfredo Mamani

Condition of Body:
- Found inside his bus at the driver's seat, decapitated.

Cause of death:
- Decapitation due to a sharp, clean severance at the neck.
- Evidence suggests decapitation occurred postmortem.

Additional Notes:
- The positioning of the body and absence of defensive wounds indicate he was likely subdued or unconscious before the fatal injury occurred.
- The interior of the bus showed no signs of struggle.

3. Gonzalo Padilla

Condition of Body:
- Found outside the crashed car, lying on the ground near the vehicle.

Cause of death:
- Blunt force trauma to the back and spinal column, resulting in a complete crushing of the thoracic region.

- Postmortem findings suggest a sudden and forceful impact caused the injuries.

<u>Additional Notes:</u>

The injuries are not consistent with a typical vehicular accident. The extent of the crushing damage raises questions about the nature of the force applied.

His police-issued firearm was recovered nearby, fully loaded, indicating no shots were fired before his death.

<u>General Observations:</u>

The crashed car showed no signs of mechanical failure. Forensic analysis of the vehicle indicated no tampering with the brakes or steering mechanism.

The boy, Hank Johnson, was found unharmed in the back seat. The absence of injuries to the child is unusual given the severity of the crash.

Eyewitness reports claim the child mentioned an "imaginary friend" assisting him, though this cannot be corroborated with physical evidence.

<u>Unresolved Questions:</u>

The precise nature of Alfredo Mamani's decapitation is unclear. The sharpness and precision of the injury suggest the use of a weapon or tool, though none was found at the scene.

The injuries sustained by Gonzalo Padilla are inconsistent with the crash dynamics and remain unexplained.

Maria Camargo's cause of death aligns with the crash; however, the overall context of the accident raises questions about the events leading up to it.

Conclusion:

The incident presents several inconsistencies that require further investigation. While the deaths of Maria Camargo and Gonzalo Padilla could be partially attributed to the crash, the decapitation of Alfredo Mamani and the absence of injuries to the child suggest the involvement of external factors.

Further analysis and interviews with witnesses, including the boy's family, may provide additional clarity. The case remains open, and updates will follow pending new evidence.

Prepared by:
Dr. Luis Fernandez
Forensic Pathologist
Cusco Forensic Department

Mary Ann Johnson's Diary
June 1, 1991

Tomorrow is Hank's 4th birthday. Michael and I agreed to keep it quiet—just the three of us at home. We'll probably buy a small cake and a gift, maybe some Lego. It seems to be popular with kids right now, and Hank would love it. A simple celebration feels right after everything we've been through.

This is the first time I've had the strength to write in my diary since the nightmare in Cusco, Peru. I don't even know where to begin—it was the most terrifying experience of my life. There was a time when I truly believed that aliens had taken Hank. I don't know if it was the fear, the sleepless nights, or just my mind breaking under the weight of it all, but I became convinced. The thought of aliens taking my son, of him talking to them—it distorted my reality and left me absolutely paralyzed with terror.

Michael has been begging me to go to therapy, and he's right. I need help. I've already booked an appointment with a family psychologist. I agreed to go, not just for myself but for Michael and Hank too. Michael seems so strong, but I know it's only because I've been falling apart. He's carrying both of us on his shoulders, and I can't let that continue.

We came back from Cusco three days ago. It feels surreal to be home again. We had to cancel our original travel plans because of Hank's abduction, and getting out of Peru was a nightmare. The police didn't want us to leave the country—they insisted on keeping us there for questioning. It was only thanks to Michael's connections that we managed to escape. He called some friends at the Australian embassy in Chile, and they intervened on our behalf. Thank God Michael has those government contacts. I don't know what we would've done without them.

As for Hank… he seems the same as ever, unaffected on the surface. But when we were alone yesterday, he started talking to his imaginary friend again. I don't know what came over me—I snapped. I screamed at him, told him to never talk to imaginary friends again, that they aren't real, and that it was his fault he got taken by bad people for saying such nonsense. The moment I said it, I regretted it. He looked so scared, and I hate myself for doing that to him.

Since then, he hasn't mentioned his imaginary friend—not in front of me, at least. I can only hope it stays that way. I just want things to be normal again. I want to be a good mother for him, and for Michael. I don't want to live in fear anymore.

Maybe tomorrow will be a small step toward normalcy. A birthday at home, with just the three of us, sounds like a good start.

June 2, 1991

Today was Hank's 4th birthday. As we planned, it was just the three of us—quiet and simple. I bought an ice cream cake, his favourite, and the way his little face lit up when he saw it made me feel like, for a brief moment, everything was normal again. We sang "Happy Birthday," and Hank laughed, clapping his hands excitedly. Seeing him so happy brought tears to my eyes. I think Michael noticed but didn't say anything. He knows I'm still fragile.

Hank spent most of the day playing with his new Lego set. He didn't talk to his imaginary friend today, not even once. Maybe it's finally over. Maybe all the terrible things that happened in Cusco are behind us now. I hope so.

Mom called again—she's been calling almost every hour since we got back, always asking how we're doing and when she can come see us. I told her "soon," but honestly, I'm not ready yet. We need time to settle, to process everything. Cheryl hasn't called, though. I suppose she doesn't know what to say, and I can't blame her. What could anyone say?

Something strange happened today. I found my old cassette recorder in Hank's little bag—the one he had with him in Cusco. I hadn't seen it in weeks and thought it was gone for good. But when I checked inside, the tape was missing. I asked Hank if he knew where it went, but he said he didn't know.

I've been obsessively watching the news since we got back.. There it was again today—our horrible story, though this time it was brief. Mom told me it was all over the news when it happened, and I guess I shouldn't be surprised. When we first arrived home, reporters from Brisbane even called our house. I still don't know how they got our number. Maybe it's in the Yellow Pages. I should probably check if we're listed.

They kept insisting on asking us questions or setting up a live interview. Michael handled it, thank God. He told them "no" firmly, and they left us alone. I'm grateful they respected our privacy. The last thing I need right now is to relive that nightmare in front of the world.

For now, I'm just glad we had this day together. Quiet. Simple. Safe. I hope it's the start of brighter days ahead.

SECOND FRIEND

CSBNC Newspaper
July 13, 1996

Headline: Cold War Escalates as China Joins Soviet Union in New Alliance

By Cameron Whitaker

The Cold War has taken a dramatic turn with the recent announcement that China has officially joined forces with the Soviet Union in a newly-formed alliance. This development comes just two days after a historic meeting between China's top leadership and Soviet officials, during which the two nations signed a formal pact to solidify their partnership.

With this agreement, the balance of global power has shifted. China and the Soviet Union, already influential on the world stage, now stand united with the United Kingdom, creating a formidable coalition. This alliance raises new questions about the strategic direction of NATO and the future of international diplomacy.

Thus far, NATO has not issued a formal response to the pact. Speculation is rampant about whether this silence indicates a measured approach or an underlying uncertainty in how to counter this new alliance. Analysts are divided on how NATO might respond, but all agree that the situation has escalated tensions in what was already a precarious geopolitical climate.

As the world watches, the question remains: What does this new alliance mean for the rest of the world? Only time will tell how NATO and other global powers will navigate this shifting landscape.

Mary Ann Johnson's Diary
September 15, 1996

It's been years since I've written in this diary. I found it today while packing our things. We're moving to Paddington—a nicer area and a bigger house, perfect for giving Hank more space. He's 9 years old now, and I can't believe how quickly time has flown.

I suppose I haven't felt the need to write because I've been going to therapy for years since the accident and everything that happened in Peru. Therapy has helped me so much. My therapist diagnosed me with chronic anxiety, something I hadn't understood about myself until those sessions. It's been a long road, but I've learned how to manage it.

One of the biggest issues I had was my obsessive habit of constantly looking at the news, always expecting the worst. I used to fixate on bad events in the world, convinced they were signs that something terrible was coming. I've stopped that now, though it wasn't easy. The last worldwide news I remember letting myself dwell on was two months ago, when I heard that China had joined the Soviet Union against NATO. The Cold War has been heating up again, and although it's hard not to worry, I try to remind myself that there's nothing I can do about it.

Overall, Hank has been doing well, with the exception of an incident that occurred two years ago. His school therapist says he has trouble making new friends because he lives in his own world. They think he might have ADD, which makes it harder for him to connect with others. I've tried not to let it bother me, and I'm grateful he's been getting help. Recently, he's been asking for a diary—he must have heard about it from his therapist. I finally bought him one. Maybe it will help him in the same way this diary has helped me.

As for Michael, he's become incredibly important over the past few years. He's climbed the ladder so quickly, and now he's the head of telecommunications in the state for the Labor Party, which was elected in March this year. I'm proud of him, but his work keeps him away from home most of the day. I'm the one who's always with Hank, taking him to and from primary school, making meals, and doing all the daily parenting.

I try to stay busy and take care of myself. I've been going to the gym regularly, mostly running on the treadmill. It helps clear my mind, but sometimes I feel like it's not enough. That's why I'm writing again. I haven't been to therapy in a long time—I just don't have the time anymore. But I think I need something to keep myself grounded, a way to let my thoughts out when they feel overwhelming.

So here I am again, filling these pages. I hope it helps.

Hank Johnson's Diary
September 18, 1996

Hi Diary,

Mom finally got me a diary! I've been asking her for so long, and now I have one! Roger Williams, this kid in my math class, told me diaries are good for keeping stuff out of your head. He says it helps him focus, so I thought I'd try it too. My brain feels all messy lately, like I can't think straight in class.

Roger's kind of okay. He talks to me a lot, even though I don't really talk back much. I'd rather draw in my notebook, but Roger keeps talking anyway. He's nice, so maybe he'll be my second friend.

My first friend is my shadow friend. He doesn't have a name—he doesn't like names. I tried giving him one before, but he got mad. He's been with me for as long as I can remember. He's strange, though. I can only see his hands and teeth. He says he has "shadow eyes," but I can't see them. He told me that he was probably born the same time as me because, when he "opened his shadow eyes," the first thing he saw was me. I think that's kind of cool, but also a little creepy.

I asked him what he is, but he doesn't know. He just said, "I don't know either." I also asked if he has a family, and he said, "Don't think so. I only know you. I'm connected to you somehow." That made me feel weird, like he's stuck with me forever.

He doesn't talk much. He says it makes him tired. When he does talk, it's really slow and quiet, like he's whispering. I sometimes have to ask him to say things again because I can't hear him. He doesn't show up all the time, though. He says he has to "sleep" a lot because keeping his form makes him tired.

Anyway, I like this diary already. Roger might be right—it feels good to write stuff down. Maybe I'll write more tomorrow.

Bye,
Hank

Hank Johnson's Diary
September 23, 1996

Hi Diary,

Dad is so busy all the time. He's always working, but today he came home earlier than usual. He said something that made me really happy—he's getting a computer! I love using the ones at school, even though we don't get much time on them because there are only a few. But having one at home? That's going to be amazing. I can't wait!

Dad has an important job in the government or something. I don't really care much about it. He talks about meetings and big decisions, but it's boring to me. There's also some sort of war going on that I've heard about for years. I don't understand it, and I'm not interested. Sometimes I see Mom looking at the newspaper with this really worried face. I think it's because of the war, but I don't ask her about it.

Something exciting happened today, though. I invited Roger to come over the weekend to play, and he said yes! I think I've decided he's my second friend now. I feel more comfortable with him, and I think he likes being my friend too. It's kind of nice having someone to talk to at school.

My shadow friend showed up a couple of times today. The first time was when I was drawing in my notebook. He told me I should draw him, that he deserves to be on a wall because he's a hero. He said he saved me from bad people when I was little. He's said that before, and it sort of makes sense because I think I heard Dad say something similar to Mom once. But Mom always changes the subject when I ask about it. I don't think she wants to admit what happened years ago. Honestly, I don't really remember much either.

I told my shadow friend I couldn't draw him. I knew it wasn't a good idea. Mom gets upset if I mention him, and besides, no one can see him anyway. I think he sort of understood when I said that.

Then he showed up again later, while I was eating dinner with Mom. I tried really hard not to look at him because I didn't want Mom to notice. But he was standing right next to her, with his big white teeth showing in that creepy smile. He didn't say a word, just stood there. Then, all of a sudden, he disappeared.

I'm glad he didn't stay too long. I don't think Mom can see him, but sometimes I worry she might notice me acting weird when he's around. I'll have to be careful.

Bye for now,
Hank

Cassette Recording
September 28, 1996

Cassette Audio Begins

Sound of shuffling and faint creaks, as if someone is shifting on a bed. A soft hum of ambient noise, indicating the room's quiet atmosphere.

Roger: (excitedly) "Hey Hank, this thing is cool. I haven't seen one of these in a while. I think my big brother still uses one. He doesn't allow me to use it though, he is mean to me."

Hank: (calmly) "Ah, yeah, it's been in my toy box for a long time, I only recently started playing with it. I even bought a new cassette for it."

Roger: (excitedly) "What about these other two cassettes, they look pretty old."

Hank: (calmly) "Yeah, I think they are my mom's. I think she used to record me and her talking. I will listen to them later. I thought it will be good to play it at school for that boring assignment."

Roger: (excited) "Yeah, I still don't know what I would do about that assignment. I prefer other classes. Hey! What classes do you like?"

Hank: (calmly) "I like science class."

Roger: (excitedly) "Science class was soooo cool yesterday, don't you think? I mean, did you see how the teacher made the volcano explode? It was, like, BOOM! I wish I could do that at home."

Hank: (calmly) "Yeah, it was cool. I liked it too… but I think computers are still my favourite."

Roger: "Oh yeah! The computers! I wish we had more at school. You know, sometimes I don't even get a turn 'cause everyone's hogging them. If I had a computer at home, I'd never stop playing."

Hank: (quietly) "We're getting one soon. My dad said so. He's important… or something."

Roger: (laughing) "Lucky! My dad says computers are too expensive, and I need to just read more books. Books are boring! Computers are the best. What are you gonna do with yours?"

Hank: "Maybe play some games… or draw things."

Roger: "Like your little notebook drawings? Those are pretty cool, Hank. I saw the monster one you did last week. Kinda creepy, but cool."

(Hank pauses, then speaks a little quieter.)

Hank: "Hey… Roger… can I tell you a secret?"

Roger: (excited) "Ooooh, a secret? Yeah, of course! I won't tell anyone, promise."

Hank: (whispering) "Remember I told you, you are my second friend?"

Roger: (whispering) "Yeah."

Hank: (whispering) "The monster I drew the other day, is my shadow friend… he's my first friend. You can't tell anyone, okay?"

Roger: (pausing, then whispering back) "Your shadow friend? What's that? Like, your imaginary friend or something?"

Hank: "Kinda… but not really. He's… real. Just no one else can see him. Only me."

Roger: (sounding intrigued) "Whoa… like, for real? What's his name?"

Hank: (quickly) "He doesn't like names. I tried to give him one, but he got mad. So, I just call him my shadow friend."

Roger: (serious, but still curious) "Okay… I believe you, Hank. I mean, why not? You're not the kind of kid to make stuff up. But, like… what does he do?"

Hank: (hesitant) "He doesn't talk much. And he usually shows up when no one's around… but he's always nice to me."

Roger: (whispering, playfully) "That's so weird, but also kinda cool. Don't worry—I won't tell anyone. It's just our secret, okay?"

Hank: (relieved) "Thanks, Roger. I trust you."

Roger: "Hey, does he ever, like… help you with homework? 'Cause I'd love to have a shadow friend for math!"

Hank: (smiling faintly) "No, he just watches me draw… sometimes."

Laughter from Roger, followed by faint scribbling noises, as if one of the boys is doodling on paper. The cassette audio ends with soft giggling and muffled chatter.

Cassette Audio Ends.

Mary Ann Johnson's Diary
September 30, 1996

Today has been a quiet and peaceful day—no bad news to weigh me down. Lately, I've been making an effort to focus on my mental health and, of course, Hank. I want to keep things positive for both of us.

I'm so happy for Hank; he finally has a friend he feels comfortable bringing home. His name is Roger, and he seems like a really good boy. I had met his mother once before—such a lovely woman who works as a nurse. Roger and Hank spent last Saturday together, and it was heartwarming to see Hank smiling and interacting so naturally.

When I asked Hank what he and Roger talked about, he was reserved. He just said Roger was "friendly" and called him his "second friend." That caught my attention, so I asked who the first friend was. Hank turned bright red, mumbled something I couldn't catch, and quickly disappeared into his room. It worried me for a moment, but then I decided it wasn't worth overthinking. Kids have their secrets, and he seemed more embarrassed than troubled.

On another note, I've been wondering if I might be able to return to work now. Hank is old enough to stay home alone for a few hours, and I've been feeling this growing itch to finally do something with my law degree. It's been sitting dormant for so long. Could it be time? I'm not sure, but the thought of picking it back up excites and terrifies me all at once.

Michael surprised us today by bringing home a computer for Hank, complete with a new game. It's some kind of fictional adventure game, but I noticed it seemed a bit violent. I asked Michael why he couldn't pick something more age-appropriate. He brushed it off, saying this is what all the kids are into these days. Hank, of course, was thrilled—he was glued to the screen as soon as it was set up.

Now I'm faced with the challenge of managing Hank's screen time. I already have so much to think about, and this feels like one more thing on my plate. I hope this game doesn't influence him in the wrong way. Maybe I'm overreacting, but I can't help worrying.

Still, today was a good day. A calm day. I'll take that as a blessing.

October 1, 1996

Mom called today in tears to tell me that Sanson, our old family dog, passed away. Poor Sanson—he was such a big part of my childhood with Cheryl. I feel sad about it, but honestly, I wish Mom would call me for something other than bad news. It's always someone passing away or another piece of drama about Cheryl.

Speaking of Cheryl, Mom mentioned she's been dating someone new and has left the boys she's supposed to be taking care of to fend for themselves again. Those poor boys—they've practically raised themselves and are now working long hours to survive, according to Mom. Shane and Matthew, who are 21 and 24 respectively, didn't pursue their studies and are still working at Big W. It breaks my heart, but what can I do? Cheryl has always been reckless, and I've learned that I can't fix her. And then there's Dean who should be 19 years old. I still worry about him. He's with his dad, and none of us have seen him in such a long time. I wonder how he's doing. Is he happy? Is he safe?

On top of all that, Hank worried me today. When we came home, he seemed more reserved than ever. His eyes were red, as if he'd been crying, but he wouldn't tell me why. He just went straight to his room and stayed there until dinner, and even then, he barely said a word. The silence is hard to deal with.

The therapist has told me not to push him—to let him come to me when he's ready. I'm trying to follow that advice, but it's so difficult not to ask questions when I see him hurting. I think I'll reach out to someone at his school to see if anything happened there. Maybe they've noticed something I haven't.

It's been an emotionally draining day. Sometimes I feel like I'm being pulled in so many different directions, but I have to stay strong—for Hank, for myself, for all the things I can't control. I just hope tomorrow is a little easier.

Sunnyvale Primary School
October 1, 1996

To: Mary Ann Johnson
Subject: Concerning Incident During Class Assignment

Dear Mrs. Johnson,

I am writing to inform you about an incident involving Hank during a class assignment today. As part of the activity, the students were asked to share something from their early childhood to present to the class. Hank chose to play a recording that he claimed was from when he was a young child.

The recording was deeply disturbing and unsettling for both the students and the staff present. Upon further discussion, it became clear that the recording had been fabricated, as Roger Williams, one of Hank's classmates, disclosed that the two of them had created it together at your home last weekend. However, Hank maintained that the recording was real and accused Roger of lying.

We received complaints from several students, and we anticipate that some parents may raise concerns as well. Given the nature of the incident, I spoke with Hank at length about the importance of honesty and considering how his actions affect others. I have asked him to take the remainder of the week off as a cooling-off period.

I also want to raise some concerns regarding Hank's overall well-being. I am aware that he attends a session with the school therapist once a week, but it may no longer be sufficient given the challenges he seems to be facing. I would strongly recommend considering private therapy sessions for Hank, which could provide more consistent and intensive support than what we can offer here. The school's resources are limited, and one session per week must be shared among all students. It's crucial that we address these issues thoroughly, especially as we all remember the incident two years ago before Hank began seeing the school therapist. We want to ensure that nothing of that nature repeats.

I kindly request that you come to the school at your earliest convenience so we can discuss this matter in greater detail. We value Hank as a member of our school community and want to work together to address this incident constructively.

Please contact the school office to arrange a time for us to meet. Thank you for your understanding and cooperation.

Sincerely,
Stephen R. Haywood
Principal
Sunnyvale Primary School

Mary Ann Johnson's Diary
October 2, 1996

I don't even know how to put today into words. My heart feels like it's been shattered into a thousand pieces, and my anxiety is clawing at me like a living thing I can't escape. It all started this morning when Hank, with downcast eyes, handed me a note from the school principal. He was not wearing his school uniform, which I found strange. It was only after reading the note that I understood why—he wasn't allowed at school.

The letter detailed something I could hardly believe: Hank had played a recording during a class assignment—a recording that apparently horrified everyone in the room. And now I learn that it was something he and Roger made as a "joke." But the most gut-wrenching part? The principal mentioned that Hank insisted the recording was real and claimed it was from when he was a child.

My mind was racing, memories I had buried, flashes of the tragedy in Peru—Could this possibly connect? I confronted Hank immediately. I demanded to know what this recording was, why he hadn't told me he had my old tape recorder—the same one I thought I had lost years ago.

At first, he wouldn't meet my eyes, but then he said he didn't know. He claimed he found the tape recorder in an old box of his toys and thought it was just another thing to play with. I wanted to believe him, but I couldn't shake the feeling that he was hiding something—or maybe he was just too scared to tell me the truth.

I asked him why on earth he and Roger thought it was a good idea to create such a thing, to scare their classmates like that. His initial silence only made me angrier. Then, finally, he muttered that he thought it would be funny, a prank to get attention. A prank! I couldn't believe what I was hearing. I reprimanded him again and again, but he just stood there, sullen and quiet, like none of it was sinking in.

I told him that from now on, there would be no more video games—especially not that violent game Michael brought home. I also made it clear that he is no longer allowed to see Roger outside of school. That boy is a bad influence, and I won't have him leading Hank down this path any further.

When I pressed him again about the tape and the recorder, he said he had thrown it away. But I didn't believe him. Why would he just throw it away? Something about it doesn't add up, and it terrifies me to think there might be more to this than he's letting on.

When Michael came home, I hoped he would back me up, but instead, he just brushed it off. He spoke to Hank, but it was a brief, half-hearted talk—nothing like the firm stance I needed him to take. Michael seemed exhausted, like the weight of work and life had drained him of the energy to care about yet another problem. I understand he's tired, but I needed his support today more than ever, and I didn't feel like I got it.

I'm sitting here now, staring at this diary, trying to make sense of all this. My mind keeps circling back to that recording. What could possibly have been on it? What could Hank have heard—or thought he heard—that made him cling to the idea it was real? And why did he think it was funny?

I feel like I'm failing as a mother. Hank is slipping through my fingers, and I don't know how to stop it. The past, the present—it's all bleeding together, and I don't know where to draw the line. I just want my son to be okay, to be happy, to be safe. But right now, I don't even know where to start.

October 3, 1996

I went to Sunnyvale Primary today, as the principal requested in the letter. Sitting across from Mr. Stephen Haywood, hearing him describe what happened, left me utterly shaken. He explained that the recording Hank played for his class wasn't just a prank—it was horrifying.

The tape apparently depicted the sounds of a car accident, complete with two adults screaming and being killed by something unseen. Hank's younger voice was on the tape too, acting as though he could see the "thing" that killed them. Mr. Haywood said the entire class was frightened, and even the staff who heard it were disturbed. He called it a terrible prank and said it would go on Hank's school record, which could affect him in the future. My heart broke when he handed me a list of phone numbers for therapists and specialists who might help.

After the meeting, I briefly spoke with the school therapist, who seemed to suggest that the move to our new house might have negatively impacted Hank. It's true that he hasn't been quite himself since we came here, but hearing her words made me feel helpless. What if moving here really was a mistake?

I couldn't even speak as I left the school. My mind kept spinning around what Mr. Haywood described. The sounds on that tape… they brought back memories I've tried so hard to bury. Could this recording somehow be connected to what we experienced in Peru? I recalled that during that time, Hank had an imaginary friend and only a few days ago, he referred to Roger as his "Second Friend." The parallels are too eerie to ignore—those dead bodies we stumbled upon, the feeling of something unseen and malevolent. But I can't remember the exact details from that day in Peru. How many people were there? How did they die? Could there still be records of it?

I resolved that I need to investigate. There must be a library or archive somewhere with newspapers from that time. I don't have any materials left from Peru—I've tried to erase all of it—but maybe there's a clue out there. Something to explain what's happening.

Back at home, Hank asked me how the meeting with the principal went. I couldn't bring myself to tell him the truth. I lied. I told him everything was fine and that I would find him a better therapist, claiming the school therapist wasn't right for him. Another lie. I didn't know what else to do—I couldn't confront him, not yet.

I told him he could return to school on Monday, but when he asked if he could see Roger this weekend, I was firm. Absolutely not. I told him he's grounded from seeing Roger indefinitely. That boy is a terrible influence, and I won't let him pull Hank into more trouble.

That's when things took a turn I can't explain. Hank glared at me, his face full of anger, and shouted, "I hate you!" Before I could respond, the lights in the house went out. The sudden darkness sent a chill down my spine. This is a brand-new house in Paddington—there shouldn't be electrical issues.

I stood frozen for what felt like an eternity before the lights came back on. When I looked around, Hank wasn't there. My heart dropped. I ran upstairs, calling his name, and found his bedroom door shut. When I opened it, he was inside, sitting on his bed, staring at the wall as if nothing had happened.

Something isn't right. It's more than a prank, more than a phase. I don't know how to help him—or if I even can. I feel like I'm losing him, and the worst part is, I'm starting to feel like I'm losing myself too.

Hank Johnson's Diary
October 4, 1996

Today was the worst day ever. Mom said I can't see Roger anymore. She said he's a bad friend, but she's wrong. He's my second friend. I messed everything up at school. I called him a liar in front of the whole class. Everyone looked at me like I was a monster.

Roger was trying to help me. He told the class we made the tape together last weekend. That wasn't true, but he was just trying to protect me. I should've gone along with it, but I didn't. Now, I can't even apologize to him. I have to see him. Maybe I can sneak out this weekend and go to his house. Mom is going to Grandma's, and Dad is always busy with work. If I tell her I feel sick, maybe she'll let me stay home alone. She said I'm old enough to stay by myself for a few hours because she's looking for a job.

Something weird happened last night. The lights went out, and I know it was my shadow friend. He was standing by the stairs, looking at Mom. I think he wanted to hurt her. I ran upstairs as fast as I could, and he followed me. He always follows me. He's stuck to me, like a shadow that's alive.

I asked him why he wanted to hurt Mom. He said he was trying to protect me, just like he always has. He said he protected me when I was little, but I don't remember. I think the tape has something to do with it.

I told him he can protect me, but he can't hurt Mom, Dad, or anyone else I care about. He said okay. Then I asked if he turned off the lights. He smiled at me with his big, sharp teeth and said yes, but he didn't know how he did it. Then he disappeared.

Cassette Recording
October 5, 1996

Cassette Audio Begins

Sound of faint shuffling and creaks, the hum of a quiet house. A faint television can be heard murmuring in another room. The sound of a tape recorder clicking on, followed by soft static.

Roger: (reassuring) "Hey, Hank, you don't have to keep saying sorry. I get it, okay? I know why you came here. It's cool, really."

Hank: (quietly) "Thanks. I just… I couldn't go to Grandma's. I told Mom I was sick, but she doesn't know I'm here."

Roger: "Yeah, I figured. Mom's working late again. It's just me and my older brother Paul. He's in his room, as usual. Don't worry, though. He won't bother us."

Sound of Hank shifting, a click as he adjusts the recorder.

Roger: (curious) "So, uh, why are you recording this? Just wondering."

Hank: (hesitant) "I don't know. I guess… I wanted it to be a hobby or something. I don't really have hobbies, you know?"

Roger: (encouraging) "That's cool. I mean, it's different. I like it."

Moment of silence, faint static from the recorder.

Roger: (lowering his voice) "But hey… about that tape you played at school. What happened to those people? Did they really die?"

Hank: (pausing, then reluctantly) "I don't remember everything. But… my first friend, my shadow friend told me. You know, the one I told you about before? I think he killed them. They were bad people, Roger. I think they kidnapped me when we were overseas with my family."

Roger: (awed) "Whoa. That's insane. What else can your shadow friend do?"

Hank: (softly) "He's not always around. But when he is, he can move things. He's really strong, and… he has these sharp, white teeth."

Roger: (excitedly) "That's so cool. I wanna meet him!"

Long pause, faint shuffling as if Hank looks around nervously.

Hank: (whispering) "He's here now. He's next to you."

Roger: (giggling nervously, moving his hand through the air) "Really? Where? I don't feel anything."

Hank: (firmly) "You can't touch him. Not even I can."

Roger: (awed) "Whoa… cool. Hey, can you ask him to move the chair? The one in my room?"

Hank: (after a pause, quietly) "He says he'll do it… but only if you go knock on Paul's door. Really hard."

Roger: (hesitating) "What? No way. Paul will freak out. He told me not to bother him."

Hank: "Yeah maybe let's do something else. I don't want you to get in trouble"

Roger sighs, then there's the sound of them both getting up. Floor creaks, faint footsteps as they walk down the hall. Roger whispers nervously.

Hank: "This is a bad idea, Roger."

Roger: (whispering) "I'll do it."

Sound of a loud knock on a door, followed by silence, then angry footsteps and muffled yelling from another room. Roger and Hank run back to the bedroom, the tape recorder capturing their hurried breaths. The sound of a door slamming open echoes.

Paul: (angrily) "Roger! What the hell is wrong with you? I told you not to bother me! You little—"

Suddenly, a loud crash is heard. The sound of wood splintering and a heavy thud. Paul groans and collapses onto the floor.

Roger: (panicked) "Paul! Oh my god, Paul!"

Hank: (whispering, trembling) "The chair… he did it."

Roger's breathing quickens as he kneels by his brother. There's a long silence, filled with static and the faint sound of Paul's groans.

Roger: (shakily) "Hank… turn it off."

Sound of Hank fumbling with the recorder, and then a sharp click as the tape ends.

Cassette Audio Ends.

Paddington Police Department
Incident Report
October 5, 1996

Report Number: PP-961005-078

Reporting Officer: Officer Jonathan Reeves
Additional Officers Involved: Sergeant Linda Harper, Officer Michael Torres

<u>Incident Details</u>

Time Reported: 16:07
Reporting Party: Mary Ann Johnson
Incident Location: Paddington Police Station, 112 Main Street, Paddington
Subject of Report: Missing Person – Hank Johnson, Age 9

<u>Narrative Report</u>

At approximately 16:07 on October 5, 1996, Mary Ann Johnson entered the Paddington Police Station to report her son, Hank Johnson, missing. Mrs. Johnson was visibly distraught, shaking, and appeared to be on the verge of tears. She informed Officer Reeves at the front desk that her son had left their residence earlier in the day and had not returned.

Mrs. Johnson stated that Hank had told her he was going to his room to rest around 09:00, as he had been feeling unwell earlier. Mrs. Johnson then proceeded to visit her mother. Upon her return, she checked on him at approximately 15:30, she discovered that his room was empty and the window was open. She searched the house and surrounding area, calling out for him, but he was nowhere to be found. Mrs. Johnson emphasized that Hank had been kidnapped when he was around 3 years old in Peru. She added that in recent years, he had never disappeared like this before and described him as generally shy and introverted.

She provided the following description of Hank:

- Age: 9
- Height: Approximately 4'6"
- Weight: 80 lbs
- Hair: Brown, short
- Clothing: Last seen wearing a green hoodie, blue jeans, and white sneakers.
- Body type: Slim

Initial Police Response

At 16:15, Officer Torres was dispatched to the Johnson residence on Paddington Lane to begin a search of the immediate area. Officer Torres noted that Hank's room was neat and showed no signs of a struggle. The open window, which Mrs. Johnson mentioned, faces the backyard, leading to a quiet alley with little foot traffic.

At 16:30, Officer Reeves initiated contact with local businesses, parks, and public venues where children might frequent. Calls were made to nearby community centres, libraries, and playgrounds. Officers also began coordinating with neighbouring jurisdictions to alert them to the situation.

At 16:55, Michael Johnson, Hank's father, arrived at the police station. Mr. Johnson expressed concern but attempted to reassure his wife, who was increasingly agitated. Both parents were instructed to return home at 17:20 in case Hank returned or attempted to contact them. Officers maintained communication with the parents throughout the evening.

Search Efforts

At 17:30, officers Torres and Reeves proceeded to Paddington Mall to continue the search for Hank Johnson. Paddington Mall, being a popular hangout for local families and children, was identified as a potential location where Hank might have gone. Upon arrival, officers began a systematic search of the premises, starting with the food court. Officer Torres approached the Mall Security Desk and provided a description of Hank. Security personnel confirmed they would monitor surveillance cameras and notify officers of any sightings.

At 18:00, officers expanded the search to include Paddington Park, the surrounding streets, and the nearby Paddington Grocery Store. Patrol cars were deployed to circulate the area, broadcasting Hank's description. Officers also spoke to neighbours near the Johnson residence, though no one reported seeing Hank leave.

Resolution

At 19:13, Mary Ann Johnson contacted the Paddington Police Station to report that Hank had returned home. She explained that Hank had been with his friend, Roger Williams, and appeared unharmed, though shaken.

At 19:30, Officer Torres returned to the Johnson residence to confirm Hank's return and conduct a brief welfare check. Hank confirmed he had been with Roger but provided limited details about why he left his home without informing his mother. Roger's mother had driven Hank home.

Mary Ann Johnson expressed relief but remained concerned about her son's behaviour. She mentioned that Hank was unusually quiet and refused to answer many of her questions about the afternoon.

Follow-Up Actions

Officer Harper contacted Roger Williams's mother at 20:00 to confirm Roger's involvement. Ms. Williams apologized for the miscommunication earlier in the day and stated that Roger had mentioned being with Hank.

Officers advised Mary Ann Johnson to monitor Hank closely and contact the police if he displayed any unusual behaviour or if there were any further concerns.

The case has been classified as "Resolved – Juvenile Returned Home." However, the report will remain open for 48 hours in case additional information arises.

Reporting Officer:
Jonathan Reeves
Badge #2146
Paddington Police Department

Mary Ann Johnson's Diary
October 6, 1996

I can't shake the shock of what happened yesterday. Hank leaving the house without telling me—without a word—feels like a betrayal I never thought he was capable of. He's always been quiet, reserved, and obedient. But lately, it's like I'm looking at a stranger. I finally sat him down to ask why he left. He wouldn't meet my eyes. All he said was, "I had to see my second friend, Roger. There were things we needed to talk about."

Second friend. That phrase keeps haunting me. What does he mean by that? Is his "first friend" the imaginary one he used to talk about when he was younger? I didn't push him further because I was afraid of what he might say—or worse, what he might not say.

I called Roger's mom today, just like she asked me to last night after she brought Hank home. She was calm, almost dismissive, like there was nothing to worry about. She told me that Hank and Roger were just talking like kids their age normally do. She also said Roger confirmed it wasn't his idea for Hank to come over—Hank just showed up unexpectedly.

But then she mentioned something odd. Her older son, Paul, was at home too. Apparently, Paul had injured his head somehow during the time Hank was there, and he doesn't remember how it happened. Roger's mom brushed it off, saying it was probably nothing, but my gut tells me otherwise. Something happened in that house, and it wasn't just "kids talking."

My anxiety is worse than ever today. It's suffocating, clawing at me from the inside, just like it was back in Peru when Hank was abducted. I still remember the things I said back then—the way I screamed that demons had taken my child. I can't believe those words came out of my mouth, but my mind was in such a fragile state. I thought I had moved past that darkness, but now it feels like it's creeping back, wrapping itself around me again.

In an effort to help, I called one of the private therapists recommended by the school. Hank will start seeing them three times a week. I'll take him after school myself. Michael agreed to this plan, but he didn't seem as invested as I hoped he'd be.

In fact, Michael had the nerve to blame me for how Hank is behaving. He said I'm too overprotective, that I've been smothering Hank, and that he's at an age where he needs more freedom to have friends and explore the world. His words cut me deeply. I'm doing the best I can for our son. Can't he see that? We ended up having a big fight—one of the worst we've had in years. Michael is sleeping in the visitor room tonight, and honestly, I don't care. I feel too drained to even try to fix things with him right now.

Meanwhile, Hank has been locked away in his bedroom all day. He hasn't come out for food or said a word to either of us. He's just… there. Silent. Waiting. For what, I don't know.

I can't do this alone. I thought I was strong enough to handle anything after Peru, but this feels different. It's like the past and the present are colliding, pulling me under. I just want my son back—the Hank I knew, the Hank I raised.

But I don't know how to reach him. And I'm terrified that I might never be able to.

Hank Johnson's Diary
October 6, 1996

Mom is mad at me again. She says I can't see Roger anymore outside of school. I don't understand why. Roger is my friend. We didn't do anything bad. She doesn't listen to me. It makes me sad.

I like Dad more now. He says I can play video games when Mom is not around. He also says I can see Roger again. He told me he will talk to Mom. I hope he does because I miss Roger.

Today, my first friend came back. My shadow friend. He talked to me for a little while. I asked him why he threw the chair at Paul, Roger's older brother. He said he felt danger around Paul. He said Paul isn't family, so it was okay. He promised me he will never hurt my family. I didn't want to talk about it more, so I stopped asking.

I decided to draw instead. I drew my shadow friend. He asked me what I was drawing. I told him I was drawing him. He said he has never seen himself before. I pointed to the mirror and told him to look. But he didn't see anything in the mirror. That was strange.

Then he disappeared.

Mom says I have to see a new therapist tomorrow. I don't want to go. Therapy is boring. I hope the new therapist has candies like my old one at school. That was the only good thing about therapy.

I also have to go back to school tomorrow. I want to hang out with Roger again. But I don't know how my classmates will act. They might say something about the recording. I don't know if they will be nice or mean. I guess I'll find out.

"Nuclear Tensions Rise: Rumours of Soviet-Chinese Atomic Facilities Spark Global Concerns"

The world stands on edge once again as rumours swirl about a renewed nuclear arms race involving two of the largest remaining powers, the Soviet Union and China. Sources within NATO have reportedly revealed alarming intelligence suggesting the construction of multiple atomic bomb facilities across Soviet and Chinese territories, sparking fears of escalating tensions in an already fragile post-war world.

The Whistleblower's Revelations

A NATO whistleblower, speaking anonymously, has disclosed that the alliance has identified at least four nuclear sites connected to the Soviet-Chinese cooperation: two currently under construction in Soviet Union territory and two reportedly operational in China.

"These are not theoretical or experimental facilities," the whistleblower said. "These sites are designed for rapid production of high-yield atomic weapons, and their locations are strategic, likely chosen to maximize defensive and offensive capabilities in the event of global conflict."

While official confirmations are absent, the whistleblower claims NATO has monitored these developments for months, suspecting covert collaboration between the Soviet and Chinese governments. This partnership, if true, could shift the balance of power and reignite fears of nuclear conflict reminiscent of the Cold War era.

NATO's Silent Preparations?

Adding to the tension, multiple sources allege that NATO itself is ramping up its nuclear arsenal in preparation for a potential escalation. A senior military official, speaking off the record, stated, "We're not blind to what's happening. If they're building bombs, we have no choice but to ensure we're prepared to defend ourselves and our allies."

This revelation has sparked controversy, with critics accusing NATO of fuelling an arms race that could spiral out of control. However, supporters argue that deterrence remains the only effective strategy in the face of such developments.

Global Reactions

So far, global leaders have remained tight-lipped on the rumours. However, political analysts note a noticeable shift in diplomatic rhetoric. Recent speeches by NATO leaders have emphasized the need for "global stability and readiness," language often associated with military preparedness.

Meanwhile, independent experts caution that if the Soviet Union and China are indeed collaborating on nuclear weapons, the implications could be catastrophic. "The Second World War nearly destroyed our world," said Dr. Elena Morozova, an expert on international relations. "The prospect of another nuclear standoff could undo the fragile unity we've been trying to rebuild."

The Public's Growing Unease

For the average citizen, the news is a chilling reminder of the instability that has defined the last decade. Many fear that the rumours, whether confirmed or not, will only heighten tensions between East and West, bringing humanity closer to the brink of destruction.

"It feels like we just got out of the ashes of the last war, and now they're ready to start the next one," said one Melbourne resident. "How much longer can we survive this?"

What Comes Next?

As the world watches and waits, one question remains: is this just a show of strength from two superpowers, or are we witnessing the early stages of a new and dangerous era of nuclear escalation?

For now, all eyes are on NATO, the Soviet Union, and China as the global community braces for what could come next. CSBNC will continue to monitor developments closely.

Stay tuned for updates as we continue to uncover the truth behind these alarming claims.

DIAVLO

Hank Johnson's Diary
December 21, 1996

I hang out with Roger a lot now. We play games on my computer. There is a Super Nintendo emulator on it, and it works great. We take turns playing, but sometimes we try to play together. It's hard because we have to share the keyboard. Four hands on one keyboard is not easy! But it's fun.

The other day, my shadow friend showed Roger he was real again. He made some kitchen stuff move and float in the air. Roger wasn't shocked this time—he's seen him do this once before—but he was still impressed. He said my shadow friend is really cool and promised to keep it a secret. I believe him. Roger is my second friend, and he wouldn't tell anyone.

The kids at school are not nice to me. Ever since the recording thing happened, they call me names like "weirdo" and don't talk to me anymore. I try not to care because I have Roger. I don't need anyone else.

I started running a lot at school. I like it. When I run, I feel free. The gym teacher said I am fast for my age. He told me to keep running because I am good at it. I think I will keep doing it.

Mom and Dad are different now. They act normal in front of me, but I know they are not happy. They don't talk as much, and they feel far away from each other. I can see it. I'm not a little kid. I know something is wrong, but they won't tell me.

Mom says Auntie Cheryl is coming for Christmas. She invited her and my cousins. I haven't seen my cousins in a long time, so I'm excited about that. I hope they are fun to play with.

Also, both my parents and Roger's parents are planning a trip to the beach in the Sunshine Coast for New Year's Eve. I've never been there before, so I think it will be fun. Roger and I can play games, and maybe we can run on the beach too.

That's all for now. Christmas is soon. I hope it's a good one.

Therapy Session Notes
December 22, 1996

Patient: Hank Johnson
Therapist: Dr. Evelyn Hart
Location: Paddington Child and Adolescent Therapy Centre, Brisbane

<u>Session Overview</u>

Hank presented as calm and cooperative during today's session. His behavior and demeanour seem typical for a child his age, though his mother has expressed concerns about his social interactions and emotional well-being. Observations suggest mild indicators of attention-deficit disorder (ADD), a condition noted in reports from previous therapists. I plan to assess this further in future sessions for confirmation.

<u>Key Discussion Points</u>

"First Friend" Mentioned:
Hank brought up his "first friend" during our conversation today. He has mentioned Roger Williams as his "second friend" in prior sessions, so I asked about the first. He hesitated before stating it was someone he knew at another school. The hesitation and lack of detail lead me to believe this may not be entirely truthful. It's possible he is reluctant to share more at this stage. I decided not to press further, as building trust is essential for him to feel comfortable revealing the truth. I encouraged him to continue expressing himself through drawing and writing in his diary, as these seem to be effective outlets for him.

Family Dynamics:
When I asked about his parents, Hank was forthright. He said, "They're not okay. I can tell." He didn't elaborate much but seemed aware of the tension between his mother and father. This level of

awareness is notable for a child his age. The potential strain in the household may be affecting Hank's mental and emotional state, so I plan to explore this further in future sessions.

Recommendations:

Continued Self-Expression:
I encouraged Hank to continue his drawing and writing in his diary. These activities appear to be therapeutic for him and may provide insights into his thoughts and emotions.

Physical Activity:
Hank mentioned he enjoys running at school and has received positive reinforcement from his gym teacher. I advised him to keep running, as it could help him channel energy and build confidence.

Parental Involvement:
It may be beneficial to have a separate session with Hank's parents to discuss their relationship and its potential impact on Hank. Addressing family dynamics could be key to his progress.

Further Assessment of ADD:
I will observe Hank's behavior in upcoming sessions and, if needed, conduct additional assessments to confirm or rule out attention-deficit disorder.

Conclusion:

Hank appears to be a bright and thoughtful child navigating challenges in his home environment. While his behavior is largely typical for his age, underlying factors such as familial tension and possible ADD warrant further attention. Building trust with Hank will be crucial in uncovering deeper insights into his thoughts and feelings, particularly regarding his mention of a "first friend."

Signed:
Dr. Evelyn Hart
Licensed Child Psychologist
Paddington Child and Adolescent Therapy Centre

Mary Ann Johnson's Diary
December 23, 1996

Today, I received a letter from Hank's new therapist, Dr. Evelyn Hart. She's asked Michael and me to come in for a conversation—just the two of us, without Hank. She said it's not urgent, but the thought of what she might want to discuss has been gnawing at me all day. Is it something Hank said? Something she noticed? I've been worrying about everything lately, and this is just one more thing added to the pile.

And then there's the news. The conflict between the Soviet Union and NATO over nuclear weapons is getting worse. Every station is saying the Cold War is about to end, but not for the better. They keep warning about the possibility of full-scale war. It's terrifying to even think about. Haven't we already lost enough? The thought of Hank growing up in a war-ridden world fills me with dread.

I've been leaning on Cheryl a lot lately. She's changed so much in the past few months, and honestly, she's been one of my only sources of comfort. She gave me some anti-depressant pills her therapist prescribed to her. Cheryl said they worked wonders for her, though she warned me they might take weeks to start working. My own therapist doesn't think medication is the right solution for me, but I disagree. I can't keep feeling this way—like I'm drowning with no way out.

Cheryl's been different, though. She's taking better care of her boys, and she's been listening to me about everything—Hank, Michael, my career. It feels like she finally understands what I'm going through, maybe because she's been through her own struggles. I invited her and the boys to spend Christmas with us. Even Dean will be coming, which I wasn't sure about at first, but the boys are older now. Hopefully, they'll behave with Hank around.

Michael has been so distant. We haven't been intimate in two months—not since the incident with Hank and the recording at school.

I love Hank so much, but I hate how his struggles have created this wall between me and Michael. It's a strange feeling, almost guilty, like I shouldn't feel this way. But I do. I need to talk to my therapist about it. I don't know how to fix things with Michael when everything else feels so broken.

My career is on pause again. I can't focus on anything with all the chaos around me. I wanted so badly to start practicing law again, to feel like I had a purpose beyond being a mother and a wife. But how can I do that when Hank needs me so much, and Michael and I can't seem to find our footing?

Christmas is in two days. I'm trying to stay hopeful, trying to hold onto the idea that having family around will make things feel a little brighter. But it's hard. Everything feels so heavy. I don't know how much longer I can carry it all.

Cassette Recording
December 24, 1996

Cassette Audio Begins

Sound of faint shuffling and creaks, the hum of a quiet house. A faint television murmurs from another room. The click of a tape recorder being turned on, followed by soft static.

Hank: (cheerful) "Okay, so you press this button to start recording. See? It's not that hard."

Shane: (laughing) "Man, I feel old. I don't think I've ever recorded on one of these. We just listened to them when we were kids."

Matthew: "Yeah, it was all about cassettes back then. Now it's CDs and computers. I didn't even know people still used these things."

Hank: (proudly) "Well, I do. I record stuff all the time. It's fun. You can even listen to it later."

Shane: "That's pretty cool, Hank. So, what else are you up to? How's school going?"

Hank: (shrugging) "It's okay. I like gym the most. The teacher says I'm fast. I run a lot."

Matthew: "Fast, huh? Maybe you'll be a sprinter one day. What about your computer games? Still playing those?"

Hank: (excited) "Yeah! I play with Roger a lot. We use an emulator to play Super Nintendo games. It's hard, though, 'cause we have to share the keyboard."

Dean: (interrupting, teasing) "Back in my day, we didn't need emulators. We just played outside."

Shane: (laughing) "Yeah, because we didn't have a computer to play on!"

Everyone laughs softly, but then Dean's tone shifts.

Dean: "Hey, Hank… do you remember the time when I held you as a baby? On the balcony?"

Hank: (confused) "No… I don't think so. What happened?"

Dean: (hesitant) "Nothing. Well… I almost dropped you. Mom and Aunt Mary Ann freaked out. I… I'm sorry about that, kid. I was just a dumb kid myself. You were so little. I guess you don't remember, huh?"

Hank: (softly) "No, Mom never told me about it."

Dean: (sighing) "Yeah, well, after that, everything went downhill for me. Mom sent me to therapy. I hated it. Then I had to live with Dad. You know what he's like? A drunk who didn't give a crap about me."

Shane: (gently) "Dean, maybe we don't need to—"

Dean: (interrupting, voice rising) "No, let me talk! You know how hard it was? All of that because of him."

Hank: (confused) "What? What did I do?"

Dean: (angry) "Everything! You don't even know, do you? Look at this."

Dean pulls his shirt down to reveal a scar on his shoulder.

Dean: "You see this? A knife, Hank. A knife that you sent flying my way when you were a baby. Mom said it wasn't your fault, but I saw it happening. You've been a freak since day one!"

Hank: (shaken) "It wasn't me. I didn't do that."

Shane: (calmly) "Dean, stop. That was years ago. Let it go."

Matthew: (whispering) "Keep it down, Dean. You're gonna wake Mom, and you know how she gets."

Dean: (mocking) "I don't care. I don't live with her anymore. What's she gonna do?"

The room grows tense as Dean steps closer to Hank. The atmosphere feels heavy.

Dean: (angrily) "You've ruined my life, Hank. And you don't even know it!"

Suddenly, the lights in the house flicker and go out, plunging the room into darkness. There's a moment of silence, then a loud scream from Dean.

Dean: (panicked, shouting) "What the hell was that?! Something is moving me!"

The lights flicker back on. Dean is no longer standing in front of Hank. He is outside the bedroom, leaning against the hallway wall, wide-eyed and pale.

Shane: (rushing to Dean) "What happened? Are you okay?"

Dean: (stammering) "I... I don't know. Something... something grabbed me and threw me out here!"

Matthew: (firmly) "Dean, that's enough. Come on, let's go. Hank, don't say anything about this. Please."

Shane: (almost begging) "Yeah, Hank, don't tell anyone. Dean's had a rough time. He doesn't need more trouble."

There's a tense pause before the sound of footsteps as Shane and Matthew lead Dean away. The room falls quiet again, except for the faint hum of the television in the background.

The recorder clicks off.

Cassette Audio Ends.

Hank Johnson's Diary
December 28, 1996

I got a new online game called "Lucifer", and it's the coolest game I've ever played! It's a multiplayer game where I can choose my character's class and level them up, get armour, and gain awesome powers. My character is a warrior, and I just got a new sword that looks like it's on fire. Roger told me he got a computer for Christmas, and now he wants his mom to get the same game "Lucifer" so we can play together online. I think playing games online with Roger would be so much fun—it's a new thing, and I can't wait for him to get it.

The other night, when Dean got mad, it was weird. I'm used to people calling me names like "weirdo" or "freak." Kids at school do it all the time, but hearing it from family felt different. It hurt. But I know what happened wasn't my fault. My shadow friend carried Dean out of the room, and I keep wondering how strong he really is.

I asked my shadow friend about it. I also asked him about what Dean said, the thing with the knife when I was a baby. My shadow friend told me it was him. He said he's the one who made the knife fly to protect me from Dean who seemed violent at that time. About carrying him out of the room, my first friend promised not to hurt my family again, but he didn't say anything about dragging them out of places. That made me laugh. He's funny sometimes.

I found my favourite pizza place! It's called Tartufo Classic Italian, and they make the best pizzas ever. My favourite is a spicy one called "Pizza Diavolo." It's super hot, but I love it.

I also decided it's time to give my shadow friend a name. I thought about it a lot, and since I love the game "Lucifer" and the pizza "Diavolo," I thought Diavolo would be a good name for him. He's all dark and kinda scary, with his sharp white teeth, but not to me. He's my friend.

When I told him the name, though, he couldn't pronounce it properly. It was like he's my age or something and couldn't say new words right. He kept saying "Diavlo, Diavlo." So, I decided that's his name now. Diavlo. He said he's okay with it.

Diavlo is a cool name. I think he likes it too.

Therapy Session Notes
December 29, 1996

Patients: Michael and Mary Ann Johnson (Parents of Hank Johnson)

Therapist: Dr. Evelyn Hart

Location: Paddington Child and Adolescent Therapy Centre, Brisbane

<u>Session Overview</u>

This special session with Michael and Mary Ann Johnson was held to address potential familial factors impacting their son, Hank Johnson. It became apparent during the session that the parents are experiencing significant relational issues that extend beyond their concerns for Hank. These unresolved tensions may be contributing to Hank's behavior and emotional well-being.

<u>Key Observations</u>

Parental Disagreements:

Michael expressed frustration with Mary Ann, stating that her overprotective parenting style is a primary reason for Hank's behavioural challenges. He believes Mary Ann's constant hovering and strictness are stifling Hank's independence and making him more socially withdrawn.

Mary Ann, in turn, remained relatively quiet in front of Michael but conveyed a sense of being misunderstood. She mentioned briefly that her actions stem from her desire to protect Hank, especially given past traumas the family has endured. However, she did not elaborate further, which may indicate she feels unable to fully express herself in Michael's presence.

Family Dynamics and Impact on Hank:

It was clear that the tension between Michael and Mary Ann is palpable, even in this setting. Their strained communication and differing parenting approaches are likely influencing the atmosphere at home. While they both affirmed their love and concern for Hank, their inability to present a united front may be causing confusion or emotional distress for him, even if he cannot articulate it.

Both parents admitted that Hank has noticed the changes in their relationship. Michael downplayed the impact, while Mary Ann seemed more aware of how their issues might be affecting their son.

Therapist Recommendations

Couples Therapy:

It is strongly recommended that Michael and Mary Ann begin attending couples therapy sessions. Their issues are not hidden from Hank, and while he may not fully understand the nuances, he is likely picking up on the discord. Addressing their own relationship challenges will create a more stable and supportive environment for Hank, which is crucial for his emotional development.

Open Communication:

Both parents should work on improving their communication, both with each other and with Hank. Family discussions, without tension or blame, could help create a sense of unity and security for Hank.

Ongoing Monitoring of Hank's Emotional Health:

Hank's therapy should continue to address his emotional and social development, but it is equally important that the home environment supports his progress. Consistency in parenting and a stable relationship between Michael and Mary Ann are key factors in ensuring Hank's well-being.

<u>Conclusion</u>

The session confirmed that the Johnsons' marital issues are contributing to the stress within the household. While they both care deeply for their son, their lack of alignment in parenting and unresolved personal conflicts are creating a challenging environment for Hank. Taking steps to address these issues through couples therapy and improved communication will benefit not only their marriage but also their son's mental and emotional health.

Signed:
Dr. Evelyn Hart
Licensed Family and Child Psychologist
Paddington Child and Adolescent Therapy Centre

Cassette Recording
December 31, 1996

Cassette Audio Begins

Sound of shuffling and faint creaks as the tape recorder clicks on. The distant hum of waves crashing can be heard through an open window. Laughter and muffled talking of adults come from downstairs.

Roger: "I like it here. The beach is so cool. Did you see the sandcastle I made earlier?"

Hank: "Yeah, it was big. The water almost got it, though."

Roger: "I know! But it's fun being near the beach. What are we doing tonight?"

Hank: "We're watching scary movies. Till late. The adults are gonna be downstairs talking and drinking forever."

Roger: "Cool. Hey, I asked my mom again about the game 'Lucifer,' but she still said no. She thinks it's bad for me."

Hank: "Don't worry. I'll give you mine."

Roger: (surprised) "What? Really? But what about you?"

Hank: "I'll just tell my dad I lost it. He'll buy me a new one. He's been saying yes to everything I want lately. It's like he wants me to like him more than Mom."

Roger: "That's kinda weird, but… cool, I guess. Thanks, Hank!"

There's a brief pause, followed by the sound of Roger shifting on a bed.

Roger: "Are your parents still fighting?"

Hank: "Yeah, I think so. They don't yell or anything, but they don't talk much. It feels weird."

Roger: "That sucks. My mom is divorced, so I get it. I don't even remember my dad. He left when I was a baby."

Hank: "That's sad. Hey, guess what? I named my shadow friend."

Roger: "Really? What's his name?"

Hank: "Diavlo."

Roger: (laughing) "That's a cool name! Where is he now?"

Hank: (matter-of-factly) "He's next to me. He's just looking at me, like he's waiting for something."

Roger: (nervous laugh) "That's creepy. Aren't you scared of him? I mean, you told me about the stuff he's done—the thing in Peru, and your mom, and even Dean, your cousin. Diavlo sounds kinda dangerous."

Hank: "No. I'm not afraid. Diavlo just wants to protect me. That's all."

Roger: (sincerely) "That's cool. I wish I had someone like that. You're lucky. You're pretty much protected forever."

Hank: (chuckling) "Yeah, I guess I am."

Roger: (excited) "Hey, let's talk to him! Diavlo, can you hear me?"

Hank: (smiling) "He can hear you."

Roger: "Okay! Hi, Diavlo! Why can't you leave Hank's side?"

Hank: (pausing as if listening) "He says he doesn't know. He's kinda attached to me somehow. He doesn't know why."

Roger: "Huh. That's weird. What else can he do? I mean, he can control lights, move stuff, and he's super strong. Is there anything else?"

Hank: (pausing again) "He says he's not sure. He's still learning what he can do, just like I'm learning new things too."

Roger: (thinking) "Maybe he's like us—like, 9 years old too. He's still a kid. I bet he'll get stronger or figure out more powers when he's older."

Hank: (grinning) "Yeah, maybe."

There's a sudden knock on the door. Both boys pause.

Hank: "That's probably Dad."

The door creaks open, and a man's voice is faint in the background.

Michael: "Pizza time, boys! I got the spicy one you like, Hank—Pizza Diavolo."

Roger: (groaning) "Aw, no! I don't like spicy! But I'll try it, I guess."

Hank: (laughing) "You'll like it. It's the best!"

The tape clicks off. Cassette Audio Ends.

Cassette Recording
January 1, 1997

Cassette Audio Begins

The faint sound of waves crashing in the distance, mixed with the hum of a quiet house. The tape clicks on, followed by soft static.

Hank: (yawning) "I'm so tired. Staying up all night was fun, though. Those horror movies were awesome."

Roger: "Yeah, I couldn't stop watching, even though some of them were so creepy. That one with the doll? I'm never looking at toys the same way again."

Hank: (laughing) "I know, right? And the one with the guy who kept showing up in mirrors? That was scary."

Roger: "Yeah, but it was cool. I don't think I've ever stayed up that late. Did you see your dad? He was so sleepy when he went to bed."

Hank: "Yeah, he couldn't keep his eyes open after midnight. The adults can't handle late nights like us."

Roger: "Ha, yeah. And the beach earlier—man, I didn't want to leave. That was the best part of this trip."

Hank: "Me neither. We swam so much, and that sandcastle we made was huge. I can't believe the waves took it down."

Roger: "Yeah, it was a bummer, but at least we had fun. This trip is the best."

There's a brief pause, and the sound of Hank shifting on the bed.

Hank: "Hey, I noticed something weird today. Diavlo wasn't around much. He came for a few minutes, but then he left again. He said he feels weaker."

Roger: (curious) "Weaker? Why?"

Hank: "He doesn't know. He told me it's getting harder for him to stay. When he's not with me, it's like he's sleeping. Or something like sleeping."

Roger: "Does he eat?"

Hank: (pausing) "I… I don't know. He's never eaten anything before. He's just… there."

Roger: "Maybe that's it! Maybe Diavlo needs to eat something. I mean, we eat to stay strong, right? Maybe he does too."

Hank: (thinking) "Huh. I never thought about that. What would he even eat?"

Roger: (excitedly) "I don't know, but we should find out! I'll help you. We can try different things—like food or… I don't know, something else. We'll figure it out."

Hank: (smiling) "Yeah, maybe. Diavlo didn't say anything about eating, though. He just said it's hard to keep his form these days. Like it takes a lot of energy."

Roger: "Well, I bet we can fix that. He's your friend, right? And friends help each other."

Hank: (grinning) "Yeah. Thanks, Roger."

The sound of footsteps passing by outside the room, followed by a faint creak of the door opening slightly. The boys fall quiet for a moment, then the door closes again.

Roger: (whispering) "Think that was your mom checking on us?"

Hank: "Probably. She always does that. She's overprotective."

Roger: (laughing softly) "Yeah, moms are like that. Anyway, let's figure out what Diavlo needs. We'll make him stronger again."

Hank: (confidently) "Yeah. Diavlo's not going anywhere. We'll help him."

The tape clicks off.

Cassette Audio Ends

Sunshine Coast Chronicle
December 3, 1997

"Mysterious Shark Attack Leaves Several Dead, Survivors Baffled"
By: Elaine Carter

The usually serene waters of the Sunshine Coast turned into a scene of horror yesterday as a series of mysterious attacks left between 10 and 15 adults dead. The tragedy unfolded near Mooloolaba Beach on December 2, 1997; where families gathered to enjoy the sun and surf. Witnesses describe the incident as a sudden and violent attack by what seemed to be a shark—but the story takes a bizarre and unexplainable turn.

<u>A Day of Chaos and Courage</u>

According to witnesses, the attack began in the early afternoon when several adults, who had been swimming with their children, suddenly started screaming and thrashing in the water. Many of the children were quickly pushed toward safety by their parents, but the adults were not as fortunate.

"I was playing in the shallows when I saw adults yelling and waving us out of the water," said Roger Williams, 9, who survived the event. "They were trying to get us to run back to shore, and I didn't understand why. Then I saw the water turn red."

Another survivor, 33-year-old local resident Sarah Jensen, described the chaos as surreal. "I heard the screams, and when I turned, people were dragging their kids out of the water. It was so fast. It seemed like something huge was under the surface, but none of us actually saw a shark until it was too late."

Sarah also recounted the moment of terror when the shark's body was discovered. "After the screaming stopped, the water was quiet for a second. Then, someone saw the shark—it was floating, torn apart. Its mouth was wide open, like it had been forced that way. Its body was ripped clean in half. It didn't make any sense. No animal could do that, not even another shark."

<u>The Bizarre Discovery</u>

Rescue teams who arrived at the scene later confirmed that the body of a large great white shark was found floating not far from the site of the attack. Experts who examined the remains were baffled. The shark's jaws were unnaturally forced open, and its body was split down the middle as if torn apart by an immense force.

Dr. Peter Harmon, a marine biologist from the University of Queensland, called the discovery "unprecedented."

"A great white shark's body is incredibly strong. For it to be torn in half like this would require immense force, far beyond the capabilities of any marine predator we know," said Dr. Harmon. "We're investigating whether this could have been caused by some sort of equipment or external force, but so far, nothing adds up."

<u>Lingering Questions</u>

The deaths of the victims, the miraculous survival of the children, and the mysterious death of the shark have left the community reeling. Authorities are warning people to stay out of the water while the investigation continues. However, the lack of clear answers is sparking rumours and speculation among locals.

Some residents have suggested that this was no ordinary shark attack. "There's something strange about all this," one local fisherman said. "I've been out in these waters for 40 years, and I've never seen anything like it. It's like the shark wasn't the predator—it was the prey."

<u>A Community in Mourning</u>

The Sunshine Coast community is mourning the loss of the victims, who acted heroically to save their children in the face of unimaginable danger. Memorial services are being planned, and grief counsellors have been made available to those affected by the tragedy.

As for what truly happened in the waters of Mooloolaba, the answer remains elusive. What started as a sunny day at the beach has left behind a trail of questions, fear, and sorrow.

If you or someone you know witnessed the incident and would like to share your story, please contact Elaine Carter at the Sunshine Coast Chronicle.

Cassette Recording
January 3, 1997

Cassette Audio Begins

The faint hum of crickets chirping outside and the occasional crash of waves in the distance. The tape recorder clicks on, followed by soft static.

Roger: (voice shaky) "I still can't stop thinking about yesterday, Hank. The beach… the shark… all those people. It was horrible."

Hank: (calmly) "Yeah, it was bad. But I'm okay. You don't have to worry about me."

Roger: (confused) "How are you okay? You were in the water! You saw the shark first, right? You were closer to it than anyone!"

Hank: (hesitant) "Yeah… I saw it. I was swimming with you, and then I saw it under the water. It was so fast. It came straight at me."

Roger: "What happened? How did you get away? The shark didn't touch you."

Hank: (quietly) "I swam to the shore as fast as I could. But the shark got close. I thought it was going to bite me. I was so scared. I… I wished it was gone."

Roger: (whispering) "And then, what happened?"

Hank: (seriously) "That's when Diavlo appeared. He stopped the shark. He killed it before it could hurt me."

Roger: (shocked) "Wait, Diavlo killed the shark?!"

Hank: "Yeah. He tore it apart, Roger. He saved me. But… that's not all."

Roger: (nervously) "What else happened?"

Hank: "By the time Diavlo killed the shark, I was near the other adults. They were all trying to push us kids to shore, yelling and scared. But everything was confusing, and I… I wished they were gone too."

Roger: (softly) "Hank…"

Hank: "Then it happened. The adults… they started dying, one by one. I thought it was the shark at first, but now I'm not sure. I think… I think Diavlo did it."

There's a long pause, and the faint sound of Roger shifting nervously.

Roger: (whispering) "You think Diavlo killed them? Not the shark?"

Hank: "Yeah. It's like he did what I wanted. First the shark, then the adults. It's… it's weird. And today, he's been around me almost all day. He's stronger now. I can feel it."

Roger: (scared) "Hank, that's scary. Are you sure he's safe? Diavlo's dangerous."

Hank: (calmly) "He's not dangerous to me. He only wants to protect me."

Roger: (thinking) "But what if… what if Diavlo gets stronger by killing? The shark, the adults… maybe that's what gives him power. Food or energy or something."

Hank: "Maybe. I asked him about it earlier. He said he felt stronger only after I wished for the shark and the adults to be gone. It's like he's connected to what I want."

Roger: (whispering) "That's… really weird. And scary."

Hank: (seriously) "Yeah, but he's my friend. He won't hurt me."

Suddenly, the door creaks open, and a woman's voice interrupts them.

Mary Ann: (firmly) "Hank, Roger, it's late. You two need to go to bed now. No more talking."

Roger: (quickly) "Okay, Mrs. Johnson."

Hank: (quietly) "Goodnight, Mom."

The sound of the door closing, followed by silence for a few moments. The tape recorder clicks off.

Cassette Audio Ends

Forensic Report
January 4, 1997

Sunshine Coast Coroner's Office

Subject: Investigation into the Deaths of 15 Adults in Mooloolaba Shark Incident

<u>Overview of Incident</u>

On January 2, 1997, 15 adults were reported deceased following a suspected shark attack at Mooloolaba Beach, Sunshine Coast. Initial reports suggested a great white shark was responsible for the deaths; however, forensic examination has revealed inconsistencies with typical shark attack patterns, raising questions about the true cause of death.

<u>Victims</u>

The identities of 13 out of 15 victims have been confirmed through family contact and personal identification. The remaining two victims are currently unidentified. Efforts to locate family members or match them to missing persons reports are ongoing.

Identified Victims:

- Robert Baker (43)
- Susan Taylor (39)
- Silvia Loreal (35)
- Karen Harper (41)
- Edward Stanton (50)
- Patricia Baker (45)
- Neil Thompson (38)
- Amanda Griffiths (32)
- James Perkins (47)

- Carol Simmons (36)
- Richard Davies (40)
- Sarah Kelly (44)
- Andrew Marshall (29)

Unidentified Victims:

- Female, approximately 30-40 years old
- Male, approximately 40-50 years old

<u>Condition of the Bodies</u>

Trauma Patterns:

Most bodies exhibited severe trauma, including dismemberment of limbs and torsos.

Cuts and tears appear to have been inflicted with extreme force. The lacerations are clean in some cases, suggesting the use of immense pressure rather than natural tearing or biting by a predator.

Bite Analysis:

None of the bodies showed superficial bites consistent with a shark's jaw.

The injuries typically associated with shark predation—crushing of bone and tissue, ragged tearing—were notably absent in all cases.

Unusual Observations:

Some limbs were severed in a manner inconsistent with known predator behavior.

The bodies of several victims were found with fractures and internal injuries suggesting blunt force trauma. These injuries are not typically associated with shark attacks.

Preliminary Findings

The forensic evidence indicates that the victims did not die from shark bites or attacks, despite initial assumptions. The presence of the great white shark, found deceased and torn apart near the scene, complicates the investigation.

Shark Role:

There is no evidence of the shark interacting with the victims, the evidence suggests it was not responsible for the injuries.

Cause of Death:

The specific cause of death for the victims remains undetermined. The injuries suggest the use of immense, unnatural force, but no tools or weapons have been identified as responsible.

Environmental Factors:

No evidence has been found of additional predators or environmental conditions that could explain the nature of the injuries.

Next Steps

Unidentified Victims:

Efforts to identify the remaining two victims will continue through dental records, DNA analysis, and missing persons reports.

Further Forensic Analysis:

Conduct additional testing to determine if any environmental or chemical factors played a role in the deaths.

Review local surveillance and eyewitness testimony for further insights.

Consulting Experts:

Specialists in marine biology and forensic pathology have been contacted to provide additional input on the unusual nature of the injuries.

Conclusion

The deaths of the 15 victims at Mooloolaba Beach on January 2, 1997, remain under investigation. While a shark was initially believed to be responsible, forensic evidence does not support this conclusion. Further investigation is required to uncover the true cause of this tragedy.

Prepared by:
Dr. Eleanor Finch
Forensic Pathologist
Sunshine Coast Coroner's Office

Incident Report
January 5, 1997

Mooloolaba Police Department

Report Number: MP-970105-013

Prepared By: Detective Sergeant Ian Morrison
Location: Mooloolaba Police Station, Sunshine Coast

<u>Incident Overview</u>

On January 2, 1997, an incident at Mooloolaba Beach resulted in the deaths of 15 adults in what was initially reported as a shark attack. Forensic evidence later suggested that the injuries sustained by the victims were not consistent with a shark attack, prompting further investigation. On January 5, 1997, two children who were present during the event, Hank Johnson (9) and Roger Williams (9), were brought in for questioning alongside their parents.

Present:

Hank Johnson, 9 years old
Roger Williams, 9 years old
Mary Ann Johnson (Mother of Hank)
Michael Johnson (Father of Hank)
Rosemary Williams (Mother of Roger)

<u>Witness Statements</u>

Hank Johnson

Hank appeared calm during questioning, though his mother, Mary Ann, remained physically close to him, holding his hand tightly throughout. At one point, Hank visibly winced and complained, "Mom, you're squeezing too hard," prompting her to loosen her grip momentarily.

Hank's statement corroborated accounts from other witnesses. He stated that he and Roger were swimming in the ocean when they noticed adults yelling and moving quickly to push them toward the shore. He did not witness anything beyond what has already been reported—namely, that a shark was initially thought to be the cause of the panic.

Hank did not provide any additional details regarding the shark or the injuries sustained by the adults.

Roger Williams

Roger appeared noticeably nervous during questioning, fidgeting in his seat and avoiding eye contact at times. His mother, Rosemary, reassured him several times, encouraging him to "just tell the truth."

Roger's account was similar to Hank's. He stated that he and Hank were swimming when the adults began yelling and pushing them toward the shore. He described the water as "red" and said that he was scared but didn't see anything more than the other witnesses had described.

Roger hesitated when asked if he noticed anything unusual about the shark or the events following the attack but ultimately said, "No, I didn't see anything."

<u>Parental Observations</u>

Mary Ann Johnson:

Mary Ann appeared physically unwell during the interview. She was pale, visibly shaken, and displayed protective behavior toward Hank, holding his hand tightly throughout the questioning. She frequently interjected to clarify or reiterate Hank's statements, though her input did not add new information.

Michael Johnson:

Michael was quiet for most of the interview, offering occasional nods of support to his wife and son. He appeared calm and cooperative, though he did not speak unless addressed directly.

Rosemary Williams:

Rosemary was attentive to Roger, encouraging him to speak honestly. She seemed composed but concerned, frequently glancing at Roger during his responses.

<u>Key Observations</u>

Behavioural Notes:

Hank Johnson appeared calm but occasionally glanced at Roger as if seeking reassurance. His account aligned with other witness statements, and no additional information was provided.

Roger Williams was noticeably nervous, which could be attributed to the traumatic nature of the incident. His hesitation on certain questions raised mild suspicion but did not provide actionable leads.

Parental Dynamics:

Mary Ann Johnson's physical state and protectiveness toward Hank were noted. Her behavior, while not obstructive, suggested heightened anxiety or distress related to the event.

Rosemary Williams and Michael Johnson appeared cooperative and supportive of their children during questioning.

<u>Conclusion</u>

The statements provided by Hank Johnson and Roger Williams corroborate existing witness accounts and do not introduce new evidence. Both children stated that they were pushed to safety by adults and did not witness the full extent of the attack.

Further investigation into the incident will focus on forensic evidence and other eyewitnesses. The children's involvement in the event appears limited to their proximity to the scene, and no further questioning is deemed necessary at this time.

Prepared By:
Detective Sergeant Ian Morrison
Mooloolaba Police Department

Incident Report
January 8, 1997

Mooloolaba Police Department
Report Number: MP-970108-021

Prepared By: Detective Sergeant Ian Morrison

Location: Mooloolaba Police Station, Sunshine Coast

Incident Overview

On January 8, 1997, the Mooloolaba Police Department received new evidence related to the tragic events of January 2, 1997, at Mooloolaba Beach, where 15 adults lost their lives in what was initially reported as a shark attack. A witness, Ms. Rachel Lawson, 26, came forward with a polaroid photograph she had taken on the day of the incident. The photograph appears to capture a moment during the attack, showing a great white shark seemingly engaged in a struggle with an invisible force. In the background, a child can be seen swimming toward the shore.

Details of the Evidence

Ms. Lawson, a local resident, stated that she was sunbathing on the beach at the time of the incident. She casually took several polaroid photos of the ocean, not realizing until days later that one of the photos contained a clear image of the shark attack in progress.

The polaroid shows the shark thrashing in the water, its body positioned as if fighting against an unseen opponent. There are no other discernible figures or animals near the shark. In the background, approximately 15 to 20 meters away from the struggle, a lone child is visible, swimming hurriedly toward the shore.

<u>Investigation and Identification of the Child</u>

Police examined the photograph and were able to identify the child as Hank Johnson, 9 years old. He was a witness who was in the water at the time of the incident, alongside other children who were pushed to safety by adults.

On January 8, officers visited the address provided for the Johnson family at a beach house in Mooloolaba, where they had stayed during the holidays. Upon arrival, officers learned from Hank's grandparents, Mr. and Mrs. Ellison, that the Johnson family had returned to Brisbane shortly after the incident. The grandparents were cooperative and provided the family's Brisbane address.

<u>Next Steps</u>

Further Questioning:

Officers plan to visit the Johnson residence in Brisbane to conduct further questioning with Hank Johnson and his parents, Michael and Mary Ann Johnson, regarding the events of January 2, 1997.

Analysis of Polaroid:

The polaroid provided by Ms. Lawson will be sent to forensic analysts for further examination. The goal is to determine whether any environmental factors or anomalies might explain the unusual appearance of the shark's struggle.

Review of Evidence:

Investigators will cross-reference the new evidence with previous forensic reports, witness statements, and expert opinions to gain a clearer understanding of the sequence of events.

<u>Conclusion</u>

The discovery of this polaroid introduces new questions about the events of January 2, 1997. While initial reports attributed the deaths to a shark attack, the photograph suggests the possibility of other factors influencing the tragedy. Investigators remain committed to uncovering the truth behind this unprecedented and deeply troubling incident.

Signed:
Detective Sergeant Ian Morrison
Mooloolaba Police Department

Cassette Recording
January 11, 1997

Cassette Audio Begins

The faint hum of a quiet house, muffled noises from downstairs, and the occasional chirp of birds outside. The sound of a tape recorder clicking on, followed by soft static.

Roger: (excited) "Man, 'Lucifer' is so good. I can't stop playing it. I mean, I was up until midnight last night trying to get new armour for my character."

Hank: (laughing) "Me too! It's even better now that we can play together from our houses. I've never played a game like this before."

Roger: "Yeah, but it's way cooler being here in person. I missed hanging out like this."

Hank: "Me too. It's more fun when you're actually here. We should do this more often."

There's a pause, and Roger's tone shifts slightly.

Roger: (quieter) "Hey, Hank… sometimes I get nightmares. About the beach. About Diavlo."

Hank: (curious) "What do you dream about?"

Roger: (nervously) "I see him… in my dreams. He's… he's strangling me. I wake up scared."

Hank: (calmly) "Don't worry. I talked to him. I told him not to hurt you. He promised he wouldn't."

Roger: (hesitant) "Are you sure?"

Hank: "Yeah. He listens to me. Since the day of the attack, he's been present most of the time. I don't mind it, but sometimes he's annoying. Like when he's around my parents."

Roger: (confused) "What do you mean?"

Hank: "He asks me questions. Like, 'What are you eating? Why do you live with your parents? Why can't you go anywhere you want without permission? I want to go out. I want you to wish people gone so I can be stronger.'"

Roger: (nervously) "Wait… what? He said that?"

Hank: "Yeah. That last part made me uncomfortable too."

Roger: (sounding scared) "Hank, you know what this means, right? If he gets stronger by you wishing bad things, then you need to feed him somehow, or he might—"

Hank: (interrupting) "Might what?"

Roger: (softly) "Might die."

Hank: "I don't want to wish anyone gone. I won't. But… I need to think of a plan."

Roger: (hesitant) "Hank… maybe it's a good thing if Diavlo's gone. He could only get you in more trouble."

Hank: (quietly) "Roger…"

There's a sudden eerie silence before Hank speaks again.

Hank: (low and serious) "He's looking at you now. He's smiling at you with his teeth showing. He just said, 'Watch your mouth, boy.'"

Roger: (panicked) "Hank, stop messing with me."

The sound of the bed creaking, followed by a sudden loud rumble as if the bed is shaking violently.

Roger: (yelling) "Hank! What's happening?!"

Hank: (shouting) "Stop, Diavlo! Stop!"

The shaking stops abruptly. There's a loud knock on the door before it opens, and Mary Ann's voice cuts through the silence.

Mary Ann: (firmly) "Hank, why are you screaming? What's going on in here?"

Hank: (quickly) "Nothing, Mom! I was just excited about the new game and playing with Roger."

Mary Ann: (suspiciously) "Hank, I've told you before, I don't like that game. It's not a good influence on you boys."

Hank: (quietly) "I know, Mom. We'll stop soon."

The sound of Mary Ann sighing, followed by the door closing. The room is silent for a moment.

Roger: (whispering) "Hank, that was scary."

Hank: (softly) "Yeah... I know."

The tape recorder clicks off. Cassette Audio Ends

Mary Ann Johnson's Diary
January 12, 1997

The police from Mooloolaba came to the house today. I froze when I saw them standing at the door. Just seeing their uniforms brought all the fear back—the fear from that horrible day at the beach. I could barely breathe as they asked to speak to us. They said they had new evidence about the shark attack.

They wanted to talk to Hank again. My heart sank. Why do they keep dragging him into this? He's just a child! But I let them in, trying to stay calm. They explained they'd found a polaroid taken by someone on the beach that day. They showed the photo to us which resembled the shark struggling in the water, but it wasn't attacking anyone—it looked like it was fighting something. And there, in the corner of the photo, was Hank, swimming toward the shore.

I didn't know what to say. I stared at the photo, my hands trembling. A thousand thoughts rushed through my mind. Were they accusing Hank of something? Did they think my little boy somehow killed a shark? Or, worse, that he had something to do with those people dying? The idea was absurd, unthinkable, but the way they looked at us—like they were searching for answers they didn't want to say out loud—it terrified me.

I snapped. I couldn't help it. I told them to get out of my house. I yelled that if they wanted to talk to my son again, they better come back with a warrant. I even said I'd have a lawyer ready. And then, in my panic, I mentioned Michael—that he's important in the government. As soon as the words left my mouth, I regretted them. What if I made things worse?

After they left, I sat Hank down again. I didn't want to, but I had to. I needed to know if he saw anything else in the water that day. The memory of Peru haunted me as I asked him. I hated reliving awful times in my life, but I couldn't let this go.

Hank just looked at me with those calm, quiet eyes of his. He said, "No, Mom. I didn't see anything else." Then he went to his room, leaving me sitting there alone.

I don't know what to believe anymore.

Detective Sergeant Ian Morrison's Investigation Diaries
January 12, 1997

This morning, we went to the Johnsons' house in Brisbane to follow up on the shark attack investigation. We intended to question young Hank Johnson further and show the family the newly discovered polaroid. The photograph clearly showed the shark in a bizarre struggle in the water, appearing to fight something invisible, with Hank in the background swimming toward the shore.

Mary Ann Johnson's reaction was… explosive, to say the least. She seemed visibly distressed as soon as we explained why we were there. When we showed her the photograph, her demeanour changed entirely—she became furious. She accused us of unfairly targeting her son and practically shoved us out of the house. She told us not to return unless we had a warrant and even mentioned her husband, Michael, and his importance in the government. That comment struck me as odd and defensive, almost like she regretted saying it the moment it left her mouth.

After we left, I couldn't stop thinking about the polaroid and Hank's presence in it. The more I dwell on this case, the stranger it gets. A few days ago, I requested the department dig up any prior incidents involving the Johnson family. This morning, before heading to the Johnsons' residence, I received a file that included a newspaper article from 1991.

The article detailed an incident in Peru. Hank Johnson, just three years old at the time, had been abducted during a family trip. The story would've been unremarkable if it weren't for the bizarre details. Days after his disappearance, Hank was found unharmed near the bodies of his presumed abductors. The cause of their deaths was described as "highly unusual"—the bodies were mangled in ways that defied explanation, almost as if a wild animal had attacked them, though no animal tracks were found.

The similarities between that incident and the recent events at Mooloolaba Beach are impossible to ignore. The shark's death, the strange injuries to the victims—none of it adds up. I can't draw any conclusions yet, but my instincts tell me Hank knows more than he's letting on.

The problem is, without concrete evidence to back my suspicions, this investigation is at a standstill. We can't get a warrant based on feelings, and the Johnson family clearly isn't going to cooperate willingly. Mary Ann's outburst this morning made that clear.

Still, I'm not ready to let this go. I'm considering requesting permission from my superiors to conduct a private investigation into the Johnsons. It would need to be off the books—something discreet, without public or departmental scrutiny. If there's more to this family's story, I need to find out what it is.

For now, I'll tread carefully. Whatever is going on here, it's bigger than a shark attack.

OPERATION PEGASUS: THE CALM BEFORE THE STORM

The jet's engines hummed steadily as the team sat around the central table in the dimly lit cabin. Papers, photographs, and cassette tapes were scattered across the surface, while a digital screen displayed scanned pages from Ian Morrison's diaries. The tension was palpable as the team processed their findings.

"This is not possible," Marcus said, breaking the silence. His voice was low but firm. "How did Hank get his hands on Morrison's diaries? That man founded the entire private organization we're a part of. He was meticulous. This should've been locked away forever."

Elena adjusted her glasses, her fingers tapping rapidly on her laptop. "Meticulous doesn't even begin to cover it," she said. "I'm combing through Morrison's notes, and there's no record of them ever leaving the classified archives. Hank must've had some serious leverage to get these—or worse, he knew someone inside."

Dimitri leaned back in his chair, arms crossed over his chest. "Hank's influence runs deeper than we thought," he said grimly. "Morrison's work was sacred—untouchable. If Hank had access to that, he's been watching us, watching everyone, for decades."

Aminah picked up a photograph from the table, her brow furrowed. "It's not just the diaries," she said. "These records are damning. And this 'Diavlo'… it's not a coincidence. At first, I thought it was just a figment of his childhood imagination, but now… now I'm not so sure."

"Diavlo was real," Kira said, her voice steady but laced with unease. She held up a cassette tape labelled January 1997. "It's all here. The more I read, the more I listen, the clearer it becomes. Diavlo wasn't just an imaginary friend. He was… something else."

Jax leaned forward, his gaze fixed on the table. "Something else?" he repeated. "What are we talking about here? A spirit? A hallucination? Or something worse?"

Marcus sighed, rubbing his temples. "Whatever Diavlo is—or was—he's tied to Hank's rise to power. There's no other explanation for how one man could unite the world and end World War III. The way he consolidated power, the speed of it… it's not natural."

"What about Roger?" Elena asked. "He was Hank's best friend, right? His 'second friend,' as the diaries put it. But there's no records of him in recent years. It's like he just… disappeared."

Dimitri frowned, leaning forward to study the photograph. "I've been thinking the same thing," he said. "Roger Williams was with Hank during some of the earliest incidents, but after that, there's nothing. No records, no sightings. It's strange."

Kira narrowed her eyes. "Strange indeed," she said. "Hank was a kid back then. If Roger just vanished, someone would have noticed. His family, the authorities—someone would've raised hell. But there's no trace of him."

Aminah tapped her pen on the table thoughtfully. "It makes me wonder," she said slowly. "Did Diavlo have something to do with it? I mean, we know Hank's 'wishes' seemed to trigger Diavlo's actions. What if something happened between Hank and Roger… something Hank regretted?"

"That's a big leap. It's better if we examine all the documents. Roger might still show up in Hank's past," Jax interjected, though his tone betrayed his unease. "If Diavlo is as dangerous as these files suggest, and if he really feeds on Hank's emotions or wishes…"

Marcus cut in, his voice sharp. "Then it's something we need to figure out," he said. "Roger was part of Hank's life at a critical time. If he's gone, there's a reason— that information might still be in the files we need to explore."

The group fell into a heavy silence, each of them grappling with the unsettling implications of Roger's absence.

Elena looked up from her screen. "So, what's the next step?"

Marcus glanced at the team, his expression resolute. "We're landing in Old London soon," he said. "The base is secure, and we'll have the resources to dig deeper into this with the boss. For now, we keep analysing what we've found and continue classifying it chronologically. We need to understand how all of this fits together."

The mention of Old London brought a brief silence over the group.

"Old London," Kira said softly, almost to herself. "The first city to fall in the war. I remember watching the news when it happened. It was gone in seconds—an atomic bomb wiped it off the map."

"Now it's just ruins," Dimitri added, his voice heavy. "And our underground base beneath it."

"It's ironic, isn't it?" Aminah said. "We're investigating the man who supposedly brought peace to the world, and we're doing it from a city that was the first to be destroyed."

"Old London reminds me of Tokyo" Kira said, her voice distant. "Tokyo was the second city to fall under atomic attack during the war. I was just a kid when it happened. The city I grew up in—everything I knew—was gone in an instant."

The others turned toward her, the usual calm in Kira's voice now replaced with a quiet sadness. She continued, her gaze fixed on the cassette tape, as if speaking to it instead of the team.

"They rebuilt Tokyo after the first bombing. Called it Tokyo 2. It was supposed to be a symbol of resilience, of hope. But that didn't last. It was bombed again, just a few years later. That's when they built Tokyo 3. It was barely standing when the government decided to move everyone underground. They had intel—better than any other nation, I think. They knew the rest of the country was going to be destroyed. One city after another, all gone."

Kira's voice wavered slightly, but she pressed on. "The secret underground city… it's the only part of Japan that still exists. It's hidden, protected. Only a few people even know how to access it now. But it came too late for so many. My parents… they didn't make it. They were trying to get us to safety when the second bomb hit. I was lucky. I was taken underground with the survivors, but they…" She trailed off, her words fading into the low hum of the engines.

The team sat in silence for a moment, the gravity of Kira's story sinking in. Finally, Dimitri spoke, his voice uncharacteristically gentle. "I'm sorry, Kira. Truly. I can't imagine what that must've been like for you."

Kira looked up at him, her expression unreadable. "Thank you, Dimitri," she said softly. "But it was a long time ago. I've had a lot of time to make peace with it."

Dimitri hesitated, then added, "Before the unification of the nations… it was Russia and China that sent those bombs to Japan. My government." He shook his head, his jaw tightening. "I never agreed with them. I never saw eye to eye with what they were doing, not during the war, not ever. That's part of why I left. I couldn't… I couldn't stand by and watch them destroy everything. Innocent people, entire cities."

Kira turned to face him fully, her dark eyes meeting his. "Dimitri," she said firmly, "that was a long time ago. And it wasn't you who made those decisions. You've saved more lives than I can count since we've been working together. Don't carry the weight of what others did."

Dimitri nodded, though the tension in his shoulders didn't fully ease. "I appreciate that," he said. "But sometimes… sometimes it feels like no matter how much good I do, it'll never erase the things my country was responsible for."

Elena, who had been listening quietly, spoke up. "We've all lost something," she said, her voice softer than usual. "This war took pieces of all of us—families, homes, entire nations. The important thing is that we're here now, doing what we can to make sure something like that never happens again."

Aminah nodded in agreement, her hands still sorting through the scattered documents. "She's right. None of us can change the past, but we're here for a reason. This mission… uncovering the truth about Hank Johnson… it matters. More than anything, it matters."

Marcus cleared his throat, drawing their attention back to him. "We've all got scars," he said, his tone steady but heavy. "Some are physical, some aren't. But those scars are why we do what we do. We've seen what happens when power goes unchecked. Hank's connection with dark forces, what we are doing, we're not just uncovering history here—we're stopping a threat that could reshape the world again. And we can't afford to fail."

Kira leaned back in her seat, letting out a long breath. "You're right," she said. "We have a job to do. But… it's hard not to think about how far we've come. From Tokyo to London, from war to… whatever this is now. Sometimes it feels like the whole world is built on ruins."

Marcus looked at Kira. "That's because it is," he said. "But it's our job to make sure those ruins don't bury what's left."

The cabin fell silent again as the team returned to their work.

Marcus straightened in his seat, his tone decisive. "Let's continue examining the material. Whatever Diavlo is, whatever Hank's connection to him, we'll find out. But we need to tread carefully. The deeper we go, the more dangerous this becomes."

The team nodded in agreement, their faces a mixture of determination and unease. The jet's engines roared softly as it carried them toward their next destination, and toward answers that could change everything.

HYPNOSIS

CSBNC Newspaper
May 6, 1998

"The Soviet Union Rebrands as Russia: A New Era of Unity or Control?"

By: Cameron Whitaker

In a landmark announcement, the Soviet Union declared its dissolution and reformation into a unified nation now known simply as Russia. Under the direction of President Viktor Ivanovich Karkin, a hardline leader with a reputation for strict control and nationalistic fervour, this move is being presented as a bold step toward uniting the former Soviet republics under a single, powerful banner.

The rebranding is part of President Karkin's broader strategy to consolidate power and stabilize the region after years of cold war fragmentation. The newly unified Russia now encompasses the territories of former Soviet republics, including Belarus, Ukraine, Kazakhstan, Georgia, Armenia, Azerbaijan, Uzbekistan, Turkmenistan, Kyrgyzstan, Tajikistan, Latvia, Lithuania, and Estonia. The unification campaign, labelled the "One Russia Initiative," aims to bring these nations under a singular government structure, though not without significant resistance.

Critics argue that the move is less about unity and more about control. Reports from the region suggest that dissent within countries like Ukraine and the Baltic states has been met with harsh suppression. Many fear this is a return to the authoritarian governance that defined the Soviet Union's history.

<u>China and the UK Stay Outside the Fold</u>

Notably absent from this alliance are China and the United Kingdom, two of the most prominent players in the geopolitical landscape. While both countries are not part of Russia's new unification, they maintain a strategic alliance with Russia. This pact ensures military and economic collaboration between the three nations, a move that has raised eyebrows in the West.

China's role as a growing global power continues to influence Russia's policies, while the UK's unique position in Europe allows it to act as a mediator. Together, these alliances form a powerful bloc that NATO and its allies are watching closely.

Global Reaction

The West, particularly NATO, has expressed concern over this development. The consolidation of power in Russia, combined with its alliances with China and the UK, shifts the balance of power globally. Political analysts warn that this could further escalate tensions in an already fragile international climate.

President Karkin defended the move in a public address, stating, "We are not the Soviet Union of the past. We are a new Russia, strong, united, and committed to the prosperity of our people." Whether the world believes him remains to be seen.

CSBNC Newspaper
May 7, 1998

"China Tests Ballistic Missiles: A Provocation or a Warning?"

By: Cameron Whitaker

In a bold and highly controversial move, China launched a series of ballistic missiles into the waters near Japan yesterday. According to Chinese officials, the launches were part of a routine military test, but NATO has interpreted the act as a deliberate provocation.

The missile tests occurred in the Pacific Ocean, dangerously close to Japan's Exclusive Economic Zone (EEZ), a region already tense due to ongoing disputes over territory and resources. Japan's government condemned the action as "reckless and aggressive," demanding an explanation from Beijing.

China's Justification

A spokesperson for the Chinese government dismissed concerns, stating, "These tests are part of our ongoing efforts to modernize our defence capabilities. There is no intent to provoke or escalate tensions with any nation." However, intelligence reports from NATO suggest otherwise.

According to anonymous sources within NATO, the missile launches may be a calculated response to increased Western naval activity in the South China Sea. Some analysts believe China is signalling its readiness to defend its interests aggressively, particularly as tensions between NATO and Russia continue to rise.

NATO's Response

NATO, in turn, has wasted no time in responding. Within hours of the missile tests, a fleet of NATO battleships was deployed to international waters near China. The move is being described as a precautionary measure, but it has further inflamed an already volatile situation.

Admiral Jonathan Harkins, commander of the NATO fleet, issued a statement, saying, "While we respect every nation's right to conduct military exercises, actions that threaten regional stability will not go unanswered. NATO is committed to ensuring the safety of our allies and maintaining peace in the region."

The Risk of Escalation

This standoff between China and NATO has sparked fears of a broader conflict. With the alliance between Russia and China, and NATO increasing its military presence, the situation could escalate rapidly. Analysts warn that any misstep or miscommunication could lead to open conflict, drawing in nations from across the globe.

Japan has called for an emergency meeting of the United Nations Security Council to address the incident and de-escalate tensions. Meanwhile, China continues to defend its actions, insisting that the missile tests were purely defensive and necessary for national security.

A Fragile World

The missile tests come at a time when the world is already on edge. With Russia's recent unification efforts and its growing alliance with China, NATO and its allies are facing challenges not seen since the height of the Second World War.

As the world watches, one thing is clear: the balance of power is shifting, and the stakes have never been higher.

Therapy Session Notes
May 8, 1998

Patient: Hank Johnson

Therapist: Dr. Evelyn Hart

Location: Paddington Child and Adolescent Therapy Centre, Brisbane

<u>Session Overview</u>

It has been over a year since Hank Johnson began therapy under my care. During this time, he has shown gradual improvement in his openness, sharing more about his thoughts and experiences. However, today's session was unlike any other, leaving me nearly speechless by the end.

At the insistence of Hank's mother, Mary Ann Johnson, today's session included an attempt at hypnosis, a method I do not use lightly and only under specific circumstances. Mary Ann was adamant that Hank was either hiding something or suppressing a past trauma. She expressed a strong belief that uncovering these memories could "fix" her son.

The hypnosis session was conducted only after the appropriate legal and parental consent forms were signed, with both Mary Ann and Michael Johnson providing their authorization.

<u>Hypnosis Session Details</u>

Under hypnosis, Hank was guided through his memories, beginning with his early childhood.

Peru Incident:

Hank recalled his family's trip to Peru with vivid detail. He spoke of his abduction at the age of three, though his recollection was fragmented. He described being scared but mentioned meeting someone who made him feel safe—a "second friend" he identified as Roger, though this contradicts the timeline of when he met Roger.

Shift in Focus to "Another Friend":

As the session progressed, Hank's demeanour shifted. He began speaking about another friend, someone who had been with him long before Roger. He described this friend as strong and protective, someone who had always been there for him.

When I pressed for more details, Hank referred to this friend by name: Diavlo.

Diavlo's Nature:

Hank described Diavlo as something more than just a friend. He stated that Diavlo "feeds on bad wishes and emotions." Hank appeared calm as he explained this, as though it was a natural and unquestionable fact. He expressed a belief that Diavlo's strength came from his ability to "help" with Hank's wishes, particularly when those wishes involved wanting someone or something to go away.

Concluding the Hypnosis:

Upon hearing this, I decided to end the hypnosis session. Hank was brought back to full awareness gently and seemed unfazed by what he had shared.

<u>Therapist's Observations</u>

Hank's description of Diavlo raises significant questions about his perception of reality and his coping mechanisms. This friend, though clearly imaginary, seems to play a central role in Hank's understanding of his experiences and his emotions. The idea that Diavlo "feeds on bad wishes" may symbolize Hank's way of processing guilt, fear, or anger.

While it is too early to draw concrete conclusions, the session suggests that this imaginary friend serves as a psychological construct, possibly created to help Hank cope with past traumas, including his abduction in Peru and subsequent events.

<u>Recommendations</u>

Further Sessions:

More sessions are required to explore Hank's relationship with this imaginary friend and its implications on his mental health. It will be essential to determine whether Diavlo represents a harmless coping mechanism or something that could hinder Hank's emotional growth.

Family Involvement:

Given Mary Ann's insistence on uncovering Hank's memories, I recommend additional conversations with his parents to manage their expectations and avoid placing undue pressure on Hank.

Monitor for Patterns:

Continued observation is necessary to identify whether Hank's reliance on this imaginary figure correlates with specific stressors or life events.

<u>Conclusion</u>

Today's session provided valuable insight into Hank's inner world but also raised new concerns. Diavlo, while likely a creation of Hank's mind, holds a significant and potentially troubling role in his life. Careful and thoughtful exploration will be needed to ensure Hank's mental and emotional well-being.

Signed:
Dr. Evelyn Hart
Licensed Child Psychologist
Paddington Child and Adolescent Therapy Centre

Hank Johnson's Diary
May 9, 1998

I feel really tired today. It started yesterday after my therapist did something weird called hypnosis. I don't remember what happened, but it must've been something big because I've been feeling super sleepy since then.

I asked Diavlo if he was there when it happened. He said he was around before it started, but when the hypnosis began, he disappeared. He told me he didn't see anything during the session. It's like he was gone too. Diavlo said he came back after it was over, but even he felt tired. That's weird.

I think it's time to help him. I know he hasn't said anything, but I can feel he's not as strong as he was before. He's been quieter and not around as much. I need to feed him again, somehow.

Roger and I have a plan. Tomorrow, we're going to the park near my house. It's the one with all the birds—the ones that swoop down and peck at people on bikes. They scare everyone. Roger and I are going to try to feed them to Diavlo. Maybe that will help him get stronger again.

I hope it works. Diavlo's my friend, and I don't want him to go away.

Cassette Recording
May 10, 1998

Cassette Audio Begins

The sound of footsteps crunching on gravel, faint chirping of birds in the background, and a light breeze rustling through leaves. A tape recorder clicks on, followed by soft static.

Roger: (curious) "Hank, why are we recording this? Is it really necessary?"

Hank: (casually) "Yeah, it's for fun. We don't have to, but I like recording stuff. It's cool to listen to later."

Roger: (hesitant) "Alright, if you say so. So, where are these birds you were talking about?"

Hank: "They're usually around the big tree by the hill. Lots of people complain about them swooping and stuff. Let's check there."

The sound of footsteps grows louder as they walk toward the tree. A few birds chirp loudly overhead.

Roger: "Your mom really let you come here? She usually doesn't let you do anything alone."

Hank: (sighing) "Not really. She didn't want me to come, even though I'm ten now. She's super protective. But I complained to my dad, and they had a fight about it. After that, she let me go, but only because she was mad at him, I think."

Roger: (laughing) "Your mom's way different from mine. My mom doesn't care much as long as I'm back before dark."

Hank: "Yeah, your mom's cool like that. Mine's always watching me, like I'm still five or something."

The sound of them stopping under a tree. Birds can be heard squawking and fluttering above.

Roger: "There they are. This tree's full of them."

Hank: (looking up) "Yeah. Okay… but Diavlo's not here right now. I don't know how to call him. He just shows up whenever he wants."

Roger: "Maybe… think about the birds. Like, wish they were gone or something. Maybe that'll bring him."

Hank: (thinking) "Alright, I'll try."

There's a long pause, filled with the sound of birds chirping loudly. Then Hank speaks, his voice quieter and different.

Hank: (slowly) "He's here. He's standing right next to you, Roger. He says… you're a smart boy."

Roger: (nervous laugh) "Uh, thanks, Diavlo. I guess."

Hank: (smiling) "Okay, now I'll wish the birds were gone. Let's see what happens."

Another pause, followed by the sudden loud squawking of birds as they flutter in panic. Branches creak and crack as if under immense pressure.

Hank: (describing) "Diavlo stretched his arms—like, super long— and his hands got huge, like bigger than the tree. He grabbed the whole thing, the birds and all, and… squeezed it. Like a lemon. The tree just broke, and the birds… they're all dead now."

Roger: (shaking) "You don't need to tell me, Hank. I saw it. I couldn't see him, but... it's like the air was crushing the tree. The birds just... died."

Hank: (calmly) "Diavlo says he feels stronger now. He says thank you for that."

Roger: (to Diavlo, through Hank) "Hey, Diavlo, do you know if it's the killing that makes you stronger, or just the thought from Hank? Like, maybe you don't have to kill to feel stronger."

Hank: (pausing, as if listening) "Diavlo says... it's both. The thought from me makes him stronger, but only after it's done. So, the killing and the thought kind of... go together."

Roger: (sarcastically) "That's... great."

The sound of the boys standing in silence under the now-quiet tree. The birds are gone, the tree is creaking slightly in the wind.

Hank: (softly) "He's still here. Watching. I think he's stronger now."

Roger: "Alright, can we go now? This is kinda... freaking me out."

Hank: (grabbing the recorder) "Yeah, let's go. I think we're done here."

The sound of footsteps walking away, then the click of the recorder being turned off.

Cassette Audio Ends

Hank Johnson's Diary
May 11, 1998

Mom talked to me today. She was really mad. She said the therapist told her about what I said during the hypnosis. Something about Diavlo, and what he does, and how he feeds. I didn't know what to say, so I didn't say anything. I just stayed quiet.

Diavlo was next to me while Mom was yelling. He felt strong after the last "meal" at the park. I didn't want to think about it, and I didn't want to say anything bad because I knew he was listening too. I didn't want him to do anything to Mom.

Then Dad came home. He was mad, really mad. He started yelling at Mom. He said he never gave permission for the hypnosis. He said Mom forged his signature. I didn't know what that meant, but I think it's bad.

Dad told me to go to my room. Now I'm here, writing this. The therapist said writing helps me get rid of bad thoughts, so I'm trying.

Diavlo is still here. He's standing in the corner, just looking at me. He asked me if I was okay. I told him yes, but then he called me a liar. He looked at me for a little longer, then he disappeared.

I feel tired again. I just want everyone to stop yelling.

Cassette Recording
May 12, 1998

Cassette Audio Begins

The faint creak of a bed and the sound of muffled voices downstairs. A tape recorder clicks on, followed by soft static.

Roger: (curious) "So, why are you staying at my place for a few days? Not that I'm complaining. It's cool having you here."

Hank: (shrugging) "I don't know, really. Dad just dropped me off and talked to your mom about it. He said Mom and him need to figure some stuff out, but he didn't tell me what. Your mom's nice, though. She didn't seem to mind."

Roger: (nodding) "Yeah, my mom's chill. She likes having company. But... did something happen? Why'd your dad leave you here?"

Hank: (sighing) "Mom and Dad had a big fight. She was mad about something I said during that hypnosis thing with my therapist. She started yelling at me, but Dad got mad at her because he never gave permission for it. He said she forged his signature or something."

Roger: (thinking) "Hmm. That doesn't sound good. Maybe... maybe they're gonna get divorced."

Hank: (looking worried) "Divorced? Why would you say that?"

Roger: (quietly) "I don't know. There's this kid at school, Liam. His parents were fighting all the time, and then one day they got divorced. It's kinda the same, right?"

Hank: (frowning) "I hope not. I don't want them to split up."

There's a brief silence before Roger speaks again, trying to change the subject.

Roger: (cheerfully) "Hey, let's talk about something else. I can't wait for school to start again. Holidays are fun, but I wanna see everyone again."

Hank: (shaking his head) "I don't. The kids at school still call me names, like 'weirdo' and stuff. You're the only one who hangs out with me."

Roger: "Yeah, but gym class is fun, right? You love running."

Hank: (smiling a little) "Yeah, I do. I can't wait to run again. That's the best part."

Roger: (excitedly) "What about Lucifer? We've been playing that non-stop. I bet no one is as good as us now."

Hank: (grinning) "Yeah! The forest level is awesome. My character's almost strong enough to beat that big boss we found last night. Did you level up yet?"

Roger: "I did! I got new armour and a better sword. I can take down those wolves in two hits now."

Hank: "Cool. I'm still working on my fire spell. It's getting stronger, though. We're gonna beat that boss soon. I just know it."

The boys laugh and talk excitedly for a few moments about their game before Roger suddenly changes the topic.

Roger: (curious) "So, what was the hypnosis like? Was it weird?"

Hank: (thinking) "It was… strange. I don't remember much. I was sitting there, and the therapist started talking really slow. Then, it's like I blinked, and it was over. She said I talked about stuff, but I don't remember any of it."

Roger: (grinning) "Maybe we should try hypnosis on Diavlo!"

Hank: (looking surprised) "Hypnosis on Diavlo? Can you even do that?"

Roger: (smiling) "Why not? He's always listening, right? We could try. Maybe he'd tell us more about himself."

Hank: (nodding) "Yeah… Diavlo's here now, in the corner of your room. He's been listening to us."

Roger: (looking at the corner nervously) "What did he say?"

Hank: (pausing) "He says… it's a good idea. He wants to try it. He says he wants to know what he is, why he's always with me, and what his purpose is. He says in all the time he's been with me, he's never seen anyone else like him."

Roger: (excitedly) "Then we have to try! After dinner, we'll set it up."

Hank: "But how? I don't really know how to do it. I can't remember all the words my therapist used when she tried hypnosis on me."

There's a pause as if Hank and Roger are thinking.

Roger: (excitedly) "I remember this book my mom has on the bookshelf. I think it's about hypnosis. You know she's a nurse—maybe that book will give us instructions on how to do it."

Hank: (smiling) "Alright. Let's do it."

The sound of the boys shifting on the bed, followed by the faint sound of footsteps outside the room. The tape recorder clicks off.

Cassette Audio Ends

This is a piece of paper that seems to have been torn from a book.

Excerpt from The Psychology of Hypnosis: A Practical Guide

How to Perform Hypnosis with Words: A Step-by-Step Guide

Hypnosis is a state of focused attention and heightened suggestibility, often accompanied by deep relaxation. Using words and verbal guidance, a skilled hypnotist can lead an individual into this state to explore the subconscious or promote behavioural change. Below is a basic guide for conducting hypnosis effectively.

Step 1: Create a Calm Environment

Purpose: Minimize distractions to help the individual focus.
How: Choose a quiet room with dim lighting and comfortable seating. Ensure there are no loud noises or interruptions. The environment should feel safe and secure for the participant.

Step 2: Build Trust and Rapport

Purpose: Establish a sense of safety and cooperation.
How: Explain the process of hypnosis to the participant, emphasizing that they remain in control at all times. Address any concerns or misconceptions. Use a calm and friendly tone to foster trust.

Step 3: Use a Relaxation Induction

Purpose: Transition the participant into a state of deep relaxation.
How:
Ask the participant to sit or lie down comfortably and close their eyes.
Use calming phrases, such as:
"Take a deep breath in… and slowly let it out."

"Feel the tension leaving your body as you exhale."

Guide their attention to different parts of the body, encouraging relaxation:

"Focus on your feet. Feel them becoming heavy and relaxed. Now move up to your legs…"

Step 4: Introduce a Focus Point

Purpose: Help the participant concentrate on one thing to enhance suggestibility.

How:

Ask them to visualize something simple, like a peaceful beach or a soft light.

"Picture a soft, glowing light above you, slowly washing over you."

Alternatively, you can use a repeated phrase or object, such as:

"Focus on my voice and let all other thoughts fade away."

Step 5: Deepen the Hypnotic State

Purpose: Reinforce the state of hypnosis to access the subconscious mind.

How:

Use countdowns or repeated instructions to deepen relaxation:

"I'm going to count backward from 10 to 1. With each number, you'll feel yourself sinking deeper and deeper into calmness."

Use layered suggestions, like:

"As you feel your body relaxing, your mind becomes lighter, free to drift into a peaceful space."

Step 6: Give Suggestions

Purpose: Guide the participant toward the desired outcome or exploration.

How:

Use positive, clear, and specific language:

"You feel confident and at peace. You can explore your thoughts freely."
If exploring memories or self-discovery, ask open-ended questions:
"Think back to a time when you felt happy. What do you see?"
"Can you describe the first time you met your 'friend'?"

Step 7: Gradually Bring Them Back

Purpose: Safely transition the participant out of the hypnotic state.
How:
Use phrases to gently guide them back to awareness:
"I'm going to count from 1 to 5. As I count, you'll begin to feel awake and refreshed."
Slowly bring them back with physical cues:
"Wiggle your fingers and toes. Feel the energy returning to your body."

Step 8: Debrief

Purpose: Discuss the participant's experience to understand insights and reinforce progress.
How:
Ask how they felt during the session and if they remember anything significant.
Reassure them about the process and provide positive reinforcement for participating.

Key Points to Remember

- Stay Calm and Patient: Hypnosis is a natural process, but each individual responds differently.
- Use Positive Language: Avoid negative phrasing to ensure a constructive experience.
- Never Push Beyond Comfort: The participant should always feel safe and in control.

- Respect Boundaries: If the participant seems uncomfortable, stop the session.

Hypnosis can be a powerful tool when used responsibly. The guide above offers a structured approach for beginners but should always be adapted to the needs of the individual.

Cassette Recording
May 12, 1998

Cassette Audio Begins

The soft hum of a tape recorder starts, followed by faint shuffling sounds and the boys whispering. The creak of a bed can be heard as they settle in Roger's bedroom.

Roger: (excitedly) "Okay, Hank, are we really doing this? I mean, it's Diavlo… will it even work?"

Hank: (determined) "Yeah, we're doing it. The steps seem easy enough. We just have to follow them. Diavlo said he's curious about himself too, remember? He's okay with it."

Roger: (nervous) "Alright. Let's start then. Step one… uh, make the room calm, right?"

Hank: "Yeah, I'll turn off the light."

The sound of a switch clicks, and the room dims. Outside noises fade as the boys settle into silence.

Roger: (calmer now) "Okay. Now step two… trust. Diavlo already trusts you, doesn't he?"

Hank: (nodding) "Yeah, he's been with me forever. I told him we're just doing this to understand him better. He's okay with it."

Roger: "Alright, step three is relaxing. Does Diavlo get relaxed? Do we still do it?"

Hank: "We'll guide him anyway. Let's just talk softly. Diavlo, relax your... um... hands?"

The boys giggle softly before quieting down again.

Hank: (seriously) "Step four. Focus. Diavlo, think about me and Roger. Only us. Focus on what we're saying and nothing else."

Roger: "Good. Now step five… uh, go deeper. Let's count backward like it said in the steps."

Hank: (calmly) "Okay. Diavlo, we're counting back from ten. Each number means you'll remember more about yourself. Ten… nine… eight…"

The boys take turns counting softly, and a faint shiver in Hank's voice suggests something is happening. Then a sudden thud is heard.

Roger: (whispering) "Hank… are you ok? You just lay on the bed."

Diavlo (through Hank): (voice slow and deep) "He is not here, I am Diavlo."

Roger: (whispering) "Ok… well, I guess, let's continue. Can you hear me well?"

Diavlo (through Hank): (voice slow and deep) "I hear you."

Roger: (excited) "Okay! Diavlo, what's the first thing you remember? What did you see when you first saw Hank?"

Diavlo (through Hank): "I see a tiny face. A baby. It's Hank, staring at me. His eyes are big. Curious. He doesn't cry."

Roger: (quietly) "That's Hank, I guess… what else do you see, Diavlo?"

Diavlo (through Hank): "A room. Bright lights. A doctor. Nurses. Hank's mother is there too. She looks tired, but she's smiling."

Roger: "Can you look up?"

Diavlo (through Hank): (pausing, voice slower) "There is… something. An opening. It's bright and big, but it's closing. Slowly. I see others like me going up through it."

Roger: (whispering) "Others like you?"

Diavlo (through Hank): "Yes. I try to reach it, but I cannot. I am… attached to him, to Hank. The opening closes before I can get through."

Roger: (shocked) "That's… weird. Can you go to the incident in Peru now, Diavlo? When Hank got taken?"

Diavlo (through Hank): (calmer) "Yes… I see them. They don't seem dangerous at first. They are loud, but they do not scare us."

Hank: "You mean the people that took Hank?"

Diavlo (through Hank): (calmer) "Yes."

Hank: "Then why did you attack them?"

Diavlo (through Hank): "They tried to take us away from your parents. I saw it as danger. If he dies… I die. I cannot let that happen. I killed the man driving the car. I killed the woman beside him. Later, I killed an old man who tried to take us on a bus."

Roger: (stammering) "You… you killed them because you were scared of disappearing?"

There's a long pause. The room feels heavy, and Hank's breathing is louder now.

Hank: (firmly) "Stop. That's enough."

The sound of the bed creaking as Hank shifts. He exhales shakily.

Hank: "I thought you were protecting me because you cared about me. Not because you were scared of… of disappearing."

Roger: "Hank? What happened? It seemed like Diavlo took over your body back there."

Hank: "He did. It was strange—I was still in my own body, but I couldn't control it. I heard everything Diavlo and you said, though."

Roger: "Is he gone?"

Hank: (looking around) "Yeah... wait. No, he's up there!"

The sound of shifting as both boys look toward the ceiling.

Hank: (panicking) " Roger, he's there! He's trying to go up!"

Roger: (shouting) "Diavlo, what are you doing?"

Hank: (distant and echoing) "He said he needs to go up! There are others like him up there!"

Suddenly, the room begins to shake violently. Objects clatter to the floor, and Roger screams.

Roger: (yelling) "Hank, make him stop! My mom's screaming downstairs! She thinks it's an earthquake!"

Hank: (panicked) "Diavlo, stop! You're shaking everything!"

The rumbling continues, louder and more chaotic. Roger's voice becomes more desperate.

Roger: "Do something, Hank!"

Hank grabs a pen from the table. The sound of objects clattering stops for a moment.

Hank: (shouting) "Diavlo! If you don't stop, I'll hurt myself! You know what that means for you!"

The shaking stops suddenly. The room falls silent, except for the sound of both boys breathing heavily.

Roger: (whispering) "He stopped… Hank, are you okay?"

The tape recorder clicks off.

Cassette Audio Ends

Paddington Post
May 13, 1998

"Mysterious 'Earthquake' Shakes Single Paddington Home"

By: Sarah Collins

Last night, residents of Paddington were startled by an unusual and unexplained event at a house located on 23 Oakridge Lane. Neighbours reported that the house appeared to be shaking violently, as if struck by a localized earthquake, at approximately 9:00 PM. However, no seismic activity was recorded in the area, leaving residents puzzled and concerned.

The incident was described by several witnesses as lasting for about two minutes, during which the house visibly trembled while other homes in the area remained unaffected. The family residing at the address, the Williams, declined to comment on the event.

"I was sitting in my living room when I heard this loud rumbling," said Barbara Harris, a neighbour who lives two houses down. "I thought it was an earthquake at first, but then I realized my house wasn't moving. When I looked outside, it was just their house shaking like crazy. It was the strangest thing I've ever seen."

Another neighbour, Peter Doyle, who lives across the street, added, "I could see the lights flickering through the windows while the house shook. I almost thought it was going to collapse. My first instinct was to run over and check, but then it just stopped as quickly as it started."

While many residents are curious about the cause of the event, the Williams family has chosen not to speak with reporters. Attempts to reach them for comment were met with polite but firm refusals.

Local authorities have not issued a statement regarding the incident, and no emergency services were called to the scene. Speculation among neighbours ranges from an electrical issue to more outlandish theories, but as of now, the cause of the mysterious "earthquake" remains unknown.

Paddington residents are left with more questions than answers, and many are hoping for an explanation to put their minds at ease.

For more updates on this story, stay tuned to the Paddington Post.

Paddington Post
May 14, 1998

"Williams Family Explains Mysterious House Shaking: Plumbing to Blame"

By: Sarah Collins

After widespread curiosity and speculation regarding the unusual shaking at a home on 23 Oakridge Lane earlier this week, the Williams family has come forward with an explanation. According to Rosemary Williams, the incident was not caused by an earthquake or any mysterious forces but rather by an issue with the home's plumbing system.

"Our house is an old Queenslander," explained Mrs. Williams, referring to the classic wooden homes typical of the area. "It's been standing here for decades, and with age comes wear and tear. What happened the other night was due to something called 'Water Hammer.'"

Water Hammer, as described by plumbing experts, is a phenomenon where sudden changes in water flow can create a shockwave within the pipes, causing noise and vibrations. These vibrations can travel through the structure of a house, creating noticeable shaking or banging.

"Basically, if water is turned off quickly, like when a tap is shut too fast, the momentum of the water in the pipes can cause them to rattle and shake," Mrs. Williams added. "It's noisy, and in an older home like ours, it can feel dramatic."

Neighbours, who previously described the event as looking like a localized earthquake, were surprised by the explanation but seemed reassured by the clarification.

"I didn't even know plumbing could do that," said Barbara Harris, who lives two houses away. "I've heard the term before, but I've never seen it cause a whole house to shake like that. It's good to know there's an explanation, though."

Local plumber Mark Brennan explained the phenomenon further when contacted by the Paddington Post. "Water Hammer is more common than people think, especially in older homes where pipes might not be secured as tightly. If the water pressure is high or the pipes have aged, the shockwave can create enough force to cause significant vibrations in the house."

Mrs. Williams assured her neighbours that the issue was being addressed and that a plumber had already been contacted to inspect the house and fix the problem. "We've lived here for years, and this is the first time it's happened this badly. We're taking care of it, and there's no reason for anyone to worry," she said.

Despite this clarification, some neighbours remain sceptical, given the intensity of the shaking. "I've heard plumbing noises before," said Peter Doyle, a neighbour from across the street, "but I've never seen anything like that. Still, if that's the explanation, I hope they get it fixed soon."

With the Williams family confident in their explanation, the matter seems to have been resolved. However, the mysterious nature of the incident has left some Paddington residents with lingering curiosity.

For more updates on local events and news, stay with the Paddington Post.

Detective Sergeant Ian Morrison's Investigation Diaries
May 16, 1998

My superiors have finally given me permission to continue a private investigation on the Johnsons, though under strict conditions. First, the operation must remain completely clean—no leaks, no mistakes, and absolutely no public awareness. Second, I cannot use taxpayers' money for any part of this investigation. Every expense will come out of my own pocket. I didn't hesitate to agree. If I'm going to uncover the truth, I'll do it on my own terms, no matter the cost.

I've spent the past few months following the Johnson family closely. My observations have only added more weight to my suspicions. The first notable event was the shark attack at Mooloolaba Beach. Though I wasn't present during the incident itself, I've pieced together enough from police interviews and forensic reports to form a troubling picture. The manner in which the victims died is disturbingly similar to the events in Peru years ago. Both involve unexplained, violent deaths that defy logic. It's impossible to ignore the parallels. I don't believe in coincidences, and the fact that Hank Johnson was present at both incidents is deeply concerning.

Then there's the matter of the Williams house at 23 Oakridge Lane. On May 12, I was parked outside the residence, following a lead on Hank's whereabouts. I witnessed the event firsthand—a violent shaking, as if the house itself was convulsing from within. It wasn't subtle; the entire structure seemed to tremble as if under immense pressure. The local newspaper reported the Williams family blamed the incident on plumbing issues—something called "Water Hammer." But I know what I saw. This was no plumbing issue. This was something far stranger.

What's most important is that Hank Johnson was inside the house that night. I don't know what transpired within those walls, but I cannot ignore the pattern. Wherever Hank goes, unexplained phenomena seem to follow.

Still, I can't jump to conclusions. My suspicions aren't enough—I need hard, physical evidence. Something undeniable that ties these events together. For now, I'll continue to observe from the shadows and document everything. If there's a connection between Hank and these incidents, I'll find it.

This investigation is far from over.

MOTHER'S LOVE

Michael and I are separated. Not officially, but it feels like it. We're still living under the same roof, pretending for the sake of Hank—or maybe just avoiding the inevitable—but I know it's only a matter of time before we have to make it real. It's been months since I made the decision, though it feels like a lifetime ago. I remember the conversation vividly. Hank was staying at Roger's for the weekend, and it was just the two of us in the house, sitting in the kitchen where everything feels colder these days.

I told him I couldn't keep doing this—that he doesn't listen to me anymore, that we're two strangers living parallel lives. He barely responded. It was as if he was a million miles away, like he's been for years now. I'd expected a fight, maybe even some regret, but all I got was silence. And that silence was the final nail in the coffin.

I've told Cheryl and Mom. Cheryl has been wonderful, so supportive. I think she feels bad for me, especially knowing how hard it is from her own divorce. We've gotten a lot closer lately, more like friends than sisters. She's been giving me advice, helping me navigate all this mess. It feels good to have someone on my side, someone who understands. Mom, on the other hand... well, she's old school. She thinks I should just stick it out, stay in the marriage no matter how unhappy I am. She believes in duty and keeping up appearances. It makes me wonder sometimes—was she unhappy in her marriage too? Did she stick it out just because she thought she had to?

We haven't told Hank yet, though I think he knows. Kids are perceptive, more than we give them credit for. He's been acting different lately—quieter, more withdrawn. I wonder if he's waiting for us to say it, or if he's just dealing with it in his own way. Michael won't let me take him to his therapist anymore. He's forbidden it, and I don't have the strength to fight him on it. I've fought enough battles. Maybe I'm giving up, or maybe I'm just tired.

I know I've been overprotective of Hank. Even my own therapist says so. But lately, I've started to let go a little. I've backed off, given him space. He's growing up, and I can't shield him from everything. I thought protecting him was the answer, but maybe I was wrong. Maybe all I did was make him feel suffocated.

But now I need to tell him. He has to know about the separation, about the divorce that's coming. He needs to be ready. I don't want to blindside him when it happens. He deserves the truth, no matter how hard it is.

August 2, 1998

We told Hank today about the breakup. I don't know what I was expecting—maybe tears, anger, confusion—but none of that happened. He just nodded, like he already knew. I guess deep down I knew he knew too, but seeing it in his face, the way he handled it… it was like talking to someone much older than eleven.

He didn't cry, didn't ask why. Instead, he just said, "I knew," and asked, in this cold, matter-of-fact way, when we were getting a divorce. Michael was the one who spoke up, saying we still needed to talk about things, and that Hank could ask us anything. But then Hank dropped a bomb I wasn't ready for: he asked if he could stay with Michael when we finally move out.

My heart shattered right there. I could barely breathe for a moment, but I didn't let it show. I just… I just nodded and said we'd talk about it later. Michael looked as shocked as I felt. I think he was hurt too, but in a different way. It's like he wanted Hank to say he'd want to stay with me. But why would he? Michael has always been the "easy going" one. He's not on Hank's back about homework or being safe, not like me.

And I guess part of me wonders if I've pushed Hank away with all my overprotectiveness. Am I to blame?

After we finished talking with Hank, I called Cheryl. I had to. I just couldn't hold it all in. She understood—of course she did. Shane lived with his dad for a long time, so she knows exactly how this feels. She told me to keep going to therapy, that it'll help. I'm not sure if anything will help, but maybe she's right.

As for Hank and his question… we didn't answer. We said we'd talk about it later, but I know we both felt the weight of it. Michael didn't like the idea any more than I did, but for different reasons. He seemed hurt, maybe even angry that Hank didn't choose me. And me? Well, I guess I wasn't surprised. It still broke my heart, but I can't blame Hank. I've always been the stricter parent. All I've ever wanted was to protect him, but maybe I've gone too far… no, that can't be.

Tomorrow, I start my new job at the law firm. I got the Junior Lawyer position I applied for a few weeks ago. At least it'll keep me busy. Michael and I have been splitting time with Hank—Monday through Wednesday, I take him to school and pick him up, and Michael does Thursday and Friday. But I guess it's time for us to really talk about the divorce. We can't keep living in limbo forever.

Divorce Papers
August 3, 1998

To:
Mary Ann Johnson
14 Meadowbrook Street
Paddington, Brisbane, QLD 4064

From:
Michael Johnson
205/8 Willow Crescent
Paddington, Brisbane, QLD 4064

Case Number: 98-124567

NOTICE OF FILING FOR DISSOLUTION OF MARRIAGE

Dear Mary Ann,

Please be advised that a petition for the dissolution of marriage (divorce) has been filed by the undersigned in the Family Court of Brisbane, Queensland, on this date of August 3, 1998.

This petition is a formal request to dissolve the marriage between Michael Johnson (Petitioner) and Mary Ann Johnson (Respondent) on the grounds of irreconcilable differences and breakdown of the marriage. The marriage is no longer viable, and it is in the best interest of both parties to terminate it.

<u>Terms and Requests:</u>

Custody of Minor Child:

The petitioner requests joint legal and physical custody of Hank Johnson, born June 2, 1987, with a schedule to be determined for shared parenting time. Michael Johnson requests the court to consider a balanced arrangement for the welfare of the child, with the child residing equally with both parents.

Property Division:

The petitioner requests an equitable division of all marital assets and liabilities, including but not limited to the following:

- Family home located at 14 Meadowbrook Street, Paddington.
- Savings accounts, investment portfolios, and other shared financial assets.
- Any outstanding debts accumulated during the marriage.
- Spousal Maintenance (if applicable):
  - The petitioner does not seek spousal support from the respondent, and requests the court to waive any future claims for alimony from either party.

Legal Fees:

The petitioner requests that each party be responsible for their own legal fees during the divorce process.

Response Required:

You, as the respondent, are required to respond to this petition within 28 days from the date of service. Failure to do so may result in a default judgment being entered against you, granting the relief sought by the petitioner.

Legal Representation:

Michael Johnson is currently represented by the law firm of Thomas & Associates, located at 54 River Street, Brisbane.

You are entitled to legal representation, and it is recommended that you seek counsel as soon as possible to ensure your rights are protected during these proceedings.

Issued By:
Michael Johnson
Petitioner

Filed On Behalf Of:
Thomas & Associates
54 River Street, Brisbane, QLD 4000
Phone: (07) 1234 5678

Service of Process:
Served on Mary Ann Johnson in accordance with the Family Law Act, 1975.

Date of Service: August 3, 1998
Signature: ___________________________
(Official Process Server)

Court Stamp:
Family Court of Brisbane, QLD
Date of Filing: August 3, 1998
Seal: ___________________________

Notes:
Mary Ann, this is a difficult moment for us both, but I believe it is in the best interest of everyone involved, including Hank. I hope we can resolve this amicably for his sake.
– Michael

Mary Ann Johnson's Diary
August 3, 1998

I feel numb. Empty. I've been crying all day, and it feels like I'll never stop. Michael served me divorce papers this morning. I couldn't believe it—not the papers, but the way he did it. No warning, no conversation, just a piece of paper handed to me before I left for work. To make it worse, the papers listed a new address for him. A new address. How long has he been living somewhere else? I thought he was in the guest room, staying in the house while we figured things out. But no—he already has a place of his own.

The letter was the last thing I needed today. I dropped Hank off at school like I always do, trying to act normal, but the tears just wouldn't stop. I was a mess by the time I got to work—red eyes, shaky voice, the works. My boss noticed right away, of course. I tried to pull myself together, but he told me to go home. He was kind about it, but it was humiliating. My first day as a junior lawyer, and I couldn't even make it to lunch. That's not the impression I wanted to make, but I couldn't focus. All I could think about was Michael and that letter.

When I got home, I walked in to find Michael packing his things. He wasn't expecting me to be there, and for a moment, we just stared at each other. Then it all came out. I confronted him about the papers, the new address, everything. I called him every name I could think of. I told him I felt betrayed, that I thought we were better than this. He didn't care. He just called me crazy, grabbed his bags, and walked out without another word.

After he left, I broke down. I called Cheryl, and she came over right away. She stayed with me the whole day, even picking up Hank from school so I wouldn't have to face anyone. She's been my rock through all of this, and I don't know what I'd do without her. We talked, we cried, and she reminded me that I need to pull myself together for Hank. She's right, but right now, I just feel so broken.

Hank seems fine, like nothing's changed. I don't know if that's because he's strong or because he's just used to all of this. Either way, I'm grateful for Cheryl. She made sure I ate dinner and helped me keep it together in front of him.

Tomorrow, I need to start thinking about my next steps. Cheryl said I need to talk to an attorney, and she's right. Maybe I'll find someone from my new job. I can't let this ruin me. I need to stand up, not just for myself, but for Hank. Even if I feel like a mess now, I know I have to find my strength again.

Hank Johnson's Diary
August 24, 1998

Life is weird right now. I've been living half the time at Mom's house and half the time at Dad's apartment. That's what they agreed to. I like staying with Dad way more. Mom is out of control—she watches everything I do, like she's scared I'm going to mess up or something. I can't even talk to Diavlo properly anymore because she's always watching me. Plus, there's no computer at Mom's house. How am I supposed to play my games?

Dad's apartment is small, but I don't mind it. At least he has a computer, and he lets me use it all the time. He's not even there much; he's always working. He said he'll buy a bigger house soon, and I can bring friends over when he does. That sounds cool, but I don't really have that many friends—just Roger.

I haven't seen Roger much lately, only at school. He's been busy with homework, and I guess I have too. But we still play Lucifer together. It's online, so we can play even when we're not at each other's houses. The game's still awesome. We're getting stronger and leveling up a lot.

Diavlo's been around a lot, and he's been really talkative. At least twice a week, I go to the park near school. There are birds and possums there, and I let him feed on my wishes to make them go away. And yeah, he kills them. It's kind of scary but also… normal now? I don't know.

He talks about everything I do during the day. Stuff like my homework, school, and even what I eat. Lately, he's been asking me why I put up with the bullies at school. He says I don't have to. He says with just one wish, they'd be gone. But I can't think about that too much. If I do, he might actually make them disappear, and that would be really bad for me.

I'm excited about October, though. There's a running competition at school, and I'm going to be in it. I've been practicing a lot, and I think I have a good chance. Running makes me feel free, like nothing else matters when I'm doing it. I can't wait.

Cassette Recording
Date: September 11, 1998

Cassette Audio Begins

The muffled sound of car tires on the road. A faint hum of the car engine fills the background. Mary Ann's voice is calm but tired, and Hank's responses are quiet and thoughtful. The recorder is faintly rustling, hidden in Hank's pocket.

Mary Ann: (gently) "Hank, do you understand what's happening today? Why we're going to court?"

Hank: (quietly) "Yeah, kinda. It's about who I'll stay with, right? You or Dad?"

Mary Ann: "That's right. I've filed a legal request for full custody of you. I don't believe your dad is fit to take care of you."

Hank: "What does that mean? He's not fit?"

Mary Ann: (sighing) "It just means he doesn't care about you or me, he is selfish and you are better with me. That's what the trial is about. It might take a few days, or longer."

Hank: (curiously) "And then the court decides?"

Mary Ann: "Yes, but the court might ask you how you feel too. You're 11 now, and your opinion matters. But I want you to know, Hank... no matter what happens, I love you, okay? And this isn't your fault. It's an adult thing, and you just got caught in the middle of it."

There's a pause. The sound of the car indicator clicking as Mary Ann turns into the parking lot.

Hank: "I know, Mom. I'm trying to be a good boy."

Mary Ann: (voice trembling) "You are, Hank. You're a wonderful boy. It's not your fault, not at all. This is just… hard."

Hank: (gently) "Why are you crying, Mom? Please don't cry."

Mary Ann: (sniffling) "I'm sorry. I just… I want you to stay with me, Hank. But more than anything, I want you to be happy. Even if that means… even if it's not what I want. I'll trust your decision, Hank. If you want to stay with your dad… I'll respect that."

Hank: (after a pause) "I love you, Mom. But… I want to stay with Dad."

The car grows silent except for the hum of the engine. Mary Ann's breathing becomes heavier as she struggles to keep her composure.

Mary Ann: (softly) "I love you too, Hank. And I want what's best for you. Even if… even if it's not me. Maybe this is what being a mother means—putting your child's happiness above your own. In that case, I will dismiss the case today."

There's a long pause. The faint sound of Mary Ann's sniffles turns into a sharp intake of breath.

Mary Ann: (suddenly alarmed) "Wait… what is that? Are you recording this, Hank?"

Hank: (panicking) "No! I mean… it's just a recorder. It's nothing."

Mary Ann: (raising her voice) "Is this your dad's idea? Did he tell you to record me? Hank, that recorder is mine! Give it to me!"

The sound of scuffling as Mary Ann tries to grab the recorder. Hank yelps in pain.

Hank: (shouting) "Mom, you're hurting me!"

Mary Ann suddenly gasps, her voice strangled, followed by choking sounds. There's a faint rustling as Hank speaks in a panic.

Hank: (yelling) "Stop, Diavlo! Stop it now!"

The choking stops abruptly, and the car door opens. Mary Ann stumbles out, her voice shrill and filled with terror.

Mary Ann: (screaming) "He's the devil! He's talking to the devil! Help me! Someone, please help!"

The sound of muffled voices outside the car as Mary Ann shouts for help in the parking lot. The tape clicks off.

Cassette Audio Ends

Court Order
September 15, 1998

Family Court of Brisbane, Queensland

Case Number: 98-563421

In the Matter Of:
Michael Johnson (Petitioner)
vs.
Mary Ann Johnson (Respondent)

<u>Order for Full Custody of Minor Child</u>

To the Parties Concerned:

Upon the filing of the petition by Michael Johnson, requesting full legal and physical custody of the minor child, Hank Johnson (DOB: June 2, 1987), the Family Court of Brisbane issues the following order:

<u>Factual Basis for Custody Petition</u>

The court acknowledges the following facts presented by the petitioner:

The minor child's mother, Mary Ann Johnson, has been admitted to a mental health institution as of September 12, 1998. Medical records provided to the court indicate she is undergoing treatment for severe mental health issues, including but not limited to emotional instability and episodes of erratic behavior, which were deemed to pose a potential risk to her own safety and the well-being of the minor child.

Mary Ann Johnson is currently under institutional care and is unable to provide adequate physical or emotional support for the minor child during her recovery period.

The petitioner, Michael Johnson, is in stable mental and physical health and has the resources, residence, and capacity to provide a safe and supportive environment for the child.

The minor child, Hank Johnson, has expressed a preference to reside with his father. While the child's preference is not binding, it is considered alongside the petitioner's evidence of suitability.

<u>Custody Determination</u>

Based on the evidence presented and in consideration of the child's welfare as the paramount concern, the court hereby grants:

Full Legal and Physical Custody of Hank Johnson to Michael Johnson.

Visitation Rights: Mary Ann Johnson may request visitation rights following her discharge from the health institution and upon providing evidence of her ability to safely interact with the child. All visitation rights will be supervised until further review by the court.

Financial Support: Michael Johnson will assume full financial responsibility for the care and well-being of Hank Johnson.

Review Period: This custody order will remain in effect unless modified or overturned by subsequent court review. The court will schedule a status hearing six months from the date of this order to assess Mary Ann Johnson's progress and consider any motions to modify custody arrangements.

<u>Conditions of the Order</u>

Educational Continuity: The petitioner is responsible for ensuring the minor child continues to attend school and participate in extracurricular activities, maintaining his routine to minimize emotional disruption.

Health and Well-Being: The petitioner will ensure the child receives necessary medical care and psychological support, as appropriate, to adjust to the change in circumstances.

Contact with the Respondent: The petitioner shall facilitate appropriate communication between the child and the respondent if and when deemed suitable by the medical team overseeing Mary Ann Johnson's treatment.

It Is So Ordered.

Date: September 15, 1998
Signed:
Judge Emily Carrington
Family Court of Brisbane, Queensland

Notice to All Parties:

This order is issued in the best interest of the child, Hank Johnson, based on the current evidence presented. Any violation of this order may result in legal consequences. For inquiries or motions related to this case, please contact the Family Court Clerk's Office at (07) 1234 5678.

Hank Johnson's Diary
September 20, 1998

Today I visited Mom at the Willowbrook Mental Health Facility. Dad said she's doing well and being treated there, but I don't really understand it. I just know I don't think I want to go back.

When I walked in, she didn't even recognize me. She looked at me, and then she started screaming. She kept shouting that I'm the devil and that I've been taken by the devil. I think it's because of what happened the other day when Diavlo tried to strangle her. It was scary, but I didn't cry. I didn't want Dad to see me upset.

Later, I talked to Diavlo about that day. I asked him—again—why he hurt Mom. I've told him so many times not to hurt my family, but he doesn't listen. He said he had no choice. He said Mom had the intention to hurt me that day, that he could "smell it." He said it's something he just discovered he could do—like he can smell bad wishes or danger.

Diavlo said he had to step in because if something happens to me, he could die too. He says he won't allow that to happen. I get why he did it, but it doesn't make me feel any better. Since then, I've been ignoring him, even though he tries to talk to me. I haven't fed him either. He's weak now, barely around. Maybe that's for the best.

But then he asks me to think bad wishes about animals, just so he can feed. He says it's no big deal, but I know better. If he gets strong, bad things will happen. I don't know what to do. Part of me feels bad for Mom, but another part doesn't want Diavlo to go away. He's been with me for as long as I can remember. What would it be like without him?

I've been talking to Roger, but not as much as before. Dad's apartment is far from Roger's house, and he can only come over when his mom can drop him off and pick him up. He can't come by himself anymore. Roger keeps saying he wants to test more of Diavlo's abilities. I think Roger sees it as some kind of game, like Lucifer. But I know better. It's not a game. Not even close. I won't do it—not for now, at least.

Patient Progress Report
October 14, 1998

Willowbrook Mental Health Facility

Patient Name: Mary Ann Johnson
Prepared By: Dr. Amelia Clarke

<u>Patient Overview</u>

Mary Ann Johnson has shown notable improvement over the past few weeks. Her mood and overall demeanour have stabilized, and she has demonstrated a willingness to engage in activities that promote her mental well-being.

<u>Religious Engagement and Spiritual Growth</u>

Mary Ann has been actively visiting the Catholic chapel located on the hospital grounds. During her sessions with the chaplain, she expressed a strong desire to connect with her faith. Mary Ann revealed that she has never been baptized, as her parents did not allow it during her childhood. She has now asked to be baptized, stating that she wants to be closer to God and find peace through her spiritual journey. This newfound connection appears to provide her with a sense of hope and purpose.

<u>Family Interaction</u>

Today, Mary Ann's sister and mother visited her at the facility. The visit was positive and filled with heartfelt conversation. Both her sister and mother appeared supportive and caring, which seemed to uplift Mary Ann significantly. She was noticeably happier and more engaged following the visit.

Prior to the visit, we advised her sister and mother not to bring up any discussions about the incidents involving her son, Hank, or her husband, Michael. This precaution was necessary to prevent potential triggers that could cause setbacks in her progress.

Medication and Treatment

Mary Ann has been prescribed Sertraline (50 mg once daily), an antidepressant to help manage her symptoms. She has been consistent with her medication regimen and has reported no adverse side effects. Her adherence to this treatment has contributed to the stabilization of her mood.

Request for Visitation

Mary Ann has expressed a desire to see her son, Hank. While she has been understanding of the current restrictions, she has stated that seeing him would mean a great deal to her. At this time, we believe it is too early to allow such visitation due to the potential emotional impact on both Mary Ann and Hank. However, if her progress continues, we may consider arranging a supervised visitation in the near future.

Conclusion and Recommendations

Mary Ann is making steady progress in her treatment and recovery. Her connection to faith, support from family, and adherence to her prescribed medication are key factors contributing to her improvement.

We recommend continued visits from family members under controlled circumstances and monitoring of her progress to determine when visitation with her son might be appropriate.

Dr. Amelia Clarke
Willowbrook Mental Health Facility
Brisbane, Queensland

**Detective Sergeant Ian Morrison's Investigation Diaries
October 21, 1998**

The Johnson case continues to pull me deeper into its web. I've been following Hank Johnson's steps, as well as keeping track of his family. The incident at the court parking lot on September 11 confirmed my suspicions that something strange surrounds this boy.

I was present that day, keeping my distance but watching carefully. Mary Ann Johnson, his mother, caused quite the scene. She screamed, over and over, that Hank was the devil. It wasn't the outburst itself that caught my attention but the sheer terror and conviction in her voice. She wasn't just shouting in anger; she truly believed it. The people around her tried to calm her down, but it was no use. From where I stood, I could see Hank sitting inside the car, frozen with fear. He looked pale, almost fragile.

Eventually, the police arrived and took Mary Ann away for fear that she might harm Hank or herself. It was chaotic, and I stayed back to avoid drawing attention to myself. Moments later, Michael Johnson showed up and took Hank away.

I've since gained access to court documents that detail the aftermath. The judge awarded Michael Johnson full custody of Hank, citing concerns over Mary Ann's mental state. It was also revealed that Mary Ann was admitted to Willowbrook Mental Health Facility shortly after the incident for treatment. The legal documents mention severe mental health issues, though the specifics remain vague.

Given what I witnessed at the parking lot, I can't say I'm surprised by the judge's decision. Mary Ann acted like a lunatic in front of her own child, during what was supposed to be a battle for custody. What I find curious, however, is that Mary Ann initiated the legal fight. She was the one who petitioned for full custody. It makes me wonder—did Michael even want Hank in the first place? Or was he pushed into this situation because of Mary Ann's actions?

This parking lot incident is yet another piece of the puzzle, another strange event to add to the growing pile surrounding Hank Johnson. There's still no concrete evidence tying all of this together, but I feel like I'm getting closer. Every new lead feels like another step forward, even if it's a small one.

My next step is to try and speak with Mary Ann. She might be unstable, but she's the closest link to understanding what's happening with Hank. Perhaps through her family—her sister Cheryl, maybe—I can find a way to approach her.

In the meantime, I'll be shifting my focus to Hank directly. I need to watch him more closely, especially at school. Children have routines, but sometimes those routines hide secrets. Maybe there's something he does at school that no one else has noticed. Something that could finally shed light on the truth.

**Cassette Recording
October 29, 1998**

Cassette Audio Begins

The faint sounds of children chatting and shuffling papers fill the classroom. Hank's voice is upbeat, brimming with excitement, while Roger speaks with his usual curiosity. The tape recorder rustles faintly, hidden on Hank's desk.

Hank: (excitedly) "I still can't believe it, Roger. First place! Me! Everyone was clapping. Maybe… maybe they won't call me a weirdo anymore."

Roger: (enthusiastically) "Congrats, Hank! You ran so fast. It was like you flew or something. Hey, was Diavlo there? Did he see it?"

Hank: (shaking his head) "No. He's been… gone a lot lately. I don't mind, though."

Roger: (worriedly) "That's not good, Hank. Diavlo is your protector. What if something bad happens?"

Hank: (suddenly frustrated) "Roger, stop! Don't ask about him anymore! Diavlo only causes me trouble. I don't want to talk about him!"

Roger: (calmly) "Okay, okay. But Hank, you know your mom's problems weren't because of him. He was just protecting you."

There's a long pause. The faint sound of a chair creaking is heard.

Hank: (quietly) "He's here now… looking at you. He's smiling."

Roger: (nervously) "Smiling?"

Hank: (pausing, then whispering) "He says he likes you."

Roger: (nervously) "Uh… okay. Thanks, Diavlo?"

Roger chuckles nervously, but the sound of his laughter is cut short.

Hank: (voice tense) "Wait… he says he smells danger. Someone is watching us. Outside the window."

Roger: (alarmed) "I… I saw someone! Just for a second! Hiding behind that bush out there."

Hank: (worried) "Who could it be? Why would someone—"

Suddenly, a new voice interrupts.

Mary Ann: (calmly) "Hi, Hank. So, you're still using my recorder."

The boys gasp. The sound of a chair scraping against the floor echoes as Hank stands abruptly.

Hank: (shocked) "Mom? What are you doing here? I thought you were sick."

Mary Ann: (softly) "I've been cured, Hank. The Lord has healed me."

Roger: (curious) "What's that cross in your hand, Mrs. Johnson?"

Mary Ann: (firmly) "Don't worry about that, Roger. Hank, I just wanted to say how proud I am of you. I saw you win the running competition. You were amazing."

Hank: (hesitantly) "Mom… it's good to see you, but… I think I should talk to Dad. He's outside waiting for me."

Mary Ann: (voice growing sharper) "Before that, Hank, I need to do something."

Suddenly, Roger's voice breaks into a panicked shout.

Roger: (yelling) "Let Hank go! Let him go!"

Mary Ann: (screaming) "I love my son! This is me loving my son!"

There's a scuffling sound. Hank's voice is muffled, gasping, as if he's struggling to breathe.

Mary Ann: (yelling) "This cross on your neck, it will banish the devil from inside you! I saw you talking to him—the devil! But you must pray to the Lord! Get out of my son, devil!"

Roger's voice becomes frantic as Hank cries out in pain.

Roger: (screaming) "Let him go! You'll kill him!"

Roger: (desperately) "Diavlo, you must do something! Just don't kill her!"

A loud thud is heard, followed by silence. A faint groan echoes, as if someone has fallen hard to the ground.

Hank: (panting) "Is… is she dead?"

Roger: (terrified) "I don't know…"

Hank: (crying) " Why? why, Mom, why?"

The tape clicks off abruptly. Cassette Audio Ends

Incident Report
October 30, 1998

Brisbane Police Department
Case Number: 98-46721

<u>Incident Details</u>

Date of Incident: October 29, 1998
Time of Incident: Approximately 2:15 PM
Location: Sunnyvale Primary School, Brisbane

<u>Involved Parties</u>

- Hank Johnson (11 years old, student)
- Mary Ann Johnson (38 years old, mother of Hank Johnson)
- Reporting Officer: Senior Constable Andrew Marks

<u>Summary of Events</u>

On October 29, 1998, officers responded to a disturbance at Sunnyvale Primary School following reports of an altercation between Mary Ann Johnson and her son, Hank Johnson, inside a classroom.

According to staff and witness statements, Mary Ann Johnson entered the school premises without prior authorization. She proceeded directly to Hank Johnson's classroom. Witnesses reported that Mary Ann appeared agitated and was holding a small wooden cross in her hand.

Upon entering the classroom, Mary Ann began shouting at her son, accusing him of being "possessed by the devil." Witnesses stated she attempted to approach Hank, who appeared frightened and backed away. Hank's friend, Roger Williams, was present and tried to intervene. Mary Ann allegedly restrained Hank, pressing the cross against his neck while shouting prayers.

During the struggle, Mary Ann slipped and fell, hitting her head on the edge of a desk.

Injuries

Mary Ann Johnson: Severe head injury. Transported to St. Mary's General Hospital by ambulance. Medical staff later confirmed she sustained a concussion and remains in a vegetative state.

Hank Johnson: No physical injuries reported, but he appeared distressed and shaken.

Witness Statements

Roger Williams:

"She was yelling and saying Hank was talking to the devil. She wouldn't let him go, and then she slipped and fell. I told her to stop, but she didn't listen."

School Administrator (Name Withheld):

"Mary Ann had no authorization to be on school grounds. She looked very upset. After the incident, we immediately called the police and emergency services."

Additional Information

Mary Ann Johnson had been recently been admitted to Willowbrook Mental Health Facility, where she was receiving treatment for severe mental health issues. Police records indicate she escaped the facility prior to the incident.

Hank Johnson is under the legal custody of his father, Michael Johnson, as per a prior court order. Mary Ann Johnson was not permitted unsupervised contact with Hank at the time of the incident.

<u>Conclusion</u>

Based on witness accounts and preliminary findings, it appears that Mary Ann Johnson's actions were the result of ongoing mental health struggles. There is no evidence to suggest premeditation or intent to cause severe harm.

The case remains open pending further investigation, though initial evidence suggests Mary Ann's injury was accidental and self-inflicted during the altercation.

Filed By: Senior Constable Andrew Marks
Badge Number: 45678
Brisbane Police Department

Therapy Session Notes
November 2, 1998

Patient: Hank Johnson
Therapist: Dr. Evelyn Hart

Location: Paddington Child and Adolescent Therapy Centre

<u>Session Overview</u>

Hank has returned to therapy for a couple of weeks now, following the traumatic incident involving his mother. His father, Michael, has expressed deep concern that the event may have left a lasting emotional impact on Hank.

The incident, in which Mary Ann Johnson attempted to strangle Hank, has understandably shaken him. Mary Ann, under severe mental distress, believed that Hank was possessed by the devil. This belief culminated in a violent episode that Hank witnessed and endured firsthand.

<u>Patient's Current State</u>

Hank has been noticeably quieter since his return to therapy. He avoids initiating conversation and seems reluctant to share his thoughts and feelings. This is a shift from his previous demeanour, where he was more forthcoming. While his reluctance to talk is expected after such a significant trauma, it is a reminder that recovery will take time and patience. I've made a conscious effort to avoid pushing him too hard during sessions, allowing him to open up at his own pace.

<u>Session Progress</u>

Today's session marked a small but notable improvement. After several sessions of near silence, I gently shifted the conversation toward Hank's friendships and social life. This topic seemed to resonate with him, and he began to talk about a close friend named Roger.

Hank spoke about Roger with fondness and described him as a good friend who he trusts. While Hank did not elaborate on specific details, the fact that he spoke freely about Roger is encouraging. It suggests that his friendship with Roger provides him with a sense of stability and normalcy amidst the chaos of his family life.

<u>Therapist's Notes</u>

Hank's recovery is likely to be slow, and it is important to approach his sessions with patience and care. The trauma he experienced with his mother is significant, and it is understandable that he is struggling to process it.

While today's conversation about Roger marks a step forward, Hank remains guarded about other aspects of his life. He still shows signs of emotional withdrawal, and it may take several more sessions before he feels comfortable discussing deeper issues.

I will continue to focus on building trust and creating a safe space for Hank to express himself. Additionally, I recommend ongoing support at home from his father and a stable routine to help him feel secure.

Prepared By:
Dr. Evelyn Hart
Paddington Child and Adolescent Therapy Centre

**Detective Sergeant Ian Morrison's Investigation Diaries
November 7, 1998**

The deeper I dive into the Johnson case, the stranger it gets. For weeks now, I've been following Hank's routine closely. His life, on the surface, appears remarkably ordinary for a child his age. Every morning, he arrives at school, spends his day there, and is picked up immediately after by his father. Most afternoons, he's either alone at Michael Johnson's apartment or spending time with his friend Roger Williams. Either Roger's mother drops him off at Hank's place, or Michael drops Hank off at Roger's home.

But a few days ago, during a school competition, something shifted. Hank participated in a running competition and won first place. The boy's speed was incredible, even uncanny, and the entire school seemed to celebrate his victory. I took the opportunity to observe him more closely that day, hiding outside his classroom. That's when things took a turn.

I watched through the window as Hank and Roger sat together, seemingly talking to someone—or something—that wasn't visible. The way they gestured, the way their heads moved, it was as if there was a third presence in the room. I instinctively took a picture, but when I later reviewed it, there was nothing unusual in the frame. Maybe I was imagining it, but my gut told me otherwise. Then, Roger glanced toward the window. For a brief moment, I was certain he saw me, though I quickly ducked away before he could identify me.

The following day, news broke about Mary Ann Johnson. I'd learned from police reports that she had escaped from the Willowbrook Mental Health Facility. In her desperation, she had attempted to strangle Hank. The report stated she claimed her son was possessed by the devil and was trying to drive it out of him using a cross pressed to his neck.

It seems Mary Ann had recently embraced religion—something out of character for her past behavior. But the police report mentioned her saying "the devil is inside him," which struck me.

The events surrounding Mary Ann's breakdown are blurred. What is clear is that during her attempt to strangle Hank, she fell and suffered a severe concussion. According to medical records I accessed, she's now in a vegetative state, lying unresponsive at St. Mary's General Hospital.

When police questioned Hank and Roger about the incident, their stories aligned perfectly. Both claimed Mary Ann slipped and hit her head on the ground. The uniformity of their accounts kept the police from investigating further, but I couldn't shake the feeling that the truth is far darker. This was another bizarre and inexplicable event in the growing pile of mysteries surrounding Hank Johnson.

Earlier today, I decided to visit Mary Ann at the hospital. I felt it was safe to approach her now that she's in this state. The nurse let me into her room and left me alone. Mary Ann's eyes were open, but her body was entirely unresponsive. I knew she couldn't answer me, but I had to try. I leaned close and whispered to her, "What is your son, Mary Ann? I believe you—something is very wrong with Hank."

Her body didn't move, but tears began streaming from her open eyes. It was all the confirmation I needed. Even in her unresponsive state, Mary Ann knew. She knew there's something deeply wrong with her son.

I can't stop now. There's more to this case, and I'm closer than ever to uncovering it. Whatever is happening with Hank, it's not just the product of an overactive imagination or coincidence. This goes far beyond that, and I intend to find out the truth—even if it takes everything I have.

GOOD BYE FRIEND

Paddington Post
May 15, 2000

By: Sarah Collins

"Mystery Surrounds Animal Deaths in Local Parks"

Residents of Paddington have been increasingly alarmed by a puzzling phenomenon that has been unfolding over the past year—the unexplained deaths of animals in local parks. The victims include a variety of wildlife such as possums, birds, and even a few stray cats. Despite investigations, authorities remain baffled, with no clear cause or culprit identified.

The incidents, which began sporadically last year, have become more frequent in recent months, with sightings of deceased animals reported in parks across the area. Most recently, a group of children playing in Hollywell Park stumbled upon three dead magpies near a large tree. Just two days earlier, a local jogger discovered the body of a possum on the footpath near Elderberry Reserve, its condition described as "unusual and distressing."

No Clear Cause

Veterinary pathologists who examined some of the animals noted that the deaths do not seem to follow a consistent pattern. While poisoning was initially suspected, tests have come back inconclusive. Similarly, there are no signs of predation or physical trauma that would indicate attacks by other animals.

Dr. Karen Wilson, a wildlife specialist consulted by local authorities, commented, "The lack of clear evidence makes this case particularly challenging. The animals appear to simply collapse and die, with no warning signs or definitive cause. It's as if their systems just shut down suddenly."

While some speculate that environmental factors like toxins or diseases could be to blame, there is no proof to support these theories. Tests on water sources and soil in the affected areas have yielded no abnormalities.

Community Concerns

Residents are growing increasingly uneasy. Parents, in particular, are worried about the safety of their children, fearing that whatever is affecting the animals could potentially harm humans as well.

"I don't let my kids play in the parks anymore," said Paddington resident Linda Foster, who lives near Hollywell Park. "It's just too strange, and no one seems to know what's causing it. First, it's the animals—what if it spreads to people next?"

Others, however, are dismissing the concerns as unnecessary panic. "It's sad, but it's probably just nature running its course," said Tom Hargrove, a local dog walker. "Wildlife dies all the time. We're probably overthinking it."

Urban Legends and Speculation

The lack of answers has also fuelled urban legends and wild speculation among residents. Some have suggested that a rogue animal is responsible, while others have spun more supernatural explanations.

"It's almost like something invisible is hunting them," said a teenage resident who preferred to remain anonymous. "My friends and I think it might be a ghost or something. It sounds silly, but how else do you explain it?"

Others have raised concerns about the possibility of secret experiments or illegal activity in the area. "What if someone's testing something on the animals?" questioned Mark Evans, another Paddington resident. "It's not that far-fetched. We've all heard of shady things happening in the past."

Ongoing Investigations

Local authorities have urged residents to remain calm as the investigation continues. Senior Wildlife Officer Peter Collins emphasized, "We understand the community's concerns, and we are doing everything we can to uncover the truth. In the meantime, we encourage people to report any unusual animal behavior or sightings immediately."

Until a clear cause is determined, the mystery of Paddington's animal deaths remains unsolved, leaving residents with more questions than answers.

Hank Johnson's Diary
June 1, 2000

Tomorrow is my birthday! I'll be 13 years old! It feels weird saying that. Thirteen sounds so much older than twelve. Dad says we'll have a small party at the new house, which is way bigger and cooler than the apartment we used to live in. It has a backyard, and Dad said we can use it for the party.

I invited Roger, of course. He's still my best friend, and we've been playing Lucifer 2 every chance we get. It's such a fun game! The graphics are way better than the first one, and you can build your own weapons now. Roger and I are already on level 18. We keep trying to beat this crazy boss monster in the dark mountains, but it's so hard. Roger says we'll beat it soon if we keep working together. I hope we can play a little tomorrow after the party.

I also invited two other kids from school: Liam Parker and Sophie Bennett. Liam's in my gym class, and he's a really good sprinter too, though I'm still faster (hehe). He's been nice to me since we started running together. Sophie's in my science class, and she's super smart. She helped me a lot with our last project, so I thought it'd be fun to have her at the party.

It's crazy how much things have changed. Two years ago, most of the kids at school were awful to me. They'd call me names and treat me like some kind of freak. But after I won all those running competitions, they started seeing me differently. Now, people actually say I'm cool and ask me for tips on running. It's still weird to think about, but I guess it's nice not to be bullied anymore.

Roger is the only one who's stayed the same. He's always been my friend, even when nobody else was. I think that's why he's my best friend. He never cared about what other people thought.

It feels like everyone at school has forgotten about that old cassette recording I played back in primary school. The one with all the creepy stuff that made everyone call me a freak. No one talks about it anymore, not even the teachers. And the stuff with my mom? That's all in the past too. Maybe people decided it was just too weird to bring up again, or maybe they just don't care anymore. Either way, I'm glad. It's like I finally got a clean slate.

I go to Sunnyvale Secondary School now. It's the same school where most of the kids from primary moved up to for secondary level. That means I still see a lot of the same faces every day. Some of the kids who used to tease me are nicer now, probably because of all the running competitions I've won. It's kind of funny how that works. Being good at something makes people look at you differently.

Dad and I live in this new house now. It's really nice. He bought it after marrying his new wife, Emma, last year. Emma's okay. She's really different from Mom, though. She's always trying to make things perfect, like planning my party and making sure everything looks just right. She even said she's baking a cake herself instead of buying one. I think she's trying hard to be a good stepmom, but it still feels weird sometimes.

I miss Mom. The court finally made the divorce official more than a year ago, but it doesn't really matter. Mom's been in the hospital for so long now, and she's still the same. She doesn't move or talk or do anything. Dad says it's called a vegetative state. I visit her whenever I can, but it's hard. Sometimes, I sit next to her and just talk about my day. I tell her about school, running, or Roger, but she never responds. It makes me sad, but I hope she can hear me somehow.

I haven't touched this diary in almost two years. Since I stopped going to therapy, I didn't see the need. But today, I grabbed it from my desk and started reading. It's actually fun to revisit things from the past.

I feel as though someone else wrote them. I even forgot that I wrote about Diavlo.

He's been present most of the time, and we've agreed on a few things: he will never act on anything I wish for unless I give a specific oral confirmation. In exchange, I feed him almost every day. There are plenty of birds and possums where we live now, so it's surprisingly easy to find food for him.

Anyway, I should go to bed soon. Dad says I need to get up early to help Emma set up for the party. I hope tomorrow's fun. It feels strange celebrating without Mom, but I know she'd want me to have a good time.

Detective Sergeant Ian Morrison's Investigation Diaries
June 1, 2000

The Johnson investigation continues, but I'm running out of time.

Mary Ann Johnson remains in St. Mary's General Hospital, her condition unchanged. She's still in a vegetative state, with no signs of improvement or response. I visit occasionally, though my visits have become less frequent. Her cries on that one occasion still haunt me, but there's nothing else to glean from her condition.

Michael Johnson, however, has been making significant strides in his life. He remarried last year to Emma Taylor, now Emma Johnson, and they appear to be living comfortably in their new home in Paddington. Professionally, Michael's success has been outstanding. Recently, he was appointed Director-General of Queensland Health. Quite the leap for a lawyer. It's a high-profile and influential position, one that requires me to tread carefully. Any misstep in my investigation into him could trigger scrutiny from government agencies or even the secret service. So far, though, there's been nothing out of the ordinary about Michael. He seems to be focused on his career and family.

As for Hank, he appears to be living a normal life—or at least, that's how it looks on the surface. There have been no incidents or reports of strange occurrences since the incident with his mother at his school two years ago. He's even gained popularity at his school due to his achievements in running competitions. By all accounts, he's just a talented, well-adjusted kid.

However, there is one detail I can't ignore. Over the past year, I've noticed a pattern of random animal deaths in parks near Hank's new home. Birds, possums, even a stray cat—all found dead with no clear explanation. It's the kind of thing that might normally be attributed to natural causes or wild predators, but the timing and proximity to Hank's movements are suspicious. Unfortunately, I have nothing concrete to tie him to these events. It's just a hunch, and hunches won't hold up in an investigation.

My superiors are growing impatient. They've given me a long leash on this case, but their patience is wearing thin. Without solid evidence, I'll soon have no choice but to abandon the investigation.

I can't shake the feeling that I'm missing something—some critical piece of the puzzle that ties everything together. For now, I'll keep watching, keep listening, and hope that the truth reveals itself before I'm forced to walk away.

Cassette Recording
June 2, 2000

Cassette Audio Begins

The muffled sound of laughter and shuffling footsteps. The faint hum of outdoor chatter can be heard in the background, along with the occasional rustling of leaves and distant birds. Children's voices are faintly heard in the distance as the tape begins.

Hank: (excitedly) "Okay, I'm turning it on now. This is my birthday party! Roger, say something."

Roger: (laughing) "What? Uh, happy birthday, Hank! How old are you now, like twenty?"

Hank: (grinning) "Thirteen! Finally, a teenager."

Liam: (chiming in) "Better enjoy it, mate. It's all downhill from here. That's what my dad says, anyway."

Sophie: (giggling) "Oh, please. Thirteen isn't old! You're just jealous Hank's faster than you in gym class."

Liam: (mocking tone) "Hey, I let him win sometimes, okay? Gotta give the birthday boy some confidence."

Hank: (laughing) "Yeah, sure you do, Liam."

Roger: "If by 'sometimes' you mean 'always,' then yeah, you let him win."

The kids burst into laughter as the recorder clicks off briefly and resumes with the sound of plates clinking and chatter in the background.

Emma: (in the background, cheerful) "Alright, kids, cake time! Come on over!"

The sound of chairs shuffling and feet moving can be heard. The group begins singing "Happy Birthday," their voices slightly off-key but full of energy. Applause follows as Emma cuts the ice cream cake.

Hank: (excitedly) "Wow, this is awesome! Thanks, Dad, and thanks, Emma. This is the best cake ever."

Emma: (warmly) "You're welcome, Hank. I'm glad you like it."

Michael: (in the background, laughing) "Don't give me any credit. Emma did all the work. I just picked up the cake."

Liam: (muffled, mouth full) "This is so good. I could eat the whole thing."

Sophie: "Don't eat too much, Liam, or you'll explode. I mean, there's no way you'll beat Hank in gym class if you're rolling around like a balloon."

The group laughs again as the sounds of forks scraping plates and casual chatter fill the air. The recorder clicks off and resumes with the sound of footsteps near the front of the house.

Liam: (calling out) "Bye, Hank! Thanks for inviting me. It was fun!"

Sophie: "Yeah, happy birthday, Hank. I'll see you at school on Monday!"

Hank: "Thanks for coming, guys! See you later!"

The faint sound of car doors closing and engines starting can be heard as Liam and Sophie leave with their parents. The chatter fades, leaving just Hank and Roger.

Roger: (grinning) "Well, now it's just us. Ready to play some games upstairs?"

Hank: "Definitely. Let's go."

The sound of footsteps moving through the house, followed by creaking stairs, as the boys head up to Hank's room. The recorder clicks back on as the boys settle in.

Roger: "Man, that was fun. I ate way too much. I think your stepmom made, like, enough food for twenty people."

Hank: "She likes going overboard. But hey, it was good, right?"

Roger: "Yeah, definitely. And that cake was awesome. Your dad was cool for bringing it."

Hank: "Yeah, it was nice of him. I think he felt bad for showing up late after work."

The sound of a door opening and closing, followed by Roger's surprised gasp.

Roger: "Whoa! Hank, your room is massive! And this house… it's so new and shiny. It's not old and creaky like mine. Your dad really went all out, huh?"

Hank: (shrugging) "Yeah, I guess. I mean, it's nice and all, but I didn't really care that much when we moved here. It's just a house."

Roger: (laughing) "Well, I care! This place is awesome. You've got so much space. Do you even miss the old apartment?"

Hank: (thinking) "Not really. What about you? Do you miss your brother Paul?"

Roger: (hesitant) "Sometimes, I guess. But not really. He was kind of mean most of the time, you know? Always yelling at me or telling me what to do. I guess it's quieter now that he's in London."

Hank: (nodding) "Yeah, Dad said it was kind of a bad move for him to go there. He says London's part of the faction that's against Australia and NATO, and things could get messy. You heard anything like that?"

Roger: (sighing) "Yeah, my mom said something similar. But Paul wanted to go, and our family in London has money. He says he'll be better off there. They're even paying for his studies."

Hank: (quietly) "I guess that makes sense. If he's happy, I guess that's what matters."

There's a long pause, filled with the sound of shuffling feet as Hank and Roger settle onto the floor. Suddenly, Hank speaks again, his voice a little lower.

Hank: "So, uh… Diavlo's here."

Roger: (surprised) "Wait, now? Where is he?"

Hank: (pointing) "He's in the corner. Just standing there like always. Showing off his bright white pointy teeth."

Roger: (nervously) "Oh… so, what does he want?"

Hank: "He says he wants me to train him. Like, test out what else he can do. He says he's got more abilities, but he doesn't know what they are. He thinks you should help convince me."
Roger: "Well, I can give it a try."

Hank: (pausing) "I mean, you know what happened the last time I let him try something."

Roger: (defensive) "Yeah, I know. But he's not always like that. What if he can do things that could, I don't know, help people? Or at least make him… I don't know, stronger without causing trouble?"

Hank: (thoughtfully) "Okay, but what if it goes wrong? What if he loses control again? Like with mom? Or worse, what if someone sees something they shouldn't?"

Roger: (grumbling) "I know, I know. But he's not going to stop asking."

Hank: "I know. He keeps saying there's more to him than just being strong or stretching his arms."

Roger: (excitedly) "What if he can fly and take you with him? That would be awesome. We know that he can "smell" danger. Maybe he can read minds! Imagine what we could do with that!"

Hank: (sceptical) "I don't think he can read minds, only mine when I have bad wishes. But yeah, maybe. He says he doesn't know until we try. But I don't want him doing anything crazy here. If Emma sees him— or worse, Dad—I'm in big trouble."

Roger: "Then we do it somewhere else. The park worked last time, right? It's big and open, and no one really pays attention to kids playing around."

Hank: (nodding slowly) "Yeah, that could work. But only when you're around. I don't want to do this alone. And we've got to be careful, okay? If he starts acting up, we stop immediately."

Roger: (grinning) "Deal. But seriously, this could be really cool. Maybe we'll discover something amazing about him."

Hank: (smiling faintly) "Maybe. But let's keep it to the park. I'm not letting him wreck anything here. Emma would freak out."

The sound of faint laughter is heard as the boys continue chatting, their voices growing softer. A knock at the door interrupts them.

Rosemary Williams: (calling out) "Roger, time to go!"

Roger: (yelling back) "Coming, Mom!"

Hank: (whispering) "Thanks for coming today, Roger. And… for helping with this."

Roger: (grinning) "What are friends for? Let's figure out what Diavlo can do. See you tomorrow!"

The sound of footsteps and the door opening and closing. The tape clicks off.

Sunnyvale Secondary School Council Bulletin
June 3, 2000

Dear Parents, Guardians, and Students,

We hope this message finds you well as we move further into an exciting term at Sunnyvale Secondary School. Below are some key updates and announcements from our vibrant school community:

Science Fair Success

We are thrilled to announce that the annual Paddington Secondary Science Fair was a huge success! Students from all year levels showcased innovative projects, from renewable energy models to creative experiments in physics and chemistry. Congratulations to Sophie Bennett from Year 8 for winning first place with her project on eco-friendly water filtration systems. Sophie's hard work and ingenuity have made the entire school proud.

Library Renovations

Our beloved school library is undergoing renovations to provide a more modern and welcoming space for students. Once completed, the library will feature updated technology hubs, a dedicated quiet study area, and an expanded collection of books and resources. The renovations are expected to be completed by early August. During this time, a temporary book-lending station will operate in Room 3B.

Upcoming Drama Production

Mark your calendars! The drama club is gearing up for their performance of The Tempest by William Shakespeare. The students have been working tirelessly to bring this classic tale to life. Performances will be held in the school auditorium on July 15 and 16.

Tickets will go on sale next week, and proceeds will contribute to the arts program.

<u>Celebrating Hank Johnson: Paddington's Fastest Runner</u>

At just 13 years old, Hank Johnson from Year 8 has set a remarkable record in the recent interschool athletics competition, solidifying his title as the fastest runner in Sunnyvale Secondary School's history. Hank's incredible speed and dedication have inspired many, and his achievements have brought pride to the entire school community.

In a fun and spirited response, a new student fan group has been formed to celebrate Hank's success. The group, affectionately called "Team Hank," is composed mostly of Year 8 students, with a notable majority being girls. Their enthusiasm and creative cheers during the competition were hard to miss, and we applaud their efforts in supporting their fellow classmate.

Hank has expressed his gratitude for the support and looks forward to continuing his success on and off the track. We're proud to call him one of our own!

<u>Reminders and Notices</u>

- Parent-teacher interviews will be held next week. Please book your time slots through the school portal.
- Uniform checks will take place during homeroom next Monday. Please ensure students are adhering to the dress code.
- Lunch menus have been updated! Check the school website for the new healthy options available.
- Thank you for being an integral part of our school community. Together, we continue to foster a supportive and inspiring environment for our students to excel.

Sunnyvale Secondary School Council

Hank Johnson's Diary
June 4, 2000

I don't really feel like writing tonight, but I guess I need to. My therapist always said writing helps unload stuff from my brain, and right now my brain feels like it's about to explode. There's just too much going on.

So… there's this group of girls at school calling themselves "Team Hank." It's weird. I don't even know how to deal with it. They made a big deal at the last athletics meet when I won, and now it's like they're following me around. They cheer when I run in gym class, and some of them even wrote "Go, Hank!" on their notebooks. I don't get it. I mean, yeah, winning is cool, but this? This is something else.

Roger thinks I should enjoy it. He says it's awesome having fans and that I should just go with it. Easy for him to say—he's not the one being stared at during lunch. I don't think I like it, though. It's just… awkward.

Anyway, Sophie and Liam are still the same at school. Sophie's super smart, as usual. In science last week, she finished her experiment before anyone else and helped me when I messed up mine. Liam's been pretty funny lately. He keeps making up silly excuses for why he's slower than me in gym. He says he lets me win, but we both know that's not true. They're both cool to hang out with, and it's nice having more people around besides just Roger.

Speaking of Roger, he's been going on and on about testing Diavlo's abilities. He's been bugging me about it all week at school, and I finally gave in. Tomorrow, we're going to the park to see what Diavlo can really do. Roger thinks it's all just a big game, like Lucifer 2 or something. I don't think he gets how serious it could be. What if we find out something we don't like? Or worse, what if someone sees us?

I'm not sure I even want to do this, but maybe it's for the best. At least then I'll know what Diavlo is really capable of. He's been quieter lately, but I still feel like he's waiting for something.

I'll write about what happens tomorrow, I guess.

Cassette Recording
June 5, 2000

Cassette Audio Begins

The sound of children laughing and playing in the background. The faint creak of swings and the rhythmic squeak of a see-saw. Hank and Roger's voices come in, slightly muffled at first.

Roger: "You know, Hank, this whole 'Team Hank' thing at school is hilarious. I mean, a bunch of girls chanting your name during gym? That's next level."

Hank: (groaning) "Don't remind me. I don't even know what to say to them. They just follow me around like I'm some kind of celebrity or something. It's weird."

Roger: (laughing) "Weird? It's awesome! Come on, you're like Paddington's fastest kid. They love you for it. Just roll with it, man."

Hank: "Easy for you to say. You're not the one getting stared at in the lunchroom every day."

Roger: "Hey, I'd trade spots with you in a heartbeat. I mean, if you don't want the attention, maybe I'll start my own 'Team Roger.'"

Hank: (snorting) "Good luck with that."

The boys laugh as the sound of gravel crunching underfoot grows louder. The background noise of kids playing fades slightly as they walk away from the main park area.

Hank: "Alright, we're far enough. No one's going to bother us here. Are you ready?"

Roger: "Yeah, let's do it. Is anyone around?"

The sound of footsteps stopping. A moment of silence.

Hank: "Nope, we're alone. And yeah, Diavlo's here. He's in front of us, smiling like usual."

Roger: (quietly) " Okay, what should we test first?"

Hank: (pointing) "There, those birds in the tree. I'll ask him to get rid of them, but the tree needs to stay intact. No destroying the whole thing this time."

Roger: "Good idea. Let's see how precise he can be."

The sound of Hank inhaling sharply, followed by a long pause.

Hank: (softly) "Alright, Diavlo, do it."

There's a faint rustling sound, then the loud flapping of bird wings, followed by silence. A few branches fall to the ground with a soft crack.

Roger: "Whoa. He got them. The tree's fine, mostly. But those branches—he couldn't resist breaking a few, huh?"

Hank: (sighing) "Yeah, I told him not to destroy anything, but I guess he needs more practice."

Roger: "Maybe it's impossible for him to feed cleanly. Or maybe, like you said, he just needs more practice. What's next?"

Hank: (listening) "I hear some toads over there, near that little pool from the rain. Let's see if he can take care of them without touching the water this time."

Roger: "Alright, go for it."

Hank: (softly) "Diavlo, get rid of the toads. But don't touch the water."

There's a faint splashing sound, followed by complete silence.

Roger: (laughing) "So much for not touching the water."

Hank: "Yeah, I don't think he can help himself. He's strong, but precise? Not so much."

Roger: "Still, that was pretty cool. But we should wrap this up soon. Wait—what's wrong?"

Hank: (lowering his voice) "Diavlo says he smells danger nearby."

Roger: (whispering) "Danger? What kind of danger?"

Hank: (looking around) "I don't know. He just says he can smell it. Let's see... there's nothing here."

Roger: "Maybe ask him to check it out? We can see how far he can go from you."

Hank: "Good idea. Diavlo, go and check it out."

There's a long pause. The faint rustling of leaves in the distance.

Hank: (confused) "He says he can't go far. He's blocked somehow."

Roger: "Where is he now?"

Hank: "He's in those bushes, near the pool. That's like… four meters away? We should remember that distance."

Roger: "Yeah, definitely. So, what's the danger he's sensing?"

Hank: (pausing) "He says it's up in the tree."

Roger: (gasping) "The tree? What is it? Wait—look! Someone's up there!"

Hank: (panicked) "Who is that? What's he doing? He's trying to climb down. We can't let him get away!"

The sound of Hank running, heavy footsteps pounding on gravel. Roger's voice becomes frantic.

Roger: "Hank, what are you doing? One thing is killing animals, but hurting a person? Are you crazy?"

Hank: (yelling back) "I'm not going to hurt him! I just want to stop him. Diavlo, grab him! But don't kill him!"

There's a loud rustling sound, followed by a thud and a sharp gasp.

Roger: (panicked) "What happened? Did you get him?"

Hank: (frustrated) "No! He escaped! Diavlo couldn't hold him. It's like he… disappeared."

Roger: "What? How could he just vanish? This doesn't make sense."

Hank: (breathing heavily) "I don't know. But he's gone. And Diavlo's angry too—he couldn't catch him."

There's a long silence, broken only by the sound of the boys catching their breath.

Roger: (softly) "Hank, we need to leave. Now."

The sound of footsteps retreating quickly, gravel crunching underfoot. The tape clicks off.

Cassette Audio Ends

Detective Sergeant Ian Morrison's Investigation Diaries
June 6, 2000

I've been following Hank Johnson closely for the past few days, but yesterday, June 5, something happened that I can't easily explain. In the morning, I observed Hank and his friend Roger heading toward the park near Hank's new house, a park I've been keeping an eye on for a while now. For the first part of the morning, they stayed in the kids' section with the other children—playing, running, just acting like typical kids.

But then, they moved deeper into the park, towards a more secluded area, where the trees and bushes block out much of the sunlight. I followed at a distance, but there was no way to track them without being seen. So, I did what I had to do: I climbed one of the tall trees nearby to get a better vantage point. I thought I'd remain hidden and keep an eye on them without being noticed.

I stayed up there, watching them for a while. They eventually stopped by a small pool of water, formed from the rain the night before. That's when things took a strange turn. At first, I thought I was imagining things—maybe the heat was getting to me—but no. I saw Hank, without any visible movement, make a gesture toward a tree where a group of birds were perched. I didn't know what to make of it, but the next moment, those birds fell dead, as if something had struck them from the inside out. There was no visible cause, no predator, no sounds of an attack. Just... dead birds.

Before I could even process what I had just seen, Hank turned his attention to a group of toads near the water. Again, he made a motion, and, to my horror, those toads stopped moving and just... died. There was no sign of injury, no explanation. They just stopped moving.

I was so stunned that I forgot to take any pictures. I know I should have, but something about it... I couldn't bring myself to act, to do anything except watch. What I witnessed felt too unreal to be caught in a photograph. I need something concrete, something that will make others believe me. Without proof, no one will take me seriously.

As I was trying to regain my composure, the boys spotted me from a distance. It was too late to leave unnoticed. I tried to duck out of sight and hid in the bushes, hoping they didn't see where I was going. But as I crouched down, trying to stay hidden, I could feel something coming toward me.

Then it happened. I watched, frozen, as the bushes around me rustled. Something invisible was moving through them, getting closer. It was like the air itself had weight. I thought it was the end, that whatever had taken those birds and toads would come for me too. But then, I saw my own notebook and pen lift off the ground. I could see them float in the air as though a hand was lifting them. My pen moved, writing something on the page as if it had a mind of its own. Then, both the pen and the notebook dropped back to the ground.

The message on the page read:
"I've been watching you for a long time. Stay away or next time I'll KILL YOU."

I could barely believe my eyes. This wasn't just a coincidence anymore. Whoever, or whatever, Hank was connected to—Diavlo, as he called it—was aware of me. It was as if this... entity had been watching me, waiting for the right moment to send me a message.

After that, Hank and Roger spoke to each other. I couldn't hear their words clearly, but I did catch the part where they said something about Diavlo not being able to "find me." They then left the area, heading back toward the park's entrance.

"Diavlo" — the name struck me. It sounded like "Diablo," the devil in many religions, the fallen angel cast out of heaven. Was this the same force Mary Ann was referring to? The devil she claimed was inside Hank? It felt too much like a warning. The thought that Hank, or whatever force controlled him, could be linked to something as dark as that… it made my blood run cold.

I have no solid evidence to accuse Hank of anything yet. But this—what I just witnessed—it's not just a coincidence anymore. This entity, whatever it is, knows I'm watching.

I'm scared. But at the same time, I can't stop. There's something here, something more than just a troubled kid with a weird imaginary friend. I need to know what it is. And maybe, just maybe, I'll find the answers I'm looking for.

Hank Johnson's Diary
June 6, 2000

I can't stop thinking about the man we saw at the park yesterday. Who was he? What did he see? What if he tells someone about Diavlo? I don't even know who he is—I've never seen him before. It's like he just showed up out of nowhere.

I asked Diavlo if he's seen him before, but Diavlo said no. That doesn't make me feel any better. Diavlo's supposed to protect me, but if he doesn't know who the man is, how can he protect me from him?

Even Roger's scared. He said maybe the guy is from the media. Now that Dad's getting famous with his new job, Roger thinks reporters or journalists might be looking into our family. That idea makes me even more nervous. What if they find out about Diavlo? What if they find out about me?

I don't know what to do. Roger said we should just wait it out and see what happens. I guess that's all I can do for now. The man hasn't done anything since he saw us, so maybe he won't say anything. Maybe he didn't see enough to make sense of it. At least, I hope so.

I visited Mom today, earlier in the afternoon. She's still the same. No change. I brought her flowers. She just stared, like always. I told her about school and the running competition, the nurse says she can hear me. It felt strange talking to her like that. I don't even know if she knows I'm there, but I keep going anyway.

I just hope things get back to normal soon. Whatever "normal" is supposed to mean for me.

Sunnyvale Secondary School Council Bulletin
June 9, 2000

Dear Parents, Guardians, and Students,

We hope this bulletin finds you well as we move closer to an exciting mid-year term. Below are some important updates and news from Sunnyvale Secondary School:

1. Preparing for the August Marathon Interschool Competition

We are thrilled to announce that preparations are underway for the much-anticipated Interschool Marathon Competition for Year 7 students, scheduled for October. Our school is incredibly proud to have Hank Johnson representing us. Known for his speed and dedication, Hank has been training tirelessly, and the whole school is rooting for him to bring home another victory.

Hank's fan club, fondly known as "Team Hank," has been a source of enthusiasm and encouragement during his practice sessions. We appreciate their positive spirit and hope it inspires all our students to support their peers in upcoming events. Go Team Paddington!

2. Missing Toads Mystery Still Unresolved

The case of the missing toads intended for the science department's Year 8 biology class is still under investigation. Last week, several toads meant for educational observation disappeared from their enclosure in the science lab. While there are no clear leads yet, the school is taking this matter seriously. We ask all students to report anything they may know about this incident to the school office.

3. New Library Resources

We're excited to share that our recently renovated library has received a shipment of new books and learning materials. These resources include updated science encyclopedias, new fiction titles, and a special section dedicated to Australian history. Students are encouraged to visit the library during breaks and make use of these materials.

4. Drama Club Shines in Regional Competition

Congratulations to our talented drama club for winning second place in the Sunshine Coast Regional Drama Festival! Their performance of The Tempest by William Shakespeare received high praise from the judges for its creativity and emotional depth. A big round of applause for all the students and teachers who worked so hard to bring this production to life.

Reminders and Notices

- Parent-teacher interviews are scheduled for next Thursday. Please book your time slot via the school portal.
- The tuckshop has added new healthy snack options! Be sure to check them out during lunch breaks.
- The school's athletic track will be closed for maintenance next week. Alternative training areas will be arranged for PE classes.

Thank you for your continued support of our school and its activities. Let's keep striving for success together!

Warm regards,
Sunnyvale Secondary School Council

Cassette Audio Begins

The faint hum of fluorescent gym lights can be heard in the background, accompanied by the occasional echo of a basketball bouncing in the empty gym. The sound of sneakers squeaking lightly against the polished floor fades in and out as Hank sets up the recorder on the bench.

Roger: "Alright, is it on? I think it's a good idea, you know. If we miss anything, we can go back and listen later."

Hank: (quietly) "Yeah, it's on. You're right, better to have a record of this. Just in case."

Roger: (excitedly) "Okay, let's do this. The gym's empty, no one's going to bother us. I told you this was the perfect spot!"

Hank: "Yeah, you were right. No one's interrupting my 'personal training.' My dad was happy I wanted more time for the marathon. He has no idea what we're actually doing here."

Roger: (laughing) "He'd probably freak out if he knew. Okay, let's start simple. Diavlo, can you move that basketball over there?"

There's a faint rustling sound, and the basketball near the hoop starts to roll. It moves across the gym floor slowly at first, then suddenly darts forward.

Roger: "Whoa! That's cool. It's like it knows exactly where to stop. You can see him, right? What's he doing?"

Hank: "Yeah, I can see him. He's just smiling. That weird, sharp-tooth smile of his."

Roger: "Creepy, but cool. Okay, what else can we try? Oh! Can he destroy the ball? Like, make it disappear or something?"

Hank: (hesitating) "Destroy it? That's easy for him. But it might make noise."

Roger: "Come on, no one's here. Just do it."

Hank: (sighing) "Alright. Diavlo, get rid of the ball."

There's a sudden loud pop as the basketball explodes, sending rubber fragments flying across the gym. The noise echoes loudly.

Roger: (laughing nervously) "Okay, that was louder than I thought. Good thing this place is soundproof!"

Hank: "Yeah, let's not do that again. What next?"

Roger: "I've got an idea. Ask Diavlo to lift you. Like, make you float or something."

Hank: "Lift me? Alright, Diavlo, can you lift me?"

There's a pause, followed by a faint whooshing sound. Hank's voice becomes distant.

Hank: (laughing nervously) "Roger, I'm floating! This is insane!"

Roger: (awed) "I can see it! You're just... levitating. It's like you're flying. This is crazy!"

Hank: (excitedly) "Alright, Diavlo, let's take it up a notch. Fly me around the gym."

The faint sound of wind picks up as Hank's voice moves in and out of range. His laughter echoes through the gym.

Roger: "You look like Superman! This is unbelievable. Diavlo's amazing. Can he do the same to me?"

Hank: (laughing) "Let's find out. Diavlo, your turn—lift Roger."

There's a pause, then Roger lets out a startled yelp.

Roger: (panicked at first) "Whoa, whoa, WHOA! Okay, this is… this is weird. But awesome!"

Hank: (laughing) " It's cool!"

The sound of light thuds as both boys gently land back on the gym floor. There's a moment of silence as they catch their breath.

Hank: "Alright, I think that's enough for today. We learned a lot about what Diavlo can do. I'm just glad no one saw us."

Roger: (quietly) "Yeah… but Hank, I need to tell you something."

Hank: "What is it?"

Roger: (hesitating) "It's about my mom. She's been talking about moving. To London. To live with Paul. She says it's for my education, and that Paul's doing really well there. She wants us to leave next month."

Hank: (shocked) "Oh..."

There's a long pause, and the sound of the recorder being fiddled with, before it abruptly stops.

Cassette Audio Ends

Hank Johnson's Diary
August 11, 2000

I feel so tired today. Not the kind of tired where you just need to sleep, but like everything inside me feels drained. Ever since Roger told me he's moving to London, I haven't felt like myself. Roger's my second friend after Diavlo. Losing him feels like I'm losing a part of myself. I don't want him to go. Even though I still have Liam and Sophie, it's not the same. Roger's different. He's the only one who really knows about me—about Diavlo—and he doesn't run away.

I told my stepmom about Roger moving, and she said his mom is probably doing what she thinks is best for him. She also said moving to London right now is risky, with all the tension between countries. I know she's trying to make me feel better, but it didn't help. I can't shake the feeling that something bad could happen to Roger over there. At least when he's here, I can protect him. With Diavlo around, no one can hurt him. But what about when he's far away?

Roger noticed I was sad after he told me the news. He kept saying not to worry, that we'd still play games online, and that I could even visit him in London. I didn't know what to say to that. London feels so far away, and with everything going on in the world, I don't think my dad would ever let me travel there. It feels impossible.

Writing it all down helps, though. If I didn't, my brain might explode. I think I feel a little better now.

Diavlo's been with me all day. He hasn't left my side since I heard the news. Even now, he's standing next to me, watching me write. Earlier, he kept asking me questions: "Why are you sad? Why do you care about Roger so much? Why do humans have feelings like this?" It was like he was trying to figure me out, trying to understand what makes humans… human.

I didn't know how to answer him. I guess that's something I'm still trying to figure out myself.

Order of Imprisonment
August 15, 2000

Gold Coast Police Department
Order Number: GC-12784-2000

To Whom It May Concern,

This document serves as the official order for the imprisonment of
Dean Coopla, aged 23, residing in Gold Coast, Queensland, who has
been convicted of Grand Theft Auto (Car Theft) under Section 408A of
the Queensland Criminal Code.

Case Details:

- Name of Offender: Dean Coopla
- Age: 23
- Charge(s): Theft of a motor vehicle, unlawful possession of
  stolen property
- Conviction Date: August 15, 2000
- Court of Jurisdiction: Southport Magistrates Court, Gold Coast,
  Queensland

Sentence Details:

- Term of Imprisonment: 7 years
- Facility Assigned: Arthur Gorrie Correctional Centre
- Sentence Start Date: Pending apprehension
- Eligibility for Parole: N/A until custody

Summary of Crime:

Dean Coopla has been convicted in absentia for the theft of a 1999
Ford Falcon XR8. Evidence presented during the trial revealed that
Coopla had forcibly removed the vehicle from a private residence in

Southport and attempted to sell it to a third party. Despite being sentenced to 7 years of imprisonment, Coopla has evaded capture and remains at large.

Current Status:

The Gold Coast Police Department has issued an arrest warrant for Dean Coopla. Officers are actively pursuing leads to locate and apprehend him.

Request for Assistance:

The Gold Coast Police Department is urging members of the public, as well as family and acquaintances of Dean Coopla, to provide any information regarding his current whereabouts. Individuals with relevant information should contact the Gold Coast Crime Stoppers at 1800 333 000 or the local police station. All tips will remain confidential.

Directive:

By the authority of the Southport Magistrates Court and the Gold Coast Police Department, upon apprehension, Dean Coopla is to serve his sentence of 7 years at the Arthur Gorrie Correctional Centre. Law enforcement officers are to transport him to the correctional facility immediately after his arrest.

Signed,

Detective Inspector Sarah Morgan
Gold Coast Police Department
Contact: (07) 5555 1234

Note: This imprisonment order remains in effect until the subject is apprehended and remanded into custody.

Hank Johnson's Diary
August 11, 2000

Yesterday, I went to visit Mom at the hospital with Grandma. Nothing has changed. She's still the same as she's always been, just lying there, staring at nothing. I brought her some flowers, like I always do, but she didn't even notice them. Sometimes I wonder if she will be in that state forever.

On the way back, before Grandma dropped me off at home, she mentioned something about Dean. She said he's in serious trouble and that the police are looking for him. She said they might even come to our house to ask about him. I didn't really know what to say. I haven't seen Dean in years, and honestly, I'm not sure what kind of trouble he's in. Grandma seemed worried, though, like she knows more than she's telling me.

This morning, what Grandma said came true. The police came to the house right before Dad was about to drop me off at Roger's. I was planning to spend the whole day at Roger's house. With him leaving for London in September, we're trying to hang out as much as we can. I'm still struggling with the idea of him moving away, but I guess I'm starting to get used to it. Kind of.

Anyway, the police asked to talk to me and Dad. They said they found an old police report from years ago that mentioned me and Dean. I couldn't remember anything about it, but apparently, it was from when I was just a baby. That's when I started thinking about the last time I saw Dean, a few years ago. He said some strange things back then, but I didn't think much of it at the time. Now I'm starting to wonder if there was more to it.

Dad told the police we haven't seen Dean, and I said the same. It's the truth—we really haven't. The police left their number and said to contact them if Dean gets in touch. I doubt he will, though. If he's in as much trouble as they say, I bet he's hiding somewhere far away.

I don't know what Dean did, but I hope it doesn't bring more trouble to our family. We've had enough of that already.

Cassette Recording
September 3, 2000

Cassette Audio Begins

The hum of airport announcements and faint chatter of travellers fills the background. The occasional sound of a suitcase rolling by can be heard. The recorder clicks on, faint rustling indicating Hank has hidden it in his pocket.

Roger: (smiling) "Hank, I am gonna miss these recording sessions of yours"

Hank: "Haha."

Sophie: "So, Roger, have you looked up what school you're going to in London? Is it fancy? I heard they wear uniforms everywhere."

Roger: (laughing) "Yeah, it's called Westfield Academy. And yeah, we have to wear ties and blazers. My mom says I'll look very proper, but it sounds annoying."

Liam: "Ties every day? That sounds awful. Australia's heat might be bad, but at least we don't have to dress like penguins."

Hank: "It's not always hot in London, though. They've got cold weather, right?"

Roger: "Yeah, my mom said it'll start getting colder as soon as we arrive. I'll probably have to buy a coat. You know, real winter clothes."

Sophie: "Well, at least you won't have to worry about sunburn. I heard it rains all the time there."

Roger: (laughing) "Yeah, my mom said I should get used to grey skies. But hey, I'll finally see snow! That's kind of exciting."

Hank: "Snow would be cool to see, but it'll be weird not having you here. How are we supposed to play games when you're so far away?"

Roger: "Easy, Hank. We'll still play online. I'm not giving up on Lucifer 2. I'll just have to log in at different times. We'll figure it out."

Liam: "Yeah, but don't forget to write letters too. Emails are great, but old-school letters are fun."

Roger: "Sure, Liam. I'll write you all postcards or something."

Roger's mom calls him over to buy some food before boarding. Then, Roger and Hank wander off toward a nearby candy store while the others stay back.

Hank: (quietly) "I'm gonna miss you, Roger. Things won't be the same without you here."

Roger: (sighing) "I'll miss you too, Hank. And Diavlo. Is he around right now?"

Hank: "Yeah, he's here. He's been… quiet lately, though. I haven't seen that creepy smile of his in a while. The one with the sharp teeth."

Roger: (looking around) "Well, I wish I can see that with my own eyes. Bye, Diavlo. Don't cause too much trouble for Hank."

Hank: (smiling) "He heard you. He's standing right next to me."

Roger: "Don't forget, Hank. Keep testing Diavlo's abilities. You need to figure out everything he can do."

Hank: "I will. But it's gonna be harder without you around. You always had the ideas."

Roger: "You'll manage. And I'll still help when we talk online. Hey, you know what we talked about the other day at school? About how Diavlo acts?"

Hank: "Yeah, I still don't know. Sometimes it feels like he only does what I think or wish, but other times it's like he's acting on his own. I asked him, but even he's not sure. He said sometimes he's tied to me, and other times he feels free to act on his own. It's weird."

Roger: (thoughtfully) "We'll figure it out. Just keep testing. There's gotta be an answer..."

Hank: (voice breaking) "Roger… I'm gonna miss you so much. You're my second best friend."

Roger: (sniffling) "You used to call me that when we first met. I'll miss you too, Hank. But we'll keep in touch. I promise."

The sound of both boys crying softly fills the tape. Footsteps approach as Roger's mom calls for him to get ready to board. The recorder clicks off.

Cassette Audio Ends

**Detective Sergeant Ian Morrison's Investigation Diaries
September 29, 2000**

It has been some time since I've followed Hank Johnson directly. After my last engagement, I realized that it would be best to keep my distance from Hank for now. However, this investigation is far from over.

To expand the scope and keep things discreet, I've decided to involve three trusted detectives who see me as a mentor and share my belief that something about Hank and his past cannot be ignored. These detectives are among the sharpest and most reliable in the force, and they've pledged to keep this investigation absolutely confidential.

- Detective Brooke Caldwell: A brilliant investigator with a background in forensic psychology. Emma is meticulous in her observations and has an uncanny ability to piece together patterns from subtle clues.

- Detective Rachel Monroe: Known for her resourcefulness and sharp instincts. Rachel has experience working undercover, which makes her perfect for blending into environments and gathering intel without drawing attention.

- Detective Callum Hayes: A seasoned officer with a knack for surveillance and technical skills. Callum has handled some of the most challenging covert operations and is skilled at managing long-term investigations.

Over the past few weeks, they've taken over the task of following Hank's movements while reporting their findings back to me. From what they've observed so far, Hank's behavior has been normal. He attends school, spends time with his stepmother and father, and occasionally visits his mother in the hospital.

There have been no signs of him speaking to invisible friends or displaying any unusual behavior. Even his time at the park with friends seems entirely innocent now. The strange deaths of animals in nearby parks have also stopped, which is puzzling.

Still, I cannot shake the feeling that there is more beneath the surface. We will continue this investigation, regardless of how quiet things appear on the outside. My team agrees that if we wait long enough, something will surface again. It always does.

For now, we will proceed cautiously and keep this operation under the radar. We must be patient.

Cassette Audio Begins

The sound of distant chatter and cheers fills the background, along with the faint hum of a loudspeaker announcing the start of the marathon. Footsteps crunch lightly on gravel as people prepare to begin. The sound of a cassette recorder clicks on.

Michael: (mildly annoyed) "Hank, do we really need to have that thing on? You're about to start the marathon, not a radio show."

Hank: (calmly) "Yeah, Dad. It's important. I want to capture every moment—it's my hobby."

Emma: (gently) "Oh, Michael, let him. It's just a kid thing. He's not hurting anyone."

Michael: (sighs) "Alright, alright. Just focus on running and don't mess with it too much, okay?"

The sound of a horn blaring signals the start of the race. Cheers erupt from the crowd as the runners take off. The background fades into the rhythmic sound of Hank's feet pounding the pavement. His breathing becomes steady but audible.

Hank: (whispering) "Diavlo, how am I doing? Am I going fast enough? Should I push harder?"

There's a pause, the only sound being Hank's steady running and the faint breeze in the background.

Hank: (whispering again) "Can you tell if they're far behind me? I don't want to look back. I need to keep my focus. Are they catching up?"

Another pause. Hank's breathing deepens slightly as he continues running.

Hank: (quietly) "Do you think I can win this? Should I save my energy for later? I don't want to burn out too soon."

Hank remains silent for a while, only the sound of his running and distant cheering can be heard. Then, faint sirens begin to grow louder. The sounds of police officers shouting instructions cut through the background noise.

Police Officer: (distorted, in the distance) "The marathon is cancelled. Everyone, return to your homes immediately. This is an emergency. Please evacuate the area calmly and safely."

The sound of cars honking and confused voices grows louder as the police move through the crowd. Hank slows his pace, his footsteps becoming uneven.

Hank: (confused) "What's going on? Why are they cancelling the marathon?"

The sound of a car door opening and slamming shut is heard. Michael's voice comes through, slightly breathless.

Michael: "Hank, get in the car. We need to go."

Hank: (still confused) "Why? What happened? Why are the police shutting everything down?"

Michael: (hesitating) "I… I didn't want to tell you like this, but there's no easy way to say it."

Hank: (urgent) "Just tell me, Dad!"

Michael: (quietly, but firmly) "A bomb went off in London. It… destroyed the city. It happened just a few minutes ago. The government's asking everyone to stay home, the country has entered a state of alert."

There's a long pause. The sound of Hank's breathing quickens, but he says nothing at first.

Hank: (shocked, whispering) "Roger…"

The sound of the recorder clicks off abruptly.

Cassette Audio Ends

CSBNC Australia Newspaper
October 15, 2000

By Cameron Whitaker

<u>London Wiped Out in Atomic Attack: The World Holds Its Breath</u>

A catastrophic atomic bomb detonated in London on October 13, erasing nearly the entire city and leaving the world in shock. Current estimates suggest that only 5% of London's population survived the attack. The tragedy has thrown the United Kingdom into turmoil, mourning the loss of its historic capital and the countless lives lost in a single, devastating moment.

Just hours after the destruction, NATO and the United States confirmed responsibility for the bombing, citing it as a retaliation for the assassination of the U.S. President on October 14. The assassination, which occurred in undisclosed circumstances, was kept under wraps until the U.S. and NATO could determine their response. Details of the President's assassination have yet to be revealed, adding another layer of mystery to the rapidly escalating global crisis.

<u>NATO States Enter Emergency Lockdown</u>

In response to fears of retaliation from Russia and its allies, NATO nations have declared states of emergency. Curfews have been enacted, with citizens restricted from leaving their homes after 5 p.m. and only allowed to go out for essential activities between 8 a.m. and 5 p.m. These measures aim to reduce civilian exposure in case of further attacks. Countries including the United States, Australia, Canada, France, Germany, and other major NATO members have adopted the emergency measures.

Military presence has intensified in major cities worldwide, and governments have urged citizens to remain calm but vigilant. The

United Nations Security Council has called for an emergency meeting to address the escalating situation, but so far, no concrete resolutions have been made.

The UK's Response: Mourning and Isolation

The United Kingdom, devastated by the attack, has declared a period of national mourning. Vigils and memorials are being held across the remaining cities as citizens grapple with the loss of London. The UK government has condemned NATO's actions in the strongest terms, labelling the bombing "a reckless and unjustifiable attack that has plunged the world further into chaos."

In response, the UK has imposed severe penalties on NATO countries, including closing its borders to NATO-aligned nations and halting all trade and commerce with them. This decision will likely have significant economic repercussions for both the UK and its former NATO allies, further isolating the country.

What Comes Next?

With the UK reeling and NATO nations bracing for potential retaliation, the world waits to see how Russia and its allies will respond. Political analysts warn that this could lead to an unprecedented escalation in global warfare. Russia has yet to issue an official statement, but there are widespread fears that it may retaliate with nuclear force, plunging the world into an even deeper crisis.

For now, the people of London, the UK, and the world mourn the devastating loss while grappling with the uncertainty of what lies ahead. As governments scramble to contain the fallout—both literal and political—the hope for peace seems more distant than ever.

<u>Australia's Stance</u>

The Australian government has extended its sympathies to the UK and its citizens, expressing deep regret over the loss of London. However, as a NATO-aligned nation, Australia remains on high alert, preparing for possible repercussions. Prime Minister Victoria Reynolds has urged citizens to abide by the curfew and emergency measures, emphasizing that public safety is the nation's top priority.

For now, the world watches anxiously, holding its breath as tensions rise and the possibility of further devastation looms.

For updates on this developing story, stay tuned to CSBNC Australia.

CSBNC Australia Newspaper
October 17, 2000

By Cameron Whitaker

China Launches Nuclear Bomb on Tokyo: Devastation in Japan

On October 16, the world witnessed yet another horrific act of nuclear warfare. A Chinese nuclear bomb struck Tokyo, Japan, obliterating much of the city. Current estimates suggest that only 9% of Tokyo's population survived, with the rest either perishing in the explosion or succumbing to the catastrophic aftermath.

This devastating attack marks a dangerous escalation in the already volatile global conflict. Tokyo, a hub of culture, technology, and history, now lies in ruins, joining the grim fate of London just days earlier. Rescue efforts are underway, but the scale of destruction has left Japan's government and citizens in a state of shock and mourning.

The Japanese Prime Minister has issued a statement condemning the attack and vowing to rebuild while urging global leaders to find a path to peace. However, the reality of the escalating war leaves little room for optimism.

The United States Swears in a New President

In the aftermath of the assassination of the U.S. President on October 14, Vice President Nathaniel Grant was sworn in as the new President of the United States. Grant, whose previous role as Head of the FBI has shaped his reputation as a strong and decisive leader, is expected to take an aggressive stance in the ongoing conflict.

Political analysts believe Grant's law enforcement background and no-nonsense approach to security will heavily influence his strategy in this war. Early indications suggest he may push for a swift and forceful response to recent events, raising concerns about further nuclear exchanges.

In his first address as President, Grant pledged to protect the United States and its allies while holding those responsible for the assassination and attacks accountable. "The world stands on the edge of chaos, but we will not falter," he said.

<u>NATO Nations Remain on High Alert</u>

Australia and other NATO countries remain in a state of emergency, with military forces maintaining heightened vigilance around the clock. Curfews and strict regulations continue to limit civilian movement, with all non-essential activities suspended.

Prime Minister Victoria Reynolds has urged Australians to stay strong and united during these turbulent times. "Our military is prepared for any threat, and we will do everything in our power to protect our people and our allies," she said in a public address late last night.

NATO allies such as the United States, Canada, France, and Germany are stepping up defensive measures and coordinating closely to prepare for potential retaliation from China or Russia.

Meanwhile, the United Kingdom, which withdrew from NATO several years ago, has condemned the attacks and closed its borders entirely, halting all commerce with NATO countries. The UK has taken an isolationist stance since the London bombing, focusing on national recovery and security.

<u>The World on the Brink</u>

As the dust settles over Tokyo and world leaders grapple with the rapidly deteriorating global situation, the fear of further nuclear strikes looms large. Speculation abounds over whether China, Russia, or NATO will make the next move, with each side refusing to back down.

The annihilation of London and Tokyo within days of each other has marked a point of no return. The Third World War has begun, and the scale of destruction and loss of life threatens to surpass any conflict in human history. The world waits with bated breath to see what will come next.

Stay tuned to CSBNC Australia for updates on this developing story.

SWEET SIXTEEN

Hank Johnson's Diary
February 13, 2003

It's been so long since I've written in this diary. I didn't feel like I needed it for years. But tonight, I feel like I need to put this somewhere—my mom moved her pinky finger on her left hand today. The doctors said it's a promising sign. I should feel happy, and I am, I guess. But I can't stop wondering. If she gets better, will she treat me the same as she did back then? That day at school, when she called me the devil and tried to hurt me. Liam says I should be afraid of her, but I can't. Even after everything, I can't.

Roger's disappearance during the London attack three years ago still feels unreal. Things haven't been the same without him. Liam and Sophie have been there for me, and I'm grateful, but no one could ever replace Roger. For months after the bombing, Dad tried helping me search for any sign that Roger, his mom, or his brother Paul survived, but nothing. The news said there were so many bodies they couldn't identify. Sometimes, I wonder if Roger made it and is out there somewhere. But deep down, I know it's unlikely.

The world's only gotten worse since then. After London, Tokyo was hit next, and then came the endless retaliation. Russia nuked cities in Canada, NATO hit cities in China. The chaos spread, and now most of South America, Africa, and India are gone. Conquered. Destroyed. I never cared much about politics or wars before London, but after losing Roger, it's hard not to notice how messed up everything is. It's like the whole world is falling apart, and no one knows how to stop it.

After London, we didn't have school for six months. When we finally went back, everything was different. The curfew still hasn't been lifted— we have to be home before 5 p.m. It's the same in most countries now. The streets are quieter, darker. It feels like the world's holding its breath, waiting for the next bomb to fall.

Diavlo has been a good support through all of this. At first, it was hard. We couldn't go out as freely as we used to, and there were days when I didn't see him at all. He would disappear for long stretches, and I worried I might lose him too. But we found ways to "feed" him without leaving the house. Bad wishes, bad thoughts—it's not the same as before, but it works. At least I still have him.

I don't know what's going to happen next. I hope my mom keeps getting better. I hope the war ends. I hope I don't lose anyone else.

February 15, 2003

Today, I went to visit Dad at work. It's always a bit overwhelming being there. Everyone already knows me, and they all seem to respect Dad so much. He's such an important figure in the state now, working as Director-General of the Department of the Premier and Cabinet. He's always busy, always making big decisions that he says affect everyone in Queensland. Dad told me again today that he hopes I'll follow in his footsteps someday, maybe even go into politics.

Honestly, I've been thinking about it. At school, I'm already part of the School Council, and I've started liking the idea of being part of decisions, even if they're just small ones right now. I think I could be good at it, but who knows? Maybe it's too early to think about all that.

Diavlo's been asking to feed again lately. It's been harder to think of things for him. I haven't had any major bad wishes in my mind recently, so today, while I was at Dad's work, I thought, just for a second, about wishing the whole department would disappear. Then I whispered so quietly that no one could hear me, "Don't kill anyone."

It worked. Diavlo felt better after that. We've figured out that he doesn't always need to act on the bad wish to feed. Just thinking it is enough, and then I can stop him with words if I need to. I know it doesn't satisfy him as much, but it's enough to keep him around without causing any real harm. I think we're finding a way to balance it all, but I'm still careful about what I wish for.

There's another running competition coming up at school in March. I haven't been practicing as I should. After Roger disappeared, I lost my focus completely. I kept coming in second or third, and it felt like I couldn't get my head back in the game. Even the fan group I used to have closed down. I kind of miss that, in a weird way. It was embarrassing at times, but it also felt nice to have people cheering me on.

This time, though, I'm going to be number one again.

CSBNC Australia
February 16, 2003

By Cameron Whitaker

<u>Third World War Continues: Tensions Persist Across the Globe</u>

The Third World War rages on, with no end in sight. Although the devastating nuclear bombings have ceased for now, military conflicts in several regions continue to escalate, causing further destruction and loss of life.

In the Middle East, clashes between NATO-allied forces and Russian-backed militias have intensified over the past month. Cities already ravaged by years of conflict are now battlegrounds for this global war, with innocent civilians caught in the crossfire. The situation remains dire, with neither side showing signs of backing down.

Meanwhile, the Korean Peninsula is witnessing one of its worst crises in decades. North Korea, having recently allied itself with Russia, is locked in a bloody war with South Korea. The conflict has devastated communities along the border, and the South Korean government, heavily reliant on NATO support, is struggling to maintain control in the face of relentless aggression from the North.

<u>Australia and Germany Increase Military Support</u>

Countries like Australia and Germany, which have largely avoided the devastating losses experienced by others, are stepping up their involvement in the war. Both nations have pledged additional military aid to NATO, providing forces and resources to support their allies on the frontlines.

Australian Prime Minister Victoria Reynolds has reiterated her government's commitment to aiding NATO but expressed a strong desire to avoid deeper involvement. "We are providing the necessary support to our allies to ensure the protection of democratic nations, but we remain cautious of escalating our direct participation in this war," Reynolds said during a press conference yesterday.

Similarly, Germany has deployed military forces to bolster NATO's presence in Eastern Europe, though German officials have voiced concerns about becoming further embroiled in the conflict.

For now, both nations hope their involvement remains limited to military assistance and logistical support, but as the war drags on, the possibility of greater entanglement looms large.

<u>No Progress Toward Peace</u>

Despite the mounting death toll and global suffering, there are no signs of peace talks on the horizon. Diplomats from NATO and Russia have reportedly refused multiple calls to negotiate, citing irreconcilable differences and distrust. The prospect of a ceasefire remains as elusive as ever, with both sides determined to secure victory at any cost.

The international community continues to watch in despair as the war reshapes the political and geographical landscape of the world. With the lack of diplomacy and rising tensions between nations, the hope for peace seems increasingly distant.

As the world grapples with the ongoing devastation, one question remains on everyone's minds: How much more can humanity endure before it breaks completely?

Stay tuned to CSBNC Australia for updates on this developing story.

Sunnyvale Secondary School Council Bulletin
March 17, 2003

<u>Weekly Announcements and Updates</u>

Welcome back to another exciting week at Sunnyvale Secondary School! Here are the latest updates and announcements from the school council:

<u>Reminders About the Curfew</u>

A reminder to all students and families: the government-imposed curfew remains in effect, requiring everyone to be at home by 5 p.m. and allowing outdoor activity only after 8 a.m. Please ensure you are adhering to these guidelines for your safety.

In light of ongoing global tensions, we also encourage all students to take part in the emergency preparedness simulations conducted during homeroom periods. These drills are vital for ensuring everyone knows how to respond in the event of an attack. Let's stay vigilant and prepared.

<u>Running Competition – March 20, 2003</u>

The much-anticipated annual Sunnyvale Secondary School Running Competition is just around the corner! This event will take place on Thursday, March 20, and promises to be an exciting showcase of athletic talent.

This year's competitors include:

- Liam Parker, our reigning champion who has claimed the top spot for the past three years.
- Hank Johnson, who was number one for several years. Hank is determined to reclaim his title this year.

- Jessica Nguyen, a promising new competitor in Year 9 who has been practicing tirelessly.
- Ethan Moore, a strong runner from Year 10 who consistently places in the top five.

In an interview with the school council, Hank Johnson shared his thoughts about the upcoming competition:

"I'm really looking forward to the next competition. It's been a while since I've been number one, but I'm ready to give it my all. Winning isn't just about the title—it's about proving to myself that I can still do it."

Hank's fan group, affectionately known as "Team Hank," is back in action, cheering him on during practice sessions. Their enthusiasm has certainly brought extra energy to the track.

We wish all competitors the best of luck and encourage students to come and support your peers at the event!

<u>Year 11 Formal Announced</u>

We are thrilled to announce the upcoming Year 11 Formal, scheduled for October 2023. This event will be a chance for our Year 11 students to celebrate their journey at Sunnyvale in style.

Highlights of the formal will include:

- The crowning of the Year 11 King and Queen of the Formal, as voted by students.
- A live DJ, catered dinner, and plenty of opportunities for fun and dancing.
- The announcement of more details, including the venue and ticket prices, will be shared in the coming months.

This is an event you won't want to miss, so Year 11 students, start thinking about your outfits and get ready for an unforgettable evening!

Let's make this week a productive and exciting one. Stay safe, stay focused, and let's make Sunnyvale Secondary proud!

Sunnyvale Secondary School Council

**Detective Sergeant Ian Morrison's Investigation Diaries
March 19, 2003**

It has been three years since I last checked on Hank Johnson personally. The operation has become increasingly challenging due to the chaos brought by the Third World War—curfews, heightened security measures, and restrictions have made surveillance more complicated. Instead, I've relied heavily on updates from the detectives assisting me in this ongoing investigation.

Detective Brooke Caldwell has been tasked with monitoring Hank's movements to and from school. She has reported nothing unusual. Hank's routine seems to be consistent—he attends school and leaves promptly after. He doesn't linger or interact much beyond his usual circle of friends. Brooke noted that his demeanour at school is normal for a teenager, and no strange behaviours have been observed during her shifts.

Detective Rachel Monroe has been responsible for watching Hank during his non-school hours. Rachel reported that Hank rarely goes out for social purposes, which aligns with the restrictions and the aftermath of the war. She speculated that Hank's reduced social activity could also be tied to the loss of his best friend, Roger Williams, during the London attack three years ago. Roger's presumed death seems to have affected Hank deeply, as he no longer engages with others in the way he once did. Rachel's surveillance noted Hank typically spends time either at home, accompanying his dad or stepmom on grocery runs, visiting his grandmother on the Sunshine Coast, or occasionally tagging along with his father to work.

Detective Callum Hayes has been focusing on the other members of Hank's family. Callum's investigation revealed that Hank's cousin, Dean Coopla, is still on the run after being wanted for car theft. Gold Coast police have deprioritized the case due to the overwhelming demands brought on by the war. Callum also continues to monitor

Michael Johnson, Hank's father, but with extreme caution. Michael's prominent position as Director-General of the Department of the Premier and Cabinet makes him a difficult subject to follow without drawing unwanted attention. Callum reported no suspicious activity, but Michael's new role necessitates a careful and subtle approach to ensure the secrecy of this operation.

As for me, the ongoing Third World War has pulled my attention elsewhere. While Australia hasn't suffered massive casualties, the global impact of the war has created new demands on law enforcement, leaving me with less time to focus on this case. Even so, I remain committed to the investigation. Hank's behavior may appear ordinary on the surface, but the incidents I've witnessed and the patterns I've traced suggest there's more beneath the surface.

For now, we will continue our quiet vigilance, waiting for the moment when something finally breaks this case open.

Video Recording
March 20, 2003

The video begins with Emma Johnson adjusting the camera, her voice coming through warmly as she directs it toward Hank, who is stretching near the starting line.

Emma: "Alright, Hank, we're rolling. You ready for your big moment?"

Hank: (grinning) "Yeah, I'm ready. First place this time, for sure."

Emma: "That's the spirit. Your dad would love to be here, you know. He's really proud of you. He just couldn't get out of his meeting."

Hank: (shrugging but smiling) "It's fine, I know he's busy. Thanks for coming though. And don't forget to record everything!"

Emma: "Of course! And look at you, not using the tape recorder this time. Does that mean we're retiring it?"

Hank: (laughing) "Not retiring it, but for today, the camera's better. We gotta catch every moment."

From the distance, a voice calls out, "Runners to your positions!" Emma pans the camera toward the track, capturing the other runners— Liam, Jessica, and Ethan—stretching and jogging in place.

Emma: "That's your cue, champ. Go show them what you've got. I'll get it all on tape."

Hank: (nodding) "Alright, see you at the finish line."

Hank jogs to the starting line. Emma zooms in on him as the runners take their positions. The sound of the starting whistle echoes, and the runners are off. Emma follows Hank with the camera, narrating softly in excitement.

Emma: "There he goes! Come on, Hank, keep that pace. Oh, Liam's got a strong lead… but Hank's not far behind. Go, Hank!"

As Hank starts to pick up speed, a strange high-pitched noise comes from the camera. The screen flickers and blurs for a few seconds. Emma fumbles with the camera, her voice sounding concerned.

Emma: "What was that? Come on, camera, don't do this now…"

The video stabilizes just in time to show Hank sprinting ahead of Liam in the last stretch and crossing the finish line first. Cheers erupt in the background as Emma refocuses the camera on Hank, who is catching his breath and smiling widely.

Emma: "You did it, Hank! First place! That was incredible!"

Hank jogs over to Emma, panting but grinning ear to ear.

Hank: "Did you get it all? Was it good?"

Emma: "I got most of it. But… there was a weird problem with the camera right before you passed Liam. Maybe we can check it later and see if it recorded properly."

Hank: (frowning slightly) "Weird… okay. But thanks for recording it, Emma. It means a lot."

Emma: "Of course, sweetheart. Now go get your medal!"

Emma follows Hank with the camera as he walks to the podium. The school council president places the gold medal around Hank's neck while the crowd cheers. Emma pans to the group of students cheering with handmade signs that read "Team Hank!" and "Go Hank!" She zooms in on their excited faces as they chant Hank's name.

Emma: "Look at that fan club, Hank. You've got your own cheering section."

Hank waves to the group, smiling shyly but clearly enjoying the attention. Emma captures every moment, from the cheers to Hank stepping off the podium, medal shining in the sunlight.

Emma: "He's going to go far… I can feel it."

The video ends with Hank walking toward his friends, medal in hand, the sounds of cheering fading into the background.

Hank Johnson's Diary
March 21, 2003

Today was such a great day at school. Everyone was congratulating me for my win yesterday at the competition. It felt really good to be back in first place again. Even Liam, who's always been a tough competitor but also my friend, came up to me and said I did an amazing job. That meant a lot. I feel like, for the first time in years, I'm finally starting to feel better since Roger… well, since he's been gone.

Something funny happened too. When I checked my locker this morning, I found at least 20 letters stuffed inside. They were all from girls asking me to go to the Formal party with them in October. I didn't even know most of them—probably 90% of the names were unfamiliar! It was kind of overwhelming, but also a little funny. I guess this is what being "popular" feels like?

To be honest, I already know who I want to ask to the Formal. Sophie. She's been my friend for a while now, and I think she's really cute. I love how smart she is, especially when she talks about science. But I don't even know if she feels the same way about me. Lately, I've seen her hanging out with other boys, so I'm not sure. We're still friendly, but I feel like maybe she sees me as just a friend. I'll need to figure out a way to ask her.

After school, I checked out the video recording from yesterday's race. It was cool to watch it back, but unfortunately, the part where I passed Liam and won was all blurred and distorted. That's the part I really wanted to see. I found it strange, and then Diavlo started talking to me about it. He said that at the exact moment I passed Liam, he felt a huge surge of energy draining him.

I tried to think back, and I realized that right before I passed Liam, I wished really hard that I could surpass him. Could it be that Diavlo's powers were somehow passed to me? It's never happened before, at least not like that. And maybe that's why the camera glitched—it couldn't handle whatever happened at that moment.

I wish Roger were still here. He always had ideas about how to figure things like this out. Without him, I feel like I'm just guessing. I don't know what this means, but maybe I'll need to test it more carefully next time. For now, I'll just enjoy the win and keep going. It's been a good day.

March 22, 2003

Tomorrow, I'm going with Dad to a jail. It's something he has to do as part of his new job. He said he needs to assess how state policies are being implemented within the jail. I asked him if I could come, and at first, he didn't want me to. He said it's not a place for me, but I kept asking, and eventually, he said yes. I think he just gave in because he's been busy lately and feels bad about not spending as much time with me.

Today, I tried something… weird. I was thinking about what happened during the race and how it seems like I used Diavlo's powers. I wondered if I could make it happen again. So, I tried wishing for things, like, "I wish I could fly," or "I wish I could break this chair." For the chair one, I even pushed hard on it, but nothing happened. Well, nothing except me hurting my shoulder. It still stings a little.

If I didn't absorb Diavlo's powers, then what actually happened during the race? Was it just luck? Or something else? I asked Diavlo about it, but he just gave me that cheeky, smirky smile of his. He didn't say anything. Honestly, I don't even think he knows what happened.

On top of all that, I've been thinking about how long it's been since Diavlo fed. He hasn't been complaining much, but I know it's only a matter of time before he starts getting restless. I need to figure out a way to feed him again, but it's been tricky. I don't want to do anything too big or risky. For now, I'll just have to keep thinking about it.

Video Recording - Channel ATVH News
March 23, 2003
Time: 12:05 PM

The screen transitions abruptly from a morning talk show to a newsroom. Two presenters, Sarah Blake and Tom Cooper, sit at a desk with serious expressions. The words "Breaking News" flash across the bottom of the screen in bold red letters.

Sarah Blake: (speaking firmly) "We interrupt your regular programming to bring you breaking news from Brisbane. A tragic and unprecedented event has occurred at the Brisbane Correctional Facility, and we're just beginning to receive the details. This is a developing story."

Tom Cooper: (nodding gravely) "That's right, Sarah. Earlier this morning, during a scheduled visit by Queensland's Director-General of the Department of the Premier and Cabinet, Michael Johnson, a major incident took place. During the visit, alarms were triggered within the facility, and what authorities discovered was nothing short of horrifying."

The screen switches to a live feed of the Brisbane Correctional Facility, where flashing police lights illuminate the entrance, and officers can be seen setting up barriers around the area.

Sarah Blake: (voiceover) "According to initial reports, an entire cell block within the facility, housing approximately 60 inmates, was discovered dead. Authorities are calling this an 'extraordinary event' and are currently investigating the causes behind this mass tragedy."

The broadcast returns to the newsroom. Sarah looks directly into the camera, her voice steady but tinged with shock.

Sarah Blake: "The deaths have been described by officials as 'extremely rare' and unlike anything the Queensland Police Service has encountered before. Investigators are already on the scene, and the prison remains under lockdown."

Tom Cooper: (leaning forward slightly) "What's particularly concerning is the timing of this event. Director-General Michael Johnson had just about to conclude his visit to the facility when the alarms began sounding. Authorities have yet to release any further details. All we know for now is that Director-General Michael Johnson and his team are still inside the facility."

Sarah Blake: (nodding) "We've also learned that Director-General Johnson brought his son with him to the visit. It's unclear why the young boy was present, but our thoughts go out to him and his family during what must be a traumatic time."

Tom Cooper: "The Queensland Police Service has promised to provide more updates as the investigation unfolds. For now, we'll continue to monitor the situation and bring you the latest developments as soon as we receive them."

Sarah Blake: "Stay tuned to ATVH News for ongoing coverage of this breaking story."

The camera fades to the "Breaking News" banner as the broadcast transitions back to the program schedule.

Time: 8:05 PM

The screen flashes with "Breaking News" in bold red letters as the presenters, Sarah Blake and Tom Cooper, appear on-screen with sombre expressions. The atmosphere is heavy, and the newsroom background is dimly lit.

Sarah Blake: (calm but serious) "Good evening. We return with further developments on the mass deaths at Brisbane Correctional

Facility. The following images and details may be deeply disturbing. If there are children present, we strongly recommend that you put them to bed before continuing to watch this broadcast."

Tom Cooper: (nodding gravely) "Authorities have confirmed the deaths of 60 inmates earlier today, but new information has revealed the horrifying nature of their deaths. According to official reports, most of the victims were found with their guts ripped apart, as if something or someone had attempted to extract their internal organs through the skin."

The screen transitions to blurred images of the prison grounds, showing police vehicles and forensics teams entering the facility. Officers are seen speaking to staff and inmates as the investigation continues.

Sarah Blake: (voiceover) "The slaughter has sent shockwaves through the community, not only because of its brutality but also because of who was present when the tragedy unfolded. Director-General Michael Johnson, his team, and his young son were still inside the facility when the incident occurred. Authorities have confirmed that no one has been allowed to leave the premises as they continue to investigate."

Tom Cooper: (interjecting) "The sheer scale of this massacre has raised questions among the public. Could this be related to the ongoing Third World War? Some are speculating that this may be the work of a new biological weapon deployed by Australia's enemies."

The screen cuts to an interview with Detective Sergeant Ian Morrison, who is standing outside the prison gates. He appears tired but composed as he speaks into the microphone of an ATVH reporter.

Reporter: (off-camera) "Detective Morrison, what can you tell us about what's happening inside the facility?"

Detective Morrison: (clearly uneasy) "At this point, we don't have all the answers. The deaths are highly unusual, and we're conducting thorough interrogations of everyone who was inside the facility during the incident. That includes staff, inmates, and visitors. We ask the public to remain calm and avoid speculation while the investigation is ongoing."

The screen returns to the newsroom, where Sarah and Tom sit silently for a moment before continuing.

Sarah Blake: (sincerely) "Thank you, Detective Morrison, for providing what little clarity is available at this time. While the cause of these deaths remains unknown, the severity of this incident cannot be overstated."

Tom Cooper: "We'll continue to monitor the situation closely and provide updates as they come. For now, we ask the public to remain vigilant and follow any instructions from authorities. This is a time for unity and resilience as we navigate these uncertain times."

Sarah Blake: (looking directly at the camera) "Our thoughts are with the families of those affected and everyone inside the facility. Stay tuned to ATVH News for the latest developments on this deeply unsettling story."

The broadcast fades out, returning to a "Breaking News" banner as the program concludes.

Tape Recording
March 23, 2003
Time: 8:25 PM

The sound of chairs being shuffled and faint murmurs in the background. The tape recorder clicks on, followed by the steady hum of the room's atmosphere. Detective Ian Morrison speaks first, his voice calm but firm.

Detective Ian Morrison: "This is Detective Sergeant Ian Morrison, recording an official interrogation at Brisbane Correctional Facility. Present in the room are Michael Johnson, Director-General of the Department of the Premier and Cabinet, and his son, Hank Johnson. Time is 8:25 PM."

Michael Johnson: (interrupting, voice sharp) "Detective Morrison, I need to make it absolutely clear that this interrogation is entirely unnecessary. Hank is only fifteen years old. How in the world could he possibly have any involvement in the deaths of those inmates?"

Detective Ian Morrison: (calmly) "Mr. Johnson, I understand your concerns, but we need to interview everyone who was present during the incident. This is standard procedure. We're simply gathering information."

Hank Johnson: (quietly) "Dad, it's fine. I don't mind."

Michael sighs heavily but doesn't respond. The sound of a chair creaking as someone shifts in their seat.

Detective Ian Morrison: "Alright, Hank, let's begin. Can you confirm your full name and date of birth for the record?"

Hank Johnson: "Uh, yeah. It's Hank Johnson. June 2, 1987."

Detective Ian Morrison: "Thank you. Now, can you tell me why you were at Brisbane Correctional Facility today?"

Hank Johnson: "I came with my dad. He had some work here, and I wanted to see what it was like."

Detective Ian Morrison: "Were you with your father the entire time during the visit?"

Hank Johnson: "Mostly. I stayed close to him, but sometimes I just looked around on my own. I didn't go far, though."

Detective Ian Morrison: "Did you notice anything unusual before the alarms went off?"

Hank Johnson: "Not really. Everything seemed normal, I guess."

Detective Ian Morrison: "When the alarms went off, where were you?"

Hank Johnson: "I was with my dad. We were about to leave the building, and then everything just got chaotic."

Detective Ian Morrison: "Did you hear or see anything that might explain what happened to the inmates?"

Hank Johnson: "No, I didn't. I didn't even know something happened until later."

Detective Ian Morrison: "Okay. Now, Hank, I need to ask you about something specific. A witness inside the facility claims they saw you speaking to yourself during the visit. Can you explain that?"

There's a pause. The sound of Hank shifting uncomfortably in his seat.

Hank Johnson: (defensively) "That's not true! I wasn't talking to myself. Why would I do that?"

Michael Johnson: (interrupting, voice rising) "Alright, that's enough! This is absurd. My son is not some lunatic. He's a teenager! You're making a mockery of this process, Detective Morrison. I demand you stop this interrogation immediately."

Detective Ian Morrison: "Mr. Johnson—"

Michael Johnson: (angrily) "No! This ends now. I've had enough of this circus. You're wasting time harassing my son instead of finding out what really happened."

The sound of a door opening, followed by hurried footsteps as Michael calls for someone outside.

Michael Johnson: "I need my team in here. Now!"

The tape abruptly stops.

The screen cuts to the Channel ATVH News studio, where a composed news presenter, Claudia Blake, sits behind the desk. The logo "BREAKING NEWS" flashes at the bottom of the screen. Claudia's expression is serious.

Claudia Blake: "We interrupt our regular programming to bring you an update on the shocking incident at Brisbane Correctional Facility earlier today. Police have now allowed those who were present during the tragic events to leave the premises, including Queensland's Director-General of the Department of the Premier and Cabinet, Michael Johnson, his son, and members of his team. Authorities have stated there is no evidence linking them to the incident, and their presence is no longer required for the ongoing investigation."

An image of the correctional facility appears on-screen, with flashing lights from police cars and ambulances illuminating the scene.

Claudia Blake: "Biologists and other specialists remain on-site, continuing their investigation into the gruesome and mysterious deaths of sixty inmates within one of the facility's blocks. No official cause of death has been released yet, though authorities assure the public they are working tirelessly to uncover the truth behind this horrifying event."

The screen transitions to a stock photo of a detective badge overlayed with text reading "Internal Tensions."

Claudia Blake: "Meanwhile, inside sources from the facility have confirmed reports of a heated argument between Director-General Michael Johnson and Detective Sergeant Ian Morrison during the course of the investigation. The dispute reportedly arose during an interview with Mr. Johnson's son, Hank Johnson, who was among those present at the facility today. While Michael Johnson's actions as a concerned father are understandable, sources claim he leveraged his position of power to bring the interrogation to an abrupt halt. Some are already calling this an abuse of authority, raising concerns over whether this has compromised the investigation."

Claudia looks directly into the camera, her tone measured but firm.

Claudia Blake: "We will continue to bring you updates on this developing story as soon as new information becomes available. For now, our thoughts remain with the families of the victims, and we thank the specialists and authorities for their dedication in uncovering the truth. Stay tuned to Channel ATVH for more updates throughout the night."

The camera zooms out slightly, and the Channel ATVH News theme plays as the broadcast transitions to a commercial break.

Hank Johnson's Diary
March 24, 2003

I'm so tired. I didn't wake up until late today after everything that happened at the jail yesterday. They didn't let us go until way too late, and Dad and I didn't get home until around 1 a.m. Emma was worried sick about us. She said the news wouldn't stop talking about the incident, and apparently, I was even on TV. It was bizarre.

Dad told me this morning that I didn't have to go to school today, or even all week if I didn't want to. He said the news is making him out to be an abuser of power, and he's worried the kids at school might treat me badly because of it. I told him I'd skip today, but tomorrow I'm going back. A few bullies won't stop me. Plus, I've got something important to do—I need to ask Sophie to the Formal in October. I've got to act fast before someone else asks her. I've been planning this for a while, and I can't let the incident at the jail ruin everything.

But yesterday... yesterday was horrible. I've been trying to process everything. That's when I confronted Diavlo. I know it was him. He killed all those men in the jail. Sixty people. I—I don't even know how to feel about it. I remember for just a half-second thinking it would be okay if he "fed" off the inmates—they were bad people anyway. But it happened so quickly. I couldn't stop him with a verbal command like I usually do. There were people around me the whole time—they would think I'm crazy. Then, the alarms went off, and I knew. I knew it was Diavlo. And there he was, standing there with that huge, vibrant smile like he always has after he's fed.

Sixty people. Gone.

Am I to blame for this? I can't stop thinking about it. Diavlo told me it was fine, that they were bad people who did bad things and deserved punishment. And honestly, for a second, that made me feel better. But then I keep wondering—how far does this go? Is this why Diavlo is with me? To punish bad people? To help me make a difference in the world?

I don't know. I just don't know.

**Detective Sergeant Ian Morrison's Investigation Diaries
March 26, 2003**

Today, I was officially pulled off the Brisbane Jail investigation and reassigned to the Sunshine Coast Police Department. My superiors said they needed me up there, but I know it's bullshit. This has Michael Johnson's fingerprints all over it. He's punishing me for what happened to him and his son at the Brisbane Correctional Facility—and for the interrogation.

They didn't stop there. My superiors also told me to shut down the secret investigation on Hank Johnson and his family. They claimed I had no physical evidence to justify continuing. Of course, they're right— I don't have anything concrete to prove my suspicions. But I know in my gut that this entity, the one Hank calls "Diavlo," was behind the deaths of those inmates. The carnage, the precision, the sheer impossibility of it—it had to be him.

I'll admit, confronting Hank at the facility was a mistake. I pushed too hard. I wanted to see his reaction, to see if this entity would reveal itself in some way. But Diavlo didn't act, and nothing happened. Still, I could see it in Hank's eyes—he was hiding something. That moment confirmed my suspicions, even if I can't prove it.

This reassignment feels like a death blow. Without being close to Brisbane, I can't keep tabs on Hank or the Johnson family directly anymore. It's devastating. But I refuse to give up. The fight isn't over.

I still have my team—Brooke Caldwell, Rachel Monroe, and Callum Hayes. They're watching Hank and his family closely, reporting back to me regularly. The operation will continue, but now it has to be even more secretive, hidden even from my superiors.

I might have lost this battle, but the war is far from over. I'll find a way to expose the truth, no matter how long it takes. This isn't just about

Hank or his family anymore—it's about something far bigger, something that could threaten everything. I can't let it go. Not now. Not ever.

Sunnyvale Secondary School Council Bulletin
October 3, 2003

Attention Students and Staff,

As we enter October, here are some important updates and reminders for the month:

<u>Year 11 Formal Reminder</u>

We are excited to announce that the much-anticipated Year 11 Formal will take place on Saturday, October 18, 2003. This is a great opportunity to celebrate your achievements and enjoy a memorable evening with your peers.

<u>Formal King and Queen Voting</u>

Voting will close at the end of the school day next Friday, October 10, 2003. Be sure to cast your votes for the King and Queen before the deadline!

More details regarding the event will be shared in next week's bulletin.

<u>Running Competition Champion</u>

A huge congratulations to Hank Johnson of Year 11, who once again claimed first place in the annual Running Competition held on September 28, 2003.

Hank has shown exceptional dedication and perseverance, making this his second consecutive win in the competition. The school is incredibly proud of his achievement, and we hope his success inspires all our students to strive for excellence in their pursuits.

Well done, Hank!

<u>Government Curfew Reminder</u>

This is a reminder to all students that the government-mandated curfew remains in effect as part of safety measures during this challenging time.

- Students must be home by 5:00 PM.
- Outdoor activities are restricted to essential purposes only.
- Let's work together to stay safe and follow these guidelines.

We thank all our students for their continued cooperation and dedication. Stay focused, stay safe, and let's make this term a successful one!

Warm regards,
Sunnyvale Secondary School Council

Video Recording - Channel ATVH News
October 5, 2003
Time: 09:00 AM

The Channel ATVH News logo fades into view with dramatic music playing softly in the background. The screen shifts to the studio where presenter Claudia Blake sits at the desk, wearing a composed but serious expression.

Claudia Blake: "Good morning, Australia. We interrupt your usual programming with the latest updates on what many are calling one of the most disturbing phenomena in recent history. Months after the horrifying deaths at Brisbane Correctional Facility on March 20, a string of similar incidents has plagued jails across Queensland."

The screen transitions to footage of police vehicles parked outside a correctional facility, with investigators in hazmat suits entering the premises.

Claudia Blake (voiceover): "Since the first incident, where sixty inmates met a gruesome end, multiple jails across Brisbane and other areas of Queensland have reported identical deaths. The victims' internal organs were found violently ripped apart, leaving investigators baffled. Specialists from across Australia—and even from the United States—have been called in to analyse this phenomenon. However, after months of study, no concrete explanations have been uncovered."

The screen cuts to a press conference clip where scientists and government officials address the media, their expressions sombre.

Claudia Blake (voiceover): "Experts have speculated that these deaths could be caused by an advanced biochemical weapon—one so sophisticated that even the most seasoned specialists cannot decipher it. However, authorities are cautious about labelling it an act of warfare, as nations accused of involvement, including Russia, China, and North Korea, have all denied responsibility."

The screen cuts back to Claudia in the studio.

Claudia Blake: "Public concern is mounting, as fears grow that this deadly phenomenon might spread beyond correctional facilities. Citizens are demanding answers, and many are calling for more robust action from the federal government. Meanwhile, some controversial groups have voiced their support for these events, arguing that this 'phenomenon' is ridding society of dangerous individuals."

Footage plays of protests outside the Parliament building in Canberra, with banners calling for accountability and action.

Claudia Blake: "Prime Minister Victoria Reynolds has addressed these concerns, urging calm and assuring the public that every effort is being made to understand and contain the situation. However, mounting pressure has left the administration visibly strained."

The screen briefly cuts to footage of the Prime Minister speaking at a press conference.

Prime Minister Victoria Reynolds: "We are working tirelessly with domestic and international specialists to ensure the safety of all Australians. Let me be clear: we will leave no stone unturned in uncovering the cause of these incidents and ensuring they are contained."

The screen cuts back to Claudia.

Claudia Blake: "In a surprising twist, Queensland Premier Alan Hensley has announced his resignation amidst the crisis, citing personal reasons. His sudden departure has left an empty seat in leadership during these turbulent times."

The screen shows a list of potential candidates for the Premier role, with photos accompanying the names.

Claudia Blake: "Among the frontrunners to replace him is Michael Johnson, the current Director-General of Queensland Health. Johnson, who was present during the first incident at Brisbane Correctional Facility, has been vocal about the need for stronger leadership to address this crisis. Other candidates are also being considered, with the decision expected soon."

The screen transitions to a live poll showing public opinion on the resignation and potential new Premier candidates.

Claudia Blake: "The nation waits anxiously for clarity. Will these deaths be contained, or will the unknown threat spread beyond our jails? Stay tuned to Channel ATVH News for the latest updates as this story develops. And remember—stay safe."

The screen fades out with the Channel ATVH News logo, and the broadcast transitions back to regular programming.

Participants: Sophie Bennett and Hank Johnson

Hank: Hey, Sophie! Can't wait for Formal. Sorry I haven't been hanging out with you much at school lately. Been swamped with studies, running practice, and all the extra stuff with the student council.

Sophie: It's okay, Hank! I've been busy too. Prepping for exams and the science competition in November. You know, trying to keep my number 1 streak alive.

Hank: You'll crush it, like always. No one's even close to you in science.

Sophie: Aww, thanks. But hey, I heard from someone today that among the students, you and I are the favourites for King and Queen at Formal.

Hank: I've heard the same rumours.

Sophie: I don't know if I can handle that kind of attention though.

Hank: Same here. I mean, it's kinda overwhelming.

Sophie: Oh, please. You should be used to it! Don't you still have that whole fan group cheering for you everywhere?

Hank: Haha, wait, are you jealous?

Sophie: (laughs out loud emoji) Jealous? Never.

Hank: Admit it.

Sophie: No.

Hank: (happy face emoji) Anyway, are you gonna ask if I'm wearing the pyjamas you got me for my 16th birthday?

Sophie: Oh my gosh, you're such a dork. Are you?

Hank: Yep. Every day. Never wash it.

Sophie: (vomit emoji) EWWWW. Hank, seriously? That's disgusting.

Hank: (laughing emoji) Okay, okay, just kidding. But hey, are you wearing the sweater I got you for your 16th?

Sophie: (happy face emoji) Actually, yes! It's super comfy, so I wear it a lot.

Hank: Knew you'd love it. I have great taste.

Sophie: Sure, let's go with that.

Hank: Hey, quick question—has Liam been talking to you at all?

Sophie: Not really. Why?

Hank: Ever since I asked you to Formal, he's been distant. Hanging out by himself most of the time. I even noticed some bullies messing with him.

Sophie: That's awful.

Hank: Yeah, it's weird. He's been my friend for a long time, but I don't know what's going on.

Sophie: Well… there's been rumours going around school. Some kids are saying he's gay.

Hank: No way. Liam? I would've noticed. We've been close for years.

Sophie: I'm just saying what I've heard. Kids at school can be such idiots, Hank.

Hank: Yeah, they are. I should talk to him.

Sophie: You definitely should. He might need a real friend right now.

Chat End

Hank Johnson's Diary
October 17, 2003

After the jail incident where I appeared on TV, I became famous for all the wrong reasons. People at school screamed at me, calling Dad corrupt and saying he was abusing his job. It was horrible for a while, and I didn't know how to handle it. Luckily, as time passed and new stories took over the headlines, things eventually faded out. Still, it left a mark on me—I learned quickly how people could turn on you in an instant.

Tomorrow is Formal, and I'm kinda nervous. As part of the school council, I got a sneak peek at the votes, and it looks like I'll be elected King and Sophie Queen. Another thing to add to my "impressive CV," as Dad likes to call it.

After the jail incident, I've become sort of famous at school—more than I was before. Honestly, I hate it. It's made it harder to make real friends. I only really have Sophie; she is my girlfriend now. Sophie's been great, but Liam stopped talking to me after I asked Sophie to Formal. For some reasons I don't know, I guess he didn't take it well. I've thought about asking him why, but I decided it's too much effort. If he wants to talk, he'll come around.

Speaking of fame, Dad's running for QLD Premier now. That's put even more attention on me. All eyes are on me at school, which just adds to the pressure. It's like I can't go anywhere without someone watching.

And then there's Diavlo—my first friend as I used to call him. Since the first time he fed on those inmates at the jail, his power has grown immensely. Now, he can travel long distances away from me. I've been testing this out by wishing for more inmates to die in other jails, just to see if it works. It does. He disappears for a while, and then he comes back with that big grinning smile and those sharp white teeth. Sure enough, I turn on the TV, and the deaths are reported.

Diavlo said he can now sense hate in other people, even from a greater distance. And that one of the most hateful people are those held in jails. He told me he gained this ability after feeding on the 60 inmates back in March. I think he's growing, just like any other adult does.

At first, I felt so guilty. Diavlo's the one doing the killing, but I'm the one making it happen. I'm sort of commanding it. He's been around me constantly now because he's feeding so well. He keeps urging me to let him do more, and I don't think I can stop him. Honestly, I don't want to. I've resolved to use him to cleanse the world of bad people. Maybe someday I'll even try to end the third world war. For now, I'll keep testing his powers and see how far they can go.

I tried on the tuxedo Dad got me for Formal tomorrow. I look way older in it—almost like a grown-up. Even Diavlo thinks I look strange in it. He just stood there, staring at me with that mischievous smile of his, like he couldn't figure out if he liked it or not. I guess I'll find out tomorrow how everyone else reacts.

**Video Recording: Year 11 Formal
October 18, 2003**

Video Begins

The lively hum of chatter fills the air, accompanied by the soft, upbeat tones of background music echoing through the gymnasium. The gym is beautifully decorated, with strings of twinkling lights and streamers hanging from the ceiling. The faint sound of laughter and clinking glasses blends with the occasional burst of applause as the camera pans over the crowd of students dressed in formal attire.

Camera Girl: (excitedly) "Alright, everyone, this is it! They're about to announce the King and Queen of Formal! Get ready!"

The camera focuses on a small podium at the front of the gym, where a teacher holds a microphone. A hush falls over the crowd as the teacher speaks.

Teacher: "Ladies and gentlemen, the moment you've all been waiting for! Your Year 11 Formal King and Queen are... Hank Johnson and Sophie Bennett!"

Cheers erupt from the crowd as the camera zooms in on Hank and Sophie. Hank smiles confidently, walking with ease through the crowd. Sophie, blushing slightly, hesitates before following him to the podium.

Camera Girl: (whispering to herself) "Oh my gosh, they look so good together!"

The camera follows Hank and Sophie as they ascend the stage. Hank takes the microphone first.

Hank: (smiling) "Thank you, everyone. I'm really honoured. This has been an amazing year, and I couldn't have done it without all of you. Let's keep making memories together!"

The crowd cheers again as Sophie takes the microphone, visibly nervous.

Sophie: (softly) "Um… thank you. This is really unexpected. You all are amazing, and… yeah, thank you so much."

The teacher places crowns on their heads, and the gym fills with applause. The music changes to a slow, romantic song, and the camera captures Hank and Sophie stepping onto the dance floor.

Camera Girl: (whispering) "This is so sweet!"

Hank and Sophie begin to dance, surrounded by the cheers of their classmates. Soon, the rest of the crowd joins in, creating a vibrant sea of moving figures. The camera pans across the gym, capturing smiles and laughter.

Suddenly, the sound of a loud bang echoes through the gym, cutting through the music and the joyous atmosphere. Screams ripple through the crowd as the camera shakes, the operator panicking.

Student Voice: "What was that?!"

Camera Girl: (frantically) "Oh my God, what's happening?!"

The camera swings wildly, capturing students ducking behind tables and the podium. A teacher stands at the front, motioning for students to hide.

Teacher: (yelling) "Everyone, stay down! Hide wherever you can!"

Another bang rings out, and the teacher collapses. Gasps and cries fill the gym as the camera captures a figure stepping into view. The man, holding a weapon, is messy and screaming.

Man: "Hank! Where are you?!"

The camera zooms in slightly, catching Hank stepping forward cautiously from behind the podium.

Hank: (shocked) "Cousin? Dean? Is that you?"

The man, revealed to be Dean Coopla, points his weapon directly at Hank. His voice is hoarse and filled with rage.

Dean: "You ruined my life, Hank! Ever since you were a baby, you've been nothing but a curse! I know it's you! You're behind everything— the jail killings, the war, everything! You're a freak!"

Hank: (calmly) "Dean, listen to me. You're not well. Put the gun down. Let's talk about this."

Dean: "Talk? There's nothing to talk about! It ends here, Hank. I'm going to end it all right now!"

The wail of police sirens pierces the air, and the gymnasium lights suddenly go out. Screams erupt again as the camera is dropped to the floor. The lens now captures only blurred movements, shadowy figures running, and panicked cries. A loud thud echoes through the darkness, followed by an eerie silence.

The lights flicker back on, and the camera's angle reveals Hank standing in the middle of the gym, his tuxedo covered in blood. Above him, Dean's lifeless body hangs grotesquely from one of the gym's ceiling fans, his torso torn open in a horrifying display.

The sounds of distant screams and sirens filter through the gymnasium doors. Hank glances around, his expression unreadable. He looks directly at the camera, walks toward it, steadies it, and then heads toward the exit. The recording captures glimpses of the chaos— the shattered decorations, overturned tables, and streaks of blood staining the once-pristine gym floor.

As Hank pushes the double doors open, the blaring noise of sirens grows louder. The flashing red and blue lights of police cars flood the scene. Officers are running toward the building, their weapons drawn. The camera captures their shocked faces as they spot Hank.

Officer 1: (yelling) "There he is! Over here!"

A bright flash momentarily blinds the lens as a photographer takes a picture of Hank. The camera shifts as Hank lowers it slightly, revealing officers rushing toward him.

Officer 2: (firmly) "Son, put the camera down and come with us. You're safe now."

Hank doesn't speak. He keeps the camera in his hand as the officers close in. The lens wobbles as one officer gently grabs his shoulder, guiding him away from the gymnasium.

The camera captures glimpses of the outside world as Hank is escorted through the chaotic scene. The police cars are surrounded by panicked students and teachers, their faces pale and tear-streaked. The lens briefly pans over the growing crowd of onlookers beyond the police tape.

Officer 3: (softly) "Let's get you out of here, son."

The camera captures the inside of a police car as Hank is guided into the back seat. An officer closes the door behind him. The lens shifts one final time, catching the reflection of Hank's bloodied face in the car's window. His expression is distant, his eyes dark and unreadable.

The screen abruptly goes dark as the recording stops.

Video Ends

OPERATION PEGASUS: INSIDE THE STORM

The sleek jet hummed steadily through the night sky, carrying Marcus Kane and his elite team toward their underground base in the ruins of old London. The cabin was heavy with silence, broken only by the occasional rattle of weapons being checked. The team was shaken, their minds reeling from what they had just uncovered in the glass case retrieved from Hank Johnson's mansion. Diavlo wasn't just a myth, a figment of Hank's childhood imagination. The evidence was undeniable: Hank's first friend, a dark entity, was real.

"This doesn't add up," Marcus finally spoke, his sharp British accent slicing through the tension. "We've been tasked to recover this so-called proof, but why would Hank leave something so damning intact? Why not destroy it?"

Dimitri Volkov frowned; his scarred face twisted in thought. "The blood to open the glass case—Hank's blood, the boss said—it's strange. How did he even acquire it?"

The group exchanged uneasy glances.

"Maybe we're overthinking this," Jax Monroe said, though his tone lacked confidence. "But you're right, Marcus. Something doesn't sit right."

Marcus nodded grimly. "It doesn't. And when we land, I intend to challenge Liam Parker about his hidden ties to Hank Johnson. You've all read the files. He was a classmate of Hank's. That's a connection too close for comfort."

Kira Yamada chimed in, her voice low. "If Ian Morrison trusted him enough to name him successor, maybe there's more to it. Or maybe Ian never knew the full truth."

"We'll find out," Marcus said, his tone hardening. "Weapons ready, but be cautious. Something about this whole operation feels wrong."

The pilot's voice crackled through the intercom, announcing they were five minutes from their destination. The team strapped in, their fingers brushing against the cool metal of their gear. Tension mounted as the jet descended into the depths of old London, where ruins stood as a testament to the devastation of the Third World War. Beneath the ruins lay the underground base.

The jet came to a smooth stop. The team disembarked, carrying the glass case containing the proof of Diavlo's existence. The air was cold, the corridors dark and foreboding as they moved toward the base's entrance. Marcus approached the metal door, placing his eye against the square scanner. A beam of light scanned his retina, and with a metallic groan, the door slid open.

They passed through another long corridor before stepping into a brightly lit operations room. Screens lined the walls, displaying streams of data. Analysts and operators worked in silence, their fingers flying across keyboards. In the centre of the room stood Liam Parker, his expression calm, almost smug.

"Welcome back, team," Liam greeted them, his voice cool and collected. "Please follow me to my office so we can discuss."

They all followed him to his office, and as soon as they entered, they noticed an old woman sitting in a wheelchair.

"I see you've found what we were looking for. So, tell me—do you think Diavlo is real?" asked Liam.

The team hesitated, exchanging wary glances. Finally, Marcus stepped forward, his voice laced with suspicion. "You've been hiding things from us, Parker. You were Hank's classmate. Why didn't you tell us that before?"

Liam chuckled lightly. "A minor detail. Irrelevant to the operation."

Marcus's eyes narrowed. "Irrelevant? It changes everything. Ian trusted you, and now I don't. If you've hidden that, what else have you hidden?"

Liam's smile widened. "I suppose it's time for the truth, then."

Aminah Sahal, her sharp eyes scanning the room, pointed toward the old woman sitting silently in a wheelchair. "Who's she?"

Liam's tone shifted, turning cold. "She's the key to everything. Meet Mary Ann Johnson, Hank's mother."

Shock rippled through the team. "That's impossible," Dimitri muttered. "She died years ago."

"Oh, she's alive," Liam said smoothly. "And her blood was the key to opening the glass case, not Hank's. I lied to you all because I couldn't reveal her existence until now. You see, Mary Ann was the ultimate weapon against Hank."

Marcus's hand instinctively went to his holster, pulling his gun. "Enough lies. You've manipulated us from the start."

Marcus then fired at Liam; however, the bullet froze in mid-air before dropping harmlessly to the ground.

Liam raised an eyebrow, unfazed. "You're lucky this office is soundproof. Otherwise, the entire base would hear your gunfire."

A tense silence fell over the room. Kira's voice was barely a whisper. "It's Diavlo, isn't it? He's here."

Liam grinned. "Bingo. He can go wherever he pleases these days. Who do you think opened the secret corridor at the mansion for all of you to escape?"

The team drew their weapons, the sound of safeties clicking off filling the air. Without hesitation, they fired at Liam, but every bullet stopped mid-air, suspended by an unseen force, before clattering harmlessly to the ground. One by one, they screamed as their limbs were torn apart, their heads severed, their organs spilling onto the floor in grotesque heaps.

Only Marcus was left alive, his body broken, his limbs bent at unnatural angles. He gasped for breath, his voice trembling. "Since when… have you been on Hank's side?"

Liam crouched beside him, his voice almost pitying. "Let me think… I think it was right after the incident at school during the Year 11 Formal. You see, Diavlo has always been with Hank. He's grown stronger, far beyond anything you could imagine. And now, Diavlo is here with us."

Marcus's eyes darted to Mary Ann, tears streaming down her face.

"Oh, her?" Liam continued. "She can't talk yet, but her hand moves just enough to write. She's the one who gathered all this evidence against Hank with the help of our beloved Ian Morrison. God rest his soul. You see, they were about to release all this proof to the public, but our dear Mary Ann got cold feet—'mother's love,' she called it. Instead, she disappeared, and not even Ian could track her down. Then she came up with this brilliant idea: buying a mansion in Sydney under Hank's name to lure him there for a private chat about the evidence she had gathered. But I found her before she could put her little plan into action. A bit of torture from Diavlo, and she revealed everything to me— except for the other half of the evidence. Poor Ian never saw it coming either. Diavlo took care of him, just as he'll take care of you."

Summoning the last of his strength, Marcus reached into his jacket, pulling out a grenade with his teeth. His voice was a broken whisper. "I'm taking you with me."

Liam smirked. "Hank's first friend, do what you must."

As Marcus pulled the pin, his body convulsed violently, crushed by an invisible force. The grenade exploded, but the blast was confined, leaving Liam untouched. The room was silent once more, save for Liam's low, chilling laugh.

"And so, it ends," Liam said, his voice calm and deliberate. He slipped his right hand into his pocket and pulled out a small, sleek device with a glowing blue button. Holding it up for a moment, he pressed the button and asked, "Shall we prepare for the next phase?"

A chilling, otherworldly voice emanated from the device, deep and resonant, sending shivers through the air. It replied, "Yes, my new friend."

...to be continued.

AUTHOR BIO

Henry A. Salas, also known as "Henry Does," is an emerging author with a passion for crafting dark fantasy horror tales that delve into the eerie and unknown. Drawing inspiration from classic horror literature, mythology, and the shadowy recesses of the human mind, Henry builds immersive worlds brimming with ancient curses, forbidden magic, and haunting creatures.

He has published *Apocrypha Act I* and *Diavlo, My First Friend*, aiming to captivate readers with gripping narratives that delve into themes of fear, power, the thin line between reality and nightmare.

When not writing, Henry enjoys exploring abandoned places, reading gothic fiction, and indulging in a good horror film.

Learn more at henrydoes.com/books.